Coming Home

Coming Home

Vonnie Hughes

ROBERT HALE · LONDON

ISBN 978-0-7090-9005-2

Robert Hale Limited
Clerkenwell House
Clerkenwell Green
London EC1R 0HT

www.halebooks.com

2 4 6 8 10 9 7 5 3 1

Typeset in 10/12.5pt Classical Garamond
Printed in Great Britain by the MPG Books Group, Bodmin and King's Lynn

CHAPTER ONE

Portuguese Border

5 May 1811

A DUST PALL hovered over the Fuentes ridge and the distant village of Fuentes de Onoro.

Colly Hetherington stood alone, rubbing the old sabre scar that snaked down his torso beneath the ragged silver lacing on his uniform. The stiff leg and ugly scar kept his life – and imminent death – in perspective.

As he squinted through the haze, the raucous shouts of his brigade celebrating victory punctured the still air. Brigade-Major Hetherington did not regard the deaths of four officers and twenty-four soldiers as cause for jubilation, but he understood the survivors' need for the affirmation of life.

Today he'd lost yet another good friend.

Year after year the bodies piled up, and year after year he made himself the same promise: make acquaintances not friends. Year after year he broke his promise.

But today when he'd seen Lieutenant Nate Carthew's convulsing body finally lie still, something within him changed. Despair replaced the biting anger. *Enough*, something inside him cried. He'd had enough.

Stony-faced, aching inside, he heard a sergeant from the 60th scream, 'A pox on Messena!'

'May the duchess cuckold Rivoli until she's blind!' someone else chimed in.

Bottles of *aguadiente*, contributed by grateful residents from Fuentes de Onoro and Almeida, clashed together.

Colly heard someone scrambling up the slope behind him and spun around, his hand on his short sword.

'Sir, the baggage train has arrived. There's a letter for you.'

'For me?' He stared at Lieutenant Worboys in surprise. He rarely received letters. From the day his father had banished him from the family home, only his grandmother had shown any interest in his well-being. And he had heard nothing from the redoubtable old lady for months.

Then he glimpsed the thickness of the folded paper and stretched out a hand. Of course. The letter would be from John. Lord John Trewbridge had, until recently, been an exploring officer attached to the 71st. Eagerly Colly turned it over. Yes, the Trewbridge seal was affixed. John must now be living at the family estate. Lucky man. Colly had stayed for a short time at Trewbridge after the Corunna débâcle and he could not think of a more peaceful corner of England in which to live.

Slapping at the mosquitoes, he dropped to the grass and propped his back against a spindly cherrylaurel tree.

News from home. His blood surged with anticipation as he ran a dirty thumbnail through the seal and unfolded the sheet of paper.

He read it and damn near choked in shock.

Green trees and green grass. Cold ale. He was going home!

Dear Colly

We hope this letter reaches you. Knowing the vagaries of army mail, all we can do is hope.

We are writing to offer you the position of steward of the Trewbridge estates. As you grew up on a big estate we are sure you can handle the work easily. Furthermore, we trust you. The parents were greatly taken with you when you came to stay after Corunna.

Colly tried to swallow, but his dry throat closed. They trusted him.

He felt tears of weakness welling up and screwed shut his eyes, but the droplets forced themselves from beneath his eyelids. They coursed down the grooves on his face and tickled the corners of his mouth. Swiping at them with a grimy hand he thanked God there was no one around. The last time he had cried was the day his father had told him, 'We can't trust you, boy. You are lying.'

So he had left; he'd had no choice.

But now he had a chance at redemption. Not with his own family – it was too late for that – but with the Trewbridges. He snatched up the letter again.

There have been some unfortunate incidents and my older brother is dead. In due time I shall inherit, although I wish I could change the circumstances.

> *Our steward retired recently and Father and I are endeavouring*
> *to run four estates between us.*
>   *I am to be married shortly. You will remember the sheep-minded*
> *Miss Ninian.*

Colly stopped reading for a moment to savour John's phrasing. Yes, he remembered the spirited Miss Ninian very well. She had possessed an amazing affinity with animals.

> *We need you, Colly! Please say you will sell out and join us. Father*
> *requested me to point out that this tenure is for as long as you wish it.*
>   *Your friend*
>   *J.T.*

Colly stared into the distance. He was useful here. Two rapid promotions and a cash bonus attested to that. But there were others to take his place.

The Trewbridges wanted *him* specifically.

If he returned to England, and if the Fates smiled on him, (hah!) he might one day achieve his dream of owning a small estate. He gazed into the shimmering heat haze. A lot of 'ifs'.

He re-read the letter and grimaced, wondering what 'unfortunate incidents' had brought about the death of Spencer Trewbridge. The man had been a shockingly loose screw, and Colly would bet his last guinea that Spencer's demise had something to do with the dreadful people he hobnobbed with. If even half the stories told about him were true, the Trewbridges were well rid of him.

John, however, would make an excellent marquess when the time came.

Could Colly help John maintain the Trewbridge traditions and assets?

He'd give it a damned good try.

Six weeks later, his scars chafing in the vicious summer heat, Colly rode wearily into Porto and headed towards the docks. His Portuguese was execrable, so he waylaid a boy who looked to be in desperate need of a centavo or two. 'Ah ... *com licença, rapaz,*' he stammered.

The boy glanced up, grinning. He'd no doubt heard his language mangled by Frenchmen and Englishmen alike. By a mix of sign language and mentioning '*hospedaria puro*', Colly managed to explain that he was seeking clean accommodation. The boy gestured straight ahead, then curved his arm around to the right. At the same time he held out his left hand expectantly. A boy after his own heart, Colly thought. Keep it simple.

He followed the directions to a weathered, stone *hospedaria* that looked well cared for and asked – again in sign language – for a bath while his uniform was cleaned.

Before booking a berth to England, he intended to make a very important visit. He had no illusions about his appearance, but he wanted to look respectable.

As he shrugged out of his jacket he muttered, 'Please God, let Juliana still be there.' Juliana with her healing hands and dark eyes full of secrets.

Yes, he knew he wasn't fit to lick her little half-boots. But just to see her once more – he'd travel a lot further than the road between Almeida and Porto for one of those shy, imperfect little smiles from Miss Juliana Colebrook.

An hour later, feeling more like a man and less like something blown in on the wind, he strode towards Sao Nazaire Hospital and the woman who'd haunted his daydreams for months. The patients had nicknamed her 'The Angel of Sao Nazaire' and, to many injured men half-dreaming in laudanum-dulled pain, that was how she seemed – an angel. After wallowing in dust and blood for months, awaking to the graceful, competent hands of Miss Juliana Colebrook had been a miracle for many wounded soldiers.

He'd seen many invitations offered to her, both crude and sincere. And had seen them all civilly declined. His pace quickened. Head down, he nearly cannoned into a wall of red, grey and buff.

'Brigade-Major Hetherington?'

A group of injured soldiers from the convalescent home were taking the air between the town and the docks. Amongst them he spied one of his lieutenants who'd been injured during a skirmish on the Spanish border three months before.

'Ah, Lieutenant Davidson – still lolling around I see.'

The freckled youth grinned amiably.

But Colly's words were not a joke. Davidson was one of the slowest men in the army. He would not have been injured if he'd been quicker on his feet. Even more importantly, others would not have been injured. Davidson's bad leg stuck awkwardly out to one side as he stood with his good leg canted to balance his weight.

'We are waiting to be shipped home, sir.'

'Is there a ship due?' Colly asked eagerly.

'Any day now. Are you going back too, sir?'

'Yes. I've sold out.'

'*Really?*' Davidson's already protuberant blue eyes bulged even further. 'I never thought you would do that, sir.'

'Neither did I, Lieutenant.' No. He had expected to spend the remainder of a very short life on the Peninsula. And when he died, only a handful of comrades would mourn him.

Then Colly realized that all the men in the group were junior in ranking to him and were standing to attention in the scorching sun. A few were wilting. He nodded to them to stand easy and took Davidson aside.

'Anyone we know in hospital at the moment?' he asked.

Davidson smirked. 'Only the Angel, sir.'

Colly didn't know what felt worse – the quickening of his heart telling him she was within reach, or the knowing look on Davidson's face. Flushing, he saluted and strode off in search of Miss Colebrook.

CHAPTER TWO

Juliana Colebrook turned away from the narrow window where she had been gulping draughts of fresh air before plunging back into the oppressive room that housed more than fifty men. The hospital was perched halfway up a hill outside Porto. The citizens had wisely isolated their sick and injured away from the thickly populated town centre. An advantage of this was that the hospital was blessed with an occasional breeze fresh off the sea.

She gazed down the rows of beds, keeping an eye out for incipient problems and prayed that Dr Barreiro's bell would not ring again today. Now that she was the most experienced worker here, he often asked her to assist him with complicated operations such as amputations and head wounds. Three years of such work had not inured her to its horrors.

In the distance a bell tinkled imperatively. *Deus*! She was summoned. Her prayers had not been answered. Her stomach began its familiar churning.

Patting a patient's hand here and there, breathing lightly so as not to choke on the malodorous air, she hurried down the room.

But when she reached the doorway, she stopped. Striding towards her was … it was *him*. The one for whom she had broken all her personal rules. '*Thank you*,' she heard herself whispering. '*Obrigada*.'

During his hospital stay she had gone each evening to his bedside, unable to go home without assuring herself that he was safe. He had been only one brave man amongst many, yet something about the expression in Brigade-Major Hetherington's hazel eyes told her he liked her – he liked her very much – and he had no intention of doing anything about it.

Fine. She liked him too, and could do nothing about it. He must fight a war in Portugal and Spain, and she must find a way to escape from Portugal to the security of her English relatives. Besides, there was that thing in her past that meant she could never, never give herself to any man.

She had visited him at Dr Barreiro's request. 'I wish you to talk to a certain brigade-major,' he had told her. 'The one who blacked your eye when—'

'I remember,' she'd said quickly. How could she not? Even in her pain she'd seen the appalled look on the officer's face when he realized he'd struck her. He had been threshing around, struggling to fight off the hospital attendants. For some reason he was desperate to return to the battlefield.

Her eye had not hurt for long. She'd had worse.

'I am unhappy about that man,' Dr Barreiro had explained. 'He is world-weary. Physically' – and here the good doctor had spread his hands in explanation – 'he's a fine specimen, but in his heart and mind …' And Dr Barreiro had shaken his head.

It had taken her only a few minutes with Brigade-Major Hetherington to understand what Dr Barreiro meant. Well, she'd helped soldiers like this before. Sometimes a woman could achieve what all the doctors in the world could not. Although she'd visited him at Dr Barreiro's behest, from the very first evening she had enjoyed Colywn Hetherington's self-deprecating humour and quiet assurance. It was a relief to find humour in the angst-ridden atmosphere of the hospital. And oh, *how* she had missed him and worried about him when he'd gone back to the front.

Now here he was, hale and hearty. Her gabbled prayers, sandwiched between her difficult work and sleepless nights had been answered. Mr Hetherington might not know it, but he had shared many a sleepless night with Juliana.

'Miss Colebrook.'

His voice sounded just the same. Mellow and smooth and subdued, a tone that hinted at a well of sorrow beneath the easy-going façade.

'Brigade-Major Hetherington! What a pleasure to see you again.' *Inferno*! The words had bubbled out before she could claim them back. She sounded too eager, as if she had been sitting around waiting for his return.

He bowed, then smiled. His even white teeth, unlike many she saw, spoke of a strong, healthy body. But he was thinner. His face was drawn and he looked older. Much older.

He stepped forward. 'Dr Barreiro has given me permission to take you for a walk, should you wish it of course,' he added hastily. 'If you cannot bring yourself to excuse my appalling manners on our first unfortunate meeting, I shall understand.'

She smiled. He had still not forgiven himself for that incident. 'Well …' She glanced down at her feet.

He clicked his tongue. 'I'm sorry. I should have remembered those aching feet,' he said softly. Their eyes met in a shared memory of her sitting at his bedside, surreptitiously toeing off her shoes to wriggle her tired feet.

'But a cup of tea at the English tea house would be very acceptable,' she blurted out. What if he thought she didn't want to accompany him?

He laughed, and she enjoyed it.

'A tea house? Wherever will we find a tea house?' he asked, puzzled.

'I will show you.' She tugged off her apron. Oh, *how* she wished she'd known he was coming. She would have worn her best dress. 'When the English troops routed the French from Porto, an enterprising Englishwoman converted a coffee house to a tea house. There are even tea roses growing outside the door. So lovely!' She was conscious of a lightness in the air that had not been there a short while ago. Even her feet no longer hurt. She collected her parasol from behind the door and indicated with the handle. 'In this direction.' She scurried out before he could change his mind.

CHAPTER THREE

HE STOLE A surreptitious glance. What had happened to her? She was thin, much too thin. The girlishness had gone from her face and been replaced with a patient stoicism. Her deep brown-black hair was just as thick, and the magnolia skin was as smooth as ever, but the dewiness and gloss were gone. Lord, it was good to see her, still with the same accented lilt to her voice, and the natural, graceful sway of her hips that owed nothing to the careful tuition of a young ladies' academy in Bath.

'That is the trouble with the English,' he heard himself say. 'They are great travellers. But wherever they go, they wish to be back in England.'

She grimaced. 'Not my father. He liked to keep going and going.' Then she bowed her head and fiddled with the handle of her parasol.

'Why did your father want to keep going?' he asked, as they turned into the street.

There was a short pause.

'Well, antiquarians have enquiring minds. Too enquiring sometimes,' she said with acerbity. 'There was always something else to see a few miles further on.'

'The grass is always greener...?'

'Precisely.'

He wondered at the bitterness in her voice.

'I'm sorry,' she said after an uncomfortable silence. 'But because of Papa I am marooned here, desperate to return to England and unable to do so.'

'I thought your childhood was spent in Portugal,' he said.

As they entered the tea shop she said, 'And in England and Egypt as well.'

He stopped. 'What? He dragged you to all his working sites?'

'My mother also, of course,' she said, as they sat down at a delicate little gate-legged table. He could not cram his long legs under the table because his left leg was still painful to bend for any length of time. In the end he compromised by pushing the spindly chair back from the table and spreading his legs out straight.

He nodded to her to carry on with her story and she continued, gazing at the whitewashed wall, seeing the long ago. '*Mãe* was of a delicate constitution, poor darling. She begged him to let the two of us go back to Portugal to live with her parents so he could explore to his heart's content. But Papa liked to have *Mãe* at his side, to prepare his meals just the way he liked them. She was very good at making a comfortable home out of whichever hut or cave we lived in at the time. And it was not all bad. Sometimes we stayed at the homes of fellow enthusiasts and they spoiled me abominably. Of course, it then became twice as hard once we were on our own.'

Colly nodded. He knew what she meant. Sometimes after one had bivouacked in a luxurious place such as a disused *pousada* or *castelo*, it was depressing to spend the next couple of weeks on the march sleeping under hedgerows and in pig byres.

He cleared his throat, trying for a casual tone. 'You never told me – where are your parents now?'

Absorbed in pouring tea, she did not look up.

'*Mãe* died when I was ten and my maternal grandparents sent me to the convent of the Good Sisters of Hope in Coimbra. When my grandparents died of the fever, Papa took me back to Egypt with him to be his assistant.'

Colly bit into the dainty scone in front of him. Scones and jam and clotted cream here, in Porto. It was like a dream.

Or a nightmare if one took Miss Colebrook's background into account. He employed his mouth and teeth in chewing his way through three dainty scones. It was better that she thought him a greedy hog than that he opened his mouth and told her what he thought of her father.

'So why are you here?' she asked, her head tilted to one side like a robin.

Did she want a potted history of his life, or did she mean, 'Why are you here *now*?'

'I am on my way home to England,' he said baldly. She would not get a potted biography from him. He had no intention of telling her the story of his life – why he had joined the army; why he was in Portugal. She would cringe away from him if he told her the truth.

'Are you on leave?' she asked, sounding interested.

He settled back in his chair, smiling. 'I have sold out. I received an offer of employment from a friend.'

She bounced in her chair. 'How wonderful!'

'You don't know *how* wonderful, Miss Colebrook. His letter came right after the Battle of Fuentes de Onoro.'

She smothered a smile, presumably because of his appalling accent, and for a moment he was drawn out of his tale to admire the way the creamy skin pinched at the corners of her mouth.

'I think I've become battle weary,' he said. 'But I was never so relieved and excited in my life than when I received his letter.'

'It *is* what you really want, isn't it? Not just an excuse to escape? Uh ...'

'At first I asked myself that question, Miss Colebrook. But I think I'm doing the right thing. It is work I am familiar with and can assimilate quickly. And I like the family very much. Most of all, they know me and trust me.' He shut his mouth. Why on earth was he warbling on and on? He had better keep silent before he admitted just how familiar he was with estate work and why. Those fruitless years when he had worked so hard as his father's stud manager only to have his every decision questioned and countermanded still rankled.

She stared at him for a moment. Her cup was raised in the air. 'Could you take me back to England with you?'

He choked on his tea and rattled the miniscule cup back onto its saucer.

'I-I ...'

Blushing, she continued, 'I do not mean anything more than that, Brigade-Major. I am determined to go to England. I have relatives there. We corresponded when my father died, and they suggested then that I should go to stay with them, but at the time I had only just begun work at Sao Nazaire. Dr Barreiro expected me to stay at least one year. I have been stuck here ever since. I understand my cousins are in straitened circumstances, so of course I will seek employment of some sort.'

Colly opened his mouth and shut it again. He stared at the beautiful young woman in front of him. He had no idea what to say.

His appalled silence said it for him.

'I see,' she said at last. 'It is quite all right. I understand.' She traced patterns on her reticule with a gloved finger, her head lowered. 'I'm sorry to be so ... so ... unladylike. I've startled you. But I am not acquainted with any English families with whom I could travel, and I've no relatives left in Portugal.'

Without realizing what he was doing, he covered her hand with his. 'I will be sailing on a troop ship, Miss Colebrook. It is most unsuitable for a woman on her own.' He felt the gloved hand beneath his quiver.

'Most of the Englishwomen here came out on troop ships,' she argued.

Colly felt a nervous sweat break out on his neck. What did she think she was doing, putting temptation in front of him like this? 'But, Miss Colebrook, what if your relatives are unsympathetic and you find yourself in England with no one to turn to?'

'I found myself in Portugal with no one to turn to in a time of war, yet I survived. Please.'

If she hadn't tacked on that 'please' he would have been all right. He would have told her that – that what? God, he was only fooling himself. He'd given in the moment she'd said, 'Could you take me back to England with you?'

Since she wanted this so very much he would help her, but he would certainly not accompany her. He swallowed hard. 'Very well. Since you are determined upon your course, I will find an acquaintance to take you under their wing. We might be able to employ a respectable companion at the receiving office. But I am the *last* person you should look to as your protector. I am totally unsuited for the role.'

There. He'd said it. She could make of it what she wanted.

Her answer was unexpected. 'Rubbish. If you do not care for the responsibility, then say so. Do not make feeble excuses.' She lurched to her feet, snapping the handle of her parasol against the table in the process. '*Inferno*! Now see what you've made me do.'

'Sit down, Miss Colebrook. Sit!' he snapped, when she would have flounced off.

'I am not your dog, sir,' she grated.

'No, indeed. The dogs I used to own did not snarl,' he bit back. 'Very well. I shall tell you the truth. And then you will see.'

'See what?'

'Why I am not a suitable escort for you.'

She stared at him and blinked, an expression of utter confusion on her face. 'I do not understand.'

He gazed straight ahead, refusing to look at her. 'I purchased a commission in the army five years ago because I had no other choice. My father threw me out.' He drew a deep breath. 'The family disowned me because a young woman accused me of ... of raping her.'

Miss Colebrook stiffened.

Colly persevered. 'When I refused to marry her, my father—' He shrugged. There was no need to go any further. The horrified expression on her face said it all.

'Oh!' She shrank away from him, a look in her eyes part fear, part something else he could not fathom.

'*Now* do you see?' He bit the words out as if he were chewing nails.

It was exactly as he had expected. Now she feared him and knew him for the worthless animal that he was. Well, she had forced it out of him. He hoped she was happy with what she'd found.

For a minute she sat quite still, her dark eyes clouded, her hands clenched around her reticule. Then she rallied. 'I see. That puts a different complexion on things.'

He had to admire her quick recovery. 'Precisely. I'm sorry, Miss Colebrook. You must be wishing me at Jericho,' he said, scrambling to his feet.

And since this was the last time he would see her, he could damned well tell her how he really felt. 'It has been an honour to know you, Miss Colebrook. I will always remember you with ... with ...' Ah, to hell with it. He gave up, bowed stiffly and stalked away.

Getting on the ship's manifest was difficult but his seniority obtained him the last cabin.

'The *Maximus* and the *Resolution* are off the coast, sir. They're due tomorrow morning,' the clerk commented.

Colly nodded curtly. He didn't give a tinker's curse what he sailed back to England in. He just wanted to get out of here.

He returned to the inn where he'd left his horse and baggage earlier in the day and enquired where he might sell his horse. The ostler directed him to a larger inn further down the road, explaining in halting English that the larger inns always had need of horses with stamina to rent out.

'Poor Marcus,' Colly whispered to his horse as he haggled for a good price. Although the 60th was a foot regiment, most of the officers owned their own horses and Colly and Marcus had been together now for eighteen months. Marcus was exceptional. 'I'd give anything to take you back to England,' Colly told the horse, as he stroked the soft black nose for the last time. 'But I can't afford to wait for another ship. These two are packed to the gills and they refuse to take any horses. I'm sorry, old chap. So sorry.'

And he walked away without looking back. After all, it was what he was best at, wasn't it? Disappointing people and walking away without looking back.

CHAPTER FOUR

Juliana hurried along the dusty pathway beside the Douro. Mr Hetherington had given her an idea. She could not travel alone, but it might be possible to employ a companion at the English receiving office, perhaps an officer's widow. She was half-English, was she not? Therefore she was entitled to go to the English receiving office.

Her heart quickened as she thought of her narrow escape. To think the brigade-major had *admitted* to her that— She stopped walking and shook her head. Actually, he had admitted nothing. He said he'd been accused, not that he'd committed rape. Puzzled, she wondered why he'd said anything at all. She would never have known if he'd kept quiet about it.

She felt a lumpy constriction in her throat and swallowed hard to get rid of it. Brigade-Major Hetherington had been woven into the fabric of her daydreams for so long that she would find it nigh on impossible to forget him. She'd never realized that one's heart could actually ache.

She trudged on, dispirited, and felt a drop of rain on her face. '*Inferno!*' she muttered under her breath. Glancing up, she saw the lowering clouds jostling on the horizon. Just what she needed on one of the worst days of her life – a brisk five-mile walk in the rain.

By the time she arrived at the receiving office her parasol was sodden and so were her skirts and half-boots. It did not help that she'd had to grip the cracked handle of the parasol tightly to hold it together. Inside her gloves her fingers were numb.

The desk clerk eyed her. 'Yes, miss?' he enquired.

She swallowed her annoyance. In the northern part of the city she was well-known, even respected, but down here by the docks they probably thought she was a camp-follower trying to earn her fare home.

'My name is Miss Juliana Ervedosa Colebrook. I am a nurse at Sao Nazaire.'

The clerk straightened up and hastened to bring a chair. 'Do sit down, miss. I'll call Miss Ffitch, the manager.'

Miss Ffitch bustled in full of sharp good humour, but when she heard what Juliana wanted, she shook her head. 'Oh no, Miss Colebrook. None of the women here is a suitable companion for a respectable lady.'

For a moment Juliana mused whether perhaps the women were suitable companions for unrespectable ladies. She gazed about her. She'd been so intent on her quest that she had not taken particular notice of her surroundings. A number of tough-looking women sprawled on benches set around the room. *Dios*! She had never seen such a motley group, even when she'd travelled the by-roads between Coimbra and Porto. Uncertainly she asked, 'Are these the only applicants available?'

Miss Ffitch sighed. 'Yes. At the moment. All likely workers are snapped up immediately. A few of these are seeking work as scullery maids and such-like. The rest ...' Here, Miss Ffitch gave an expressive shrug that Juliana took to mean that the women would soon find themselves on the streets.

'Oh! Well, perhaps one of the scullery maid applicants might be suitable?'

Miss Ffitch stood firm. 'No, Miss Colebrook, I couldn't do it. Before you got anywhere near the ship you'd find yourself without a penny to your name and probably a black eye and broken arm as well.'

''Ere,' interrupted one of the more scrofulous applicants who was sitting on the front bench, eavesdropping. She lurched to her feet. 'This woman wants a maid!'

Suddenly Juliana found herself surrounded by an importuning, filthy rabble. Startled, she shrank back, treading on Miss Ffitch's sturdy shoes.

'Get away with you!' Miss Ffitch barked. 'Go back to your seats and wait, else you can leave.'

Grumbling, the women obeyed, some of them still eyeing Juliana hungrily.

Juliana's heart settled back to its normal rhythm.

'My dear,' Miss Ffitch said, 'why don't you talk to the booking-office clerk? He would know if any ladies booked to sail have need of a companion.'

Juliana thanked her, but she didn't hold out much hope. Those ladies already booked would have had plenty of time to find travelling companions. However, if she could secure a cabin she might be able to befriend a woman who was already on the manifest.

She *must* escape. Her work at the hospital was untenable. So much needless death. Each morning she had to steel herself to walk through the big blue doors to face another working day. Her only bastion against the horror was the chance that she might escape it one day.

And she was so alone. She *must* get a berth on a ship sailing to England as soon as possible. Her relatives would not wait forever. By now they might have written her off, since it was a twelve-month since they'd corresponded.

She plunged out into the rain once more and headed towards the docks. But the clerk at the booking office dashed her faint hope. 'I'm sorry, miss. All cabins are taken on both the *Resolution* and the *Maximus*. Some people have been waiting for weeks. We always hold one cabin in reserve and that was taken a short time ago.'

Probably taken by Brigade-Major Hetherington, Juliana thought. She shivered. Lord, she'd had a narrow escape there. So much for all her silly daydreams....

There was only one thing to do: return to the hospital and endure as best she could until the next ship arrived. She would book it in advance. At least she had a plan now, although she still had to find a reliable travelling companion.

'Miss?' the booking clerk offered, as she turned away. 'You could come by on sailing day because sometimes people don't turn up.' He shrugged as if to say that people like that were inexplicable. 'I can put you on our waiting list.'

But when Juliana signed her name, she saw there were already several names before hers. She had had no idea so many people were anxious to leave Porto. Not all the people milling about the booking office were speaking English. Some spoke German and others spoke a strange language that some of her patients had informed her was Gaelic. And it seemed that all of them wanted to reach England – the sooner the better.

'We hope that sailing day will be Wednesday,' the clerk explained. 'The ships are just outside the estuary now.'

What should she say to Dr Barreiro? How could she tell him she might be leaving his employ suddenly? And then again, she might not.

The grinding ache in her stomach began to nag again.

She plodded back along the river path, her sodden skirts clinging to her ankles. Inside her half-boots the soles of her feet felt as if she were walking on stinging nettles, but that was too bad. She had to get back to Sao Nazaire quickly. Dr Barreiro had given her permission to go out for a couple of hours, not the entire afternoon.

'What the hell are you doing?' demanded an irate voice.

Oh, God. Brigade-Major Hetherington. And she looked like a drowned rat. Not of course that it mattered when one considered what sort of person he was, but just the same …

'I – I'm going back to the hospital,' she responded with what she hoped was dignity. Her chin rose.

He fell into step beside her. 'Miss Colebrook, we are a good five miles from Sao Nazaire. Do you intend to walk all the way?'

'Why not? I walked all the way down here.' Now she sounded *really* snappish. Her feet burned and her shift stuck to her body like a family of leeches.

'Have you been down to the wharves?'

His voice had softened a little, so she risked a glance up at him. He had not offered his arm. For which, of course, she was thankful. He walked a careful couple of paces away from her. Then she saw his face twist in pain as he stumbled over the rocky edge of the path. He muffled a curse and surreptitiously rubbed his thigh.

'Here,' she said crossly. Swapping her reticule and parasol into her left hand, she held out her right arm. It was perfectly safe, she told herself. It was daylight and there were many people about.

He hesitated, then growled, 'I'm fine, thank you. I do not need your support.'

She did not bite out words like 'ungrateful' and 'idiot' because she had seen the dreadful conflict in his eyes. 'It is the weather,' she explained. 'All old wounds ache in Porto.'

He nodded brusquely, dismissing her comment.

'It is so,' she insisted. 'Dr Barreiro says that Porto's changeable weather is bad for bones and sinews that have suffered damage.'

Reluctantly he took her arm, but he kept a distance between them. Which was hopeless. He was so tall she had to trot to keep up with his paces, and when he held himself stiffly away from her the problem was compounded. She edged a little closer and, to her relief, he did not seem to notice. He was staring straight ahead, his face remote and stern.

After a few minutes he asked, 'Were you trying to get on board the *Resolution?*'

'*Sim*. But first I went to the receiving office.' And she explained the unsettling experience she'd had there.

He looked horrified. 'I'm sorry for suggesting it then. I am out of touch – hey!'

One of Porto's open carriages was winding its way down the sloping road beside the river path. Brigade-Major Hetherington inelegantly shoved two fingers in his mouth and let go a piercing whistle. The carriage halted, waiting for them.

Juliana grinned. He mightn't speak much Portuguese but he could get his message across. No doubt a whistle worked better on a battle-field than a shout.

He assisted her into the carriage and gratefully she sank on to the seat.

'To Sao Nazaire,' Mr Hetherington said to the driver, mangling the vowels. As the carriage turned around, he sat down opposite her. She was surprised to feel disappointed.

'This is wonderful,' she said shyly. 'I couldn't find a carriage when … before.' She had almost said, 'when you rushed off and deserted me at the tea shop.' Of course, she had *wanted* him to leave after his shocking revelation, but she hadn't expected to feel like a dropped package.

'What did the booking clerk say, Miss Colebrook?' He had the disagreeably portentous look on his face that all men had when they were about to lecture an unfortunate female.

Inwardly she sighed. She knew it. He was going to go on and on about how she should give up her idea of travelling to England.

'No cabins available,' she answered tersely.

'Then—'

'No! I will *not* give up!' she shouted. 'I hate it here. I'm so tired of …' And to her shame she began to sob like a child. Pressing her gloved hands to her face she leaned forward and cried and cried. Why couldn't she stop? What was happening to her? This was terrible.

CHAPTER FIVE

COLLY CLENCHED HIS fists. Her silent weeping jagged at his heart, but there wasn't a thing he could do.

Lord, he was an idiot. He should have realized she was at the end of her tether when she'd tried to persuade him to take her to England. But no, he'd let his angry pride get in the way of common sense.

'Miss C— Juliana, please don't. I can't bear it when you …' He stretched out a hand towards her then drew it back quickly. No, Hetherington. Do *not* touch her.

Struggling to gain control, she scrabbled inside her soggy reticule and produced a tiny lace-edged handkerchief. He couldn't help smiling at the dainty two-inch wisp of fabric. What good did she think that would do?

'Here.' He held out his much larger kerchief, thankful he'd changed his raiment at the inn.

She clutched at it blindly and it fluttered to the dirty floor of the carriage.

Colly picked it up. Sighing, he gave in. He stripped off his gloves and moved to sit beside her. 'Excuse me,' he said, and attempted to dab her wet face. At the first touch of his hand on her cheek, she jerked back as if she'd been burnt.

'I'm just wiping your face,' he growled. 'Sit still.'

She froze.

He carried on as if he hadn't noticed. 'The way I see it, we have two options.'

'Options?'

'Mmm.' He struggled to hide his enjoyment when his fingers brushed across her petal-soft skin. Then he crumpled up the kerchief and stuffed it back in his pocket. He moved back to the other seat. 'You could use my cabin and I can sleep on deck. I did that on the way over here.' He tried to make light of one of the worst experiences of his life. Three years ago vicious gales had swept their little flotilla from Portsmouth into Mondego Bay in record time. The majority he had purchased counted for nothing in the overcrowded ships and he had ended up sleeping on deck with the ordinary soldiers.

Which had turned out to be a fortunate thing. Seasick, green to the complex rules of army life, he had learned more up on deck from some of the old campaigners than he had ever learned at the military college at Farnham. All the same, he did not fancy a repeat experience.

'Or,' he continued, 'we could pretend we are married and share my cabin. I—'

'What?' Miss Colebrook's delightfully accented, softly modulated voice rose to the volume of a banshee's shriek.

'Damn it all! You want to go to England, don't you? You practically begged me to take you.' Indignation and embarrassment warred with each other in Colly's voice. So it wasn't to madam's liking? Well, that was the best he could bloody well suggest.

'Begged? I think not.'

'You were determined to come to England with me.'

'Well … not with you in particular. I want to get to England and you are someone I knew and trusted.'

Colly noticed she used the past tense. 'Unfortunately there are flaws in both schemes.'

'Yes, I cannot afford the price of a cabin on my own,' she agreed.

He brushed that aside. 'It's already paid for. But if you take the cabin on your own, we are back where we started. You will still need to find a companion.' He chose his next words carefully. 'If we give the impression we are married, however, that will solve the problem.' Hah, he thought. It wouldn't solve any problems for him, being around her, breathing the very air she breathed, trying to pretend an aloofness he could never feel. God, what had made him suggest such a ridiculous solution?

You know very well why you suggested it, his conscience muttered. *And, as Father said, you are the unwisest man ever born.*

Juliana sat bolt upright on her seat, clutching her reticule like a lifeline. 'Sir, I don't think—' She tried again, obviously searching for a polite way to say no. 'It wouldn't work,' she said at last.

'Juliana,' he said softly, 'do not be frightened of me. Please. I promise I would spend most of my time outside the cabin. Will you let me explain what happened when I was accused of … of rape?' There, he'd said the word that had pursued him ever since that appalling day when he'd realized that if his own father didn't believe him, then no one would.

She put out a hand in protest, as if to push him away. 'Sir, I do not—'
The carriage rocked to a halt outside the doors of Sao Nazaire. Colly
jumped down and paid the driver, then turned to take Juliana's arm.
But she had already stepped down and scuttled across the pavement
towards the big blue doors. The doors shut with a slam that echoed
around the square.

He stood on the doorstep watching the steam rising off the pavement
as the sun came out from behind the clouds.

This was the end. She was not interested in his story, not interested in
him. Even though she was desperate to leave Porto, she would endure a
loathsome job rather than travel with him. And who could blame her?

Heart in his boots, he turned to walk away.

Suddenly the door behind him opened and the fetid hospital odour
assailed his nostrils. Juliana stood there, looking at him from beneath
lowered lashes. One hand clutched the doorjamb so tightly that her
knuckles gleamed white. He could see the trace of a tear on her cheek.
She took a deep breath. 'I'm coming with you,' she said.

CHAPTER SIX

COLLY GULPED. 'I see. Good.' He regrouped as best he could. 'Ah ... as my wife?'

'Yes,' she said tersely. The door shut again.

Colly grinned and grinned and grinned. He had never before experienced the strange sensation of walking on air, but at the moment his feet did not seem to touch the ground. 'Pull yourself together, Hetherington,' he ordered himself. 'This is going to be the hardest thing you've ever done.'

But try as he might to be sensible, he couldn't quite quell the hopeful clamour inside him. He hailed another carriage and returned to the booking office.

He did not tell a straight-out lie. He mumbled just enough information to let the clerk believe that he and Miss Colebrook had married the day before, but that Miss Colebrook had not expected to be able to leave her position at such short notice. However, she had been given permission so ...

In other words, he dissembled. He deserved to be struck dead. Not that he had got through life by telling no white lies at all, but he had just told the biggest one ever.

To his embarrassment the clerk smiled indulgently. 'Congratulations, sir. May I wish you both happy?'

Colly stalked back to the inn feeling like the lowest scum in Porto. But at least he now held two tickets in the names of 'Brigade-Major and Mrs Hetherington.'

Next morning he intercepted Juliana as she rushed towards the hospital.

'I'm late,' she warned him.

He grinned. Association with him was turning Little Miss Neat and Tidy into a less-than-bandbox-perfect young lady. Yesterday she had been damp and dishevelled. This morning she looked rumpled. The poor thing had probably lain awake all night worrying, then slept late this morning. There was little point in reassuring her she had nothing to fear – not from him anyway. All he could do was keep his distance and gradually she would learn he meant her no harm.

Harm! He would give her the world if he could. 'I have the tickets,' he said. 'The *Maximus* has docked and the *Resolution* is hove-to within the harbour mouth. When they have both been provisioned we'll set sail. We must travel in convoy to avoid French privateers.'

An anxious expression crossed her face and he cursed himself for mentioning privateers. She simply wanted to get to England and hadn't given a thought to the dangers of the voyage.

'Have you told Dr Barreiro yet?' he asked.

'Yes. Last evening. I feel bad about it because he and his wife have been very kind to me.'

'So they should. Dr Barreiro will find it very difficult to replace you.' He reflected that finding another such convent-trained nurse who would work amongst filth and death uncomplainingly would be nigh on impossible. 'You are a true heroine, Miss Colebrook. But I dare say many men have told you that,' he finished, off-handedly.

She grinned, her slightly imperfect front teeth clenching on her lip. 'No. Most men either gasp for the laudanum or the ... er ... chamber pot.' Then she sobered. 'That is something I must forget when I reach England. I am sure that nice young ladies *never, ever* mention chamber pots.'

He threw his head back and laughed. 'No, Miss Colebrook. I can't say I've ever heard one mention the humble chamber pot.'

She smiled, then gasped as a bell tinkled in the distance. 'Oh! I must go.' And with a flurry of skirts she rushed out of the sunlight into the dimness of the hospital.

Colly shut the doors behind her.

CHAPTER SEVEN

FOUR DAYS LATER Juliana unpinned her apron for the last time. From habit she placed it in the sluice bucket. Dr Barreiro was unlikely to find a replacement nurse for a while, and in the meantime one of the maids would no doubt snaffle the apron. She was welcome to it and to the spare one already at the laundry.

As she pushed open the front door of Sao Nazaire for the last time, Juliana's hand shook on the doorknob. She had burnt her bridges. She was leaving the place where she had toiled for three years and was throwing in her lot with a man who had been accused of rape. She was so very frightened, but she was glad too; glad to be quitting the death and despair.

She stepped out into the street. The day was drawing in. This would be the last time she would walk these streets alone at night. Everyone living on the northern slopes near the hospital knew the nurse from Sao Nazaire who limped home late at night. She felt safe.

If it had been Lisbon, that would have been very different. For many years Lisbon had been a dirty, unsavoury place with a reputation for crime and corruption. That was why she had chosen to work in Porto. A woman alone needed to protect herself. Then she remembered a time when she had failed to protect herself and quickly thrust it out of her mind.

She stopped to look back at Sao Nazaire for the last time and a tall man crossed the cobblestones to stand beside her. Stepping into his shadow, she paced along beside him.

'Good evening, Miss Colebrook.'

'Good evening, Brigade-Major Hetherington.'

He cleared his throat. 'From now on we must dispense with "Miss Colebrook" and "Brigade-Major Hetherington". In company we had best use "Mr and Mrs Hetherington". My friends call me Colly.'

She nodded. She already knew that, and a lot more besides. In his semi-conscious state he had mumbled about many things. 'Colly is short for Colwyn, is it not?' *Deus*. She hadn't meant to say that.

'Yes. Colwyn is my mother's maiden name.'

She hurried to speak before he realized she had made enquiries about him. 'I am named for my mother and grandmother. I am Juliana Carlotta Ervedosa Colebrook.'

He paused for a moment, then resumed walking.

'Is there something wrong, sir?'

'No.'

Another pause. She could have sworn he was savouring her words.

'Do you have a portmanteau or bandbox you would like me to convey to the ship? I've paid a man to keep an eye on our belongings until we sail.'

'Thank you, sir. You must let me know how much you have remitted on my behalf. I shall repay you before we sail. I am visiting the bank in the morning.' She was conscious that her voice had risen.

He merely nodded in the half-dark.

Thank goodness. Her hackles subsided. He was not going to take advantage of the situation. Just because circumstances forced her to be *temporarily* dependent on him, she did not want him to feel responsible for her. Most men would have taken over. Then again, she had not found him to be like other men. That was why she couldn't help liking him even though it would be most unwise to trust him too far.

Colly was her only chance of making a better life for herself. He might not be perfect, but then, neither was she. Colly didn't know it but she was already ruined.

She glanced at him sideways. He prowled beside her, his long legs eating up the flagstones, his hazel eyes fixed straight ahead. She would always remember this walk – the long, smooth Portuguese dusk with him at her side. As they drew further away from the city centre the air grew cooler and tiny fireflies flicked beneath bushes in the orange-scented gardens. This was her favourite time, the only time she got to smell the fragrant flowers she loved.

Colly murmured, 'You will miss Portugal.'

'Yes. I expect to be very homesick.' She swallowed hard. 'But I know I'm doing the right thing. A woman on her own needs her relatives.'

He frowned and did not respond. Obviously his opinion of families had not changed overnight.

'Will you miss anything in Portugal, sir?' she asked, presuming she would receive a resounding 'No!'

'The bright colours,' he answered at last, 'and, of course, my horse.'

'Your horse?'

'Yes.'

Was he serious?

He was. 'He's a prime piece of horseflesh. Because of the over-crowded ships it's not possible to take him back to England. But I shall miss him. He's quite a character.'

He sounded deeply regretful. She remembered he had once told her that his father's estate housed one of the best studs in the south of England. No doubt he had been tossed on the back of a horse while he was still in leading-strings. She smiled at a mental vision of a miniature Colly Hetherington, all long legs and fierce concentration, astride a pony.

'Here,' she murmured at last. 'This is my street. And that is my house.' She pointed out the iron fretwork gate propped open to reveal a cool inner courtyard. 'Thank you for escorting me.' It would be ungrateful to say it had been unnecessary.

He brushed it aside. 'We sail on the high tide at three. After you have been to the bank, I will carry your packages down to the ship.'

She laughed. 'Sir, I have very few packages. I came to the hospital with nothing, and I shall leave with very little more.'

'But you must have mementoes of your parents and suchlike?'

'My father left everything in his will to his fellow collector in Coimbra. But I have my mother's tortoiseshell hair combs and some rings her parents gave her. That is enough.'

CHAPTER EIGHT

A ND INDEED, ON the following day when they crushed themselves into their tiny cabin on the *Maximus*, he saw that his big portmanteau and greatcoat took up a lot more space than Miss Colebrook's meagre belongings. They shuffled around trying to make room for each other, and eventually managed a compromise. When one person stood, the other sat on the bunk.

As they began to unpack there was a brisk rat-tat on the door and Juliana blushed when Colly squeezed past her, holding his breath. The decision to undergo this purgatory had been his, but he was having grave doubts about his ability to carry out the charade, and the ship had not even left port yet. He opened the cabin door to find the ship's captain standing there, cap under his arm, beaming.

'Good afternoon, sir. We sail in about an hour.' He peered around Colly. 'Mrs Hetherington, glad to have you aboard, ma'am. May I congratulate you both on your recent marriage?'

Colly felt Juliana stiffen. He nodded to acknowledge the captain's wishes and hoped the damned man would be quiet and go away. But no ...

'Lieutenant Harding and his wife are next door to you, Brigade-Major. I believe he is partial to a game of cards.'

Oh, what wondrous luck. A chatty captain and a friendly neighbour. Colly took Captain Petty's proffered hand but did not vouchsafe any personal information.

'Ah, well, I shall see you at dinner,' the captain said, and left.

Colly closed the door and turned to Juliana. 'We had best not become too friendly with Lieutenant Harding and his wife, just in case they come to suspect....'

Juliana's awkward blush receded as she straightened up from folding his greatcoat. To his surprise she tossed the coat carelessly into a corner.

'I understand, Mr Hetherington. The next few weeks will be very hard to bear if you persist in reminding me that our "marriage" is a myth. I am well aware of it. I shall do my best to make sure our charade is not discovered.' She turned aside to place her hatbox on top of her valise. 'Shall I hang a blanket down the centre of the cabin so I don't encroach on your space?'

'What the devil?' Colly demanded. 'You must do as you please, madam. I am going up on deck.' He slammed the door behind him.

Ouch. The gentleman was not amused. Well, neither was she. She was annoyed, not with Colly, but with herself. Because Colly had a light touch on the reins, she had been lulled into playing childish 'if only' games in her head. She knew better than to indulge in such silliness.

Then her delicate stomach roiled in the old, familiar pattern. Whenever her father had announced, 'Well, that's that. Nothing much in the way of artifacts on this site. We shall move on', her stomach had started up a nagging discomfort. During her years at Sao Nazaire she had found the appalling sights and sounds she endured were best coped with on an empty stomach. Even the smallest sip of tea had her stomach burning after particularly gruesome operations. Perhaps in England, supported by her relatives, she would find peace and stability and her rebellious stomach would settle.

But it would not happen today.

Timber creaked. They were under way.

She climbed on deck to watch the coastline of Porto recede. Etched against the blue sky, the tiled roofs splashed their colours like flowers. The little *Resolution* ploughed valiantly along astern of them. A fresh south-westerly blew. By evening, Portugal would be just a smudged blur on the horizon. She might never see Portugal again.

'*Adeus*,' she whispered, straining to see the cupola on the roof of the hospital perched on the distant hill. The jumble of houses and trees on the lower slopes blurred.

She wiped her eyes and went below.

CHAPTER NINE

ALTHOUGH THE FOLLOWING wind abated a little, their journey was brisk. No French vessels were sighted at any stage. True to his promise Colly spent a good deal of the voyage on deck, but intermittent rain squalls followed by several days of rough seas exacerbated the ache in his leg. He was comfortable sitting on an upturned keg playing cards with Lieutenant Davidson and Lieutenant Harding, or lying propped on one elbow swapping apocryphal war stories with the men sleeping on deck. But when he took a turn about the deck with Juliana on his arm, the uneven lurch and sway had him clenching his teeth against the hot claws of pain digging into his thigh.

Juliana watched him as anxiously as a hen with one chick, and when he was no longer able to negotiate the companionway without wincing, she said, 'Enough. Lie down on the bunk. I shall massage your leg.'

Colly closed his eyes. She wanted to *rub his leg*? Good God! He was in enough torment now without that.

But she was determined. 'You must spend more time in the cabin. It is ridiculous that you suffer so, going up and down, up and down.'

Colly gritted his teeth. 'Very well, but I shall massage my own leg.' She was a nurse, for heaven's sake. Surely she understood what would happen if she hovered over him, with her hands on his thigh?

She did. Pink in the face she collected her sewing and shot across to the other side of the cabin. Then she perched on top of his portmanteau trying to look unconcerned. But before she bowed her head he saw the fear on her face. His fists clenched. Didn't she know by now that she could trust him?

When they finally sighted Plymouth off the port bow, Colly was so grateful he damn near jumped overboard and swam ashore. He had spent the last few days in a state of extreme sexual frustration. Miss Juliana Colebrook swanned around the small cabin as if she really were his wife.

A button came off his uniform. She sewed it back on.

33

The old sabre wound on his chest itched and she produced a jar of salve. She did not offer to rub it on to his skin.

He lost several guineas dicing with the men sleeping on deck, and she pursed her mouth up in a wifely way but forbore to lecture him.

She brushed down his uniform unasked, and washed out his shirts.

Each morning the cabin boy brought her a jug of warm water for her ablutions and she dismissed Colly with a sunny smile saying, 'I shall be with you directly.'

Once he had lingered long enough to see her slide the wrapper down over her creamy shoulders, dragging her camisole with it. Delicate hollows beneath her shoulders had gleamed in the warm light filtering through the open porthole. He had bolted down the corridor as if the hounds of hell were after him. And in a way, they were.

For the subterfuge of being Juliana's husband had become an ideal he cherished above all others. He could not imagine a fate closer to his heart. Whether they promenaded around the deck arm-in-arm conversing with the other travellers, or just stood side by side leaning on the ship's rail staring into the inky blue Atlantic swells, he knew this was where he most wanted to be – beside Juliana. He stored up every moment in his mind against the lonely years. Because when they arrived at Trewbridge there would be no more Juliana and Colly.

And the nights! The nights were a peculiar mix of heaven and hell. He slept on the floor, but no amount of discomfort could distract him from sensual dreams of a soft, naked Juliana curling into his body with a pleased murmur. He was restless and throbbing from the moment he laid his head on the makeshift pillow till sun-up. Sometimes only his own surreptitious hand made the nights bearable. He had had to throw a couple of good handkerchiefs overboard. God forbid that Juliana found out what she did to him. Especially considering the charges against him. She would be terrified.

To add to his misery the weather grew hotter and the cabin was like a furnace.

After dinner he usually pretended to write in a diary while Juliana brushed her long, dark hair. Then he would leave the cabin so she could do whatever it was women took forever to do. When he returned he would find her lying in bed facing the wall.

He had fashioned a roll of bedding that he wedged on the edge of the bunk.

'What is that for?' Juliana had asked.

He had felt his face flush and hoped desperately that she didn't notice. 'It is in case the boat hits rough seas. I do not want you to be cast out of bed.' *And on top of me*, he thought. That bedding repre-sented the gulf between them, and reminded him not to attempt to cross that gulf.

Fortunately she kept the bedsheet drawn up to her neck. Even when she tossed in her sleep, and she did a lot of that – sharing a cabin with a rapist was hardly conducive to a sound night's sleep – somehow she managed to keep the sheet anchored.

Until the last evening before they docked at Portsmouth.

Humidity hung like a pall on the air. The passengers milled around on deck in the purple dusk saying their farewells. The ship already sailed in the lee of the land and was expected to dock at dawn next morning. When they went down to their cabin, Colly opened the port-hole as wide as it would go. Then he left Juliana to get ready for bed.

When he returned he found her sitting up in the bunk, fanning herself. Fine beads of sweat dotted her face and neck and she wore only a shift.

Colly swallowed hard, his Adam's apple bobbing about like corn in a hot frying pan.

'It is dreadfully hot,' she complained. 'Almost as bad as Portugal in summer.'

'Yes.' Sweat trickled down his spine and collected in the small of his back. 'But there is only one night left.' His unspoken 'thank goodness' resonated in the air between them.

'Will you mind, Col— er, Brigade-Major, if I do not wear the sheet tonight?' she asked. Her eyes begged him to make this easy for her.

Swallowing, he managed, 'No, of course not.' What else could he say?

'Thank goodness,' she muttered, and to his consternation she pulled aside the sheet and dropped it on the floor. Then she rolled over and lay on her stomach, all in one swift movement.

Oh, God. The glimpse of her dusky nipples beneath the shift had been bad enough. But the way she lay now, all sprawled out ... like a feast for his delectation.

Rubbish, he told himself. *Lust is overriding your common sense, you bloody fool.*

He rolled up the spare blanket as usual and placed it carefully along the edge of the bunk. Trying to keep his eyes averted from the smooth, neatly rounded little hillocks perilously close to his hands, he felt around until he had the barrier erected to his satisfaction. But the barrier wasn't the only thing erected by the time he'd finished.

No. This was no good. It was agony. But a 'newly married man' could not sleep up on deck. Already Davidson had commented on Colly's predilection for the company of men rather than his lovely wife.

But it was the last night, thank God. He could last one more night, couldn't he? In the half-dark he pulled off his boots and stripped down to his shirt. He reached for the folded blanket that would be his pillow – and stopped still, not daring to breathe. His fingers had encountered a warm, silky surface. Oh Lord! He leaped back and bashed his elbow against the bulkhead.

'S-sorry,' he muttered.

To his horror she *sat up*, although she had the good sense to hold her hands in front of her breasts this time. 'What are you doing?'

'Just getting the blanket. Using it for a pillow.' He seemed to be talking in abbreviated sentences, but he was afraid that if he spoke normally, his voracious desire and discomfort would leach into the words and she would *know*.

CHAPTER TEN

In the gleam of phosphorescence off the sea she saw him standing there – tall, loose-knit and *very* desirable. She had seen many naked men during the past three years, but none except this man had ever affected her. After that dreadful night when she'd been attacked, a man's body had simply become something she nursed back to health. She had nothing to fear from the incapacitated men she nursed and she had worked hard to subdue her aversion to a man's touch. As for the other sort of men, the healthy ones, she kept well away from them.

But for some reason Brigade-Major Hetherington's well-honed body nudged to life a desire she had never, in her wildest dreams, thought to feel. Perhaps she was perverse as her father used to say, in desiring the attentions of a rapist.

A wash of warmth flooded her skin, chasing away the threatening tendrils of fear. Colly was … just Colly. He was not a drunken, sadistic Frenchman bent on carnal violence. For days she had yearned for what she could not have. She had dreamed of smoothing her hands over that toughened, whipcord strength, of curving her hand around the back of his neck and tugging his face down to hers. What would it be like, pressed up against the ripple of muscle flexing beneath the shirt and breeches?

They had no future together, but one night was possible.

She had taken many risks in her life and this would be the biggest one of all. Sitting in the darkness, her hands clutching the sheet, she was overwhelmed by what she was about to do. And she *was* going to do it. Never again would she have such an opportunity.

He stood in front of her now, hers for the taking – because she saw what he didn't want her to see. Mr Hetherington's ardent erection was very impressive. Unfortunately her convent education had not prepared her for this. How did she even begin to seduce the only man in the world who made her soft and wanton?

She was a twenty-three-year-old spinster. Not quite on the shelf, but close, very close because she hadn't known one single man who had not failed her in some way or other.

Her grandfather, whom she loved, had died and left her alone in the world. Not his fault of course, but the years with her grandparents had been the happiest in her life and their deaths had overturned her safe little world.

Then her uncle had handed her over to Papa without a qualm and he and his family had gone to Brazil.

And when Papa had died leaving her nothing at all, his friend could not wait to get rid of her. For a year she had run his household, yet on her father's death he had treated her like a distasteful obligation.

Worst of all had been that dreadful night outside Porto – that night she refused to remember.

No, she would be a fool to cast her future into a man's lap.

But Colly was different somehow. She *wanted* to give herself to Colly. He'd made it very plain that he considered himself unmarriageable. Fine. So was she.

But if she could even halfway believe in a man, that man would be Colly – Colly, with his self-deprecating grin and his thoughtful ways that hid a proud stubbornness to equal hers.

She was amused and exasperated that he designated her 'a young lady' and insisted on going to extremes to keep her at arm's length. But recently there had been a glimmer of hope. Several times she had caught him staring at her hungrily, as if he were contemplating a tasty snack, or rather, an eight-course meal. She'd been unable to resist teasing him a little. Her evening hair-brushing took longer each night. Sometimes when he stepped aside from the doorway to allow her to precede him, she 'inadvertently' brushed against him. And even though she still felt that nasty little frisson of fear, she spent hours afterwards savouring the smell and feel of him. Which showed she was not the young lady he thought she was.

So ... what was she waiting for? Even if he thought her over-bold or, worse still, a trollop, she would risk everything on this throw of the dice. If she lost, nobody would ever know. Colly was so screamingly honourable that he would die rather than divulge what had happened to anyone.

Lord, she had never imagined seduction would require so much courage. Heart pumping she attempted what she hoped was a come-hither look. 'Don't be silly. There's no need to sleep on the floor tonight. I shan't bite. Sleep on the bunk.'

'Bite.' She wished she hadn't said that. Colly had flicked her such a hot glance she felt scorched from head to toe.

'Miss Colebrook, I'm not – I mean … I have just one more night left to play the gentleman. I cannot do it when you look like this,' he said helplessly. He indicated her shift.

There was a short silence.

The man was determined to save her from himself. Well, she didn't want to be saved. Just this once, she wanted to sin.

She felt a scalding blush spread over her face and neck as she begged, 'Please.'

Just one word, whispered brokenly, and she saw Colly unravel.

CHAPTER ELEVEN

JULIANA FROZE, STARTLED by his fervour. For many days she had imagined soft, seductive words. Instead she got a hard-edged lover, straining at the leash. Her heart stuttered with anxiety as he crushed her close and lavished hungry kisses on her neck. Then he settled on feeding at her mouth in a frenzy of greedy taking. She had been kissed just once in her life, and that had been by a gentle, soft-skinned Portuguese youth, who was then overcome by his own boldness. He had begged her pardon profusely. She had felt no emotion apart from surprise.

That one experience had not prepared her for such an assault on her senses as Colly's kisses. His kisses *demanded* a response. Her soft mouth capitulated under the onslaught and her skin began to sting where his beard rasped. When he cradled her flush against his hard body, she felt the telltale tremor in his muscles as he struggled to hold on to the shreds of control. He could not have made it plainer had he shouted it from the rooftops. He wanted her *now*.

Even as fear edged its way inside her, the tenor of his lovemaking changed. He planted soft butterfly kisses across one cheek and continued down over her neck … down … down. It felt so-o-o good.

Her fingers uncurled and her legs relaxed. Her skin shimmered with impatience, wanting more, demanding more. A wanton sigh escaped her as he lowered her onto the bunk. When he followed the trail of his lips with his callused fingers … oh! She wanted to do this forever. She murmured her appreciation and felt herself melting, sinking deep into the palliasse.

Carefully Colly eased down on top of her, measuring his length along hers. Mmm, how her body relished the strength and hardness of his! She felt a bulge pressing against her thigh and for an instant the memory of another man flashed through her brain. Then it was gone as Colly murmured 'Juliana' on an exhale. Something inside her tingled and throbbed in response.

She smoothed her hands across the taut width of Colly's back and stroked the rigid muscles on his upper arms. How different his skin felt from hers! Her fingers brushed over a puckered cicatrice on his back and probed a small dent in his arm. He had gathered more scars and wounds since she had attended to him after the Battle of the Douro. As his hand cupped her breast she absorbed his trembling inhalation that echoed through her, from her brain to her ecstatically curling toes.

Then it was over.

He was gone.

She was alone on the bunk, one arm reaching out for him.

He had wrenched himself away and sat, head bowed, on the end of the bunk.

'Sorry. So sorry, Juliana. Now you'll think that damned story is true,' he muttered despairingly.

And she knew right then and there that he would never coerce any woman. Heavens, why would he need to? Any woman would say, 'Yes please, Colly. More.' He had not harmed a hair on that woman's conniving little head.

He angled his body away from her to hide his face and muttered, 'I've never been so … it's just that you're—' He waved his hand vaguely. 'I can't seem to stop thinking about you, damn it.' His voice overflowed with despair and everything within her contracted.

'These last two weeks, having you here like this – it's been misery and heaven. I don't know where I am or what I'm doing.'

Her heart sank. Those silly, ignoble games she had played to tease him – how could she have been so cruel?

He rubbed his scalp tiredly. 'Mustn't do this. I am no good to any woman.'

Greatly daring, she wriggled forward and stretched her arms around his waist. Absentmindedly he grasped her hands and rubbed them against his chest. She smiled into the back of his neck.

'Colly, are you planning on remaining celibate for the rest of your life?'

In spite of everything, he snorted with amusement.

'Or is it only women like me?'

He flinched. 'It is only *ladies* I must stay away from. They expect marriage, and rightly so. You know I cannot offer that. Even if that old charge were not held against me, my prospects are not rosy. I do not have a home of my own to offer a lady.'

'Rubbish. Your prospects sound excellent to me.' She stroked the long wound knifing down from his shoulder to his stomach. The muscles flexed as her palm smoothed downwards, downwards …

He jerked upright and grabbed her hand.

But she hadn't finished fighting, not by a long shot. She would not be lucky enough to have him, but another woman might. He *deserved* to have the love of a loyal woman.

'Colly,' she argued, 'you have a job for life in elegant circumstances. What else could you wish for?'

'A home of my own,' he murmured quietly. 'My brother is fortunate. He will inherit Heather Hill.'

'Is that your family home?'

'Yes.'

It was the quiet, despairing tone in his voice that warned her to tread carefully.

'Where is it?'

She hoped he would tell her more, because she was greedy to know every little detail about him. On lonely nights when they were far apart she would be able to gloat over her little hoard of knowledge. She would take out her dreams and savour them, count them, remember them.

'It is not far from Bath. It is a manor house with several farms and a horse stud. The barony is a very old one.' He got up from the bunk, removing his tender anatomy from her inquisitive fingers.

Conceding defeat, Juliana fingered back her hair and smoothed down her crumpled shift. The clammy heat grabbed it and sucked it against her skin. There was no sense in making this more difficult for both of them, so she reached behind her and grabbed the pillow. Holding it against her stomach she told him, 'Like you, Papa was a younger son with no prospects. But you have made something of yourself whilst my father ...' She trailed off and explained, 'If he wanted to insinuate himself into some of the digs, he would offer to lecture at the Universities of Cairo and Coimbra. When they paid him in books or research materials Mãe and I were not happy.' She grimaced. 'If our financial situation became untenable he would press Mãe to apply to her parents for funds. My grandparents were comfortably off, you see. Poor Mãe hated doing that, but the Ervedosas were always generous. They were pleased that their daughter had married a man of letters.'

Colly vouchsafed no comment about her revelations but simply looked at her for a moment, his hazel eyes serious. Then he smiled ruefully and stepped away from the bunk. 'Well, Miss Colebrook. We seem to be back where we started. We had best ... that is, good night.'

He bowed ironically in her direction then lay down on the cabin floor, shoving the folded blanket beneath his head. His long body stretched right to the door. He folded his arms beneath his head and closed his eyes, feigning relaxation. The shaggy, dark brown hair fell back from the shuttered face.

Juliana smiled ruefully and lay back on the bed, stifling a sigh. He had not so much rebuffed her as gently set her aside, but it hurt – oh, how it hurt. They certainly were 'back to where they had started.' And she had lost her gamble.

She lay still, listening to the creaking timbers and the wash of the sea against the hull of the ship. If Colly had not raped that girl, who had? In fact – and here was an interesting thought – had she been raped at all? She wondered if the Colebrooks' house at Melksham was far from Bath. Then she told herself sharply to mind her own business. How many times did a man have to say 'no' before she accepted it?

She nibbled on a fingernail. Oh, he admired her, he desired her. He had admitted it. But he had no intention of doing anything about it. She had already twisted his arm to make him bring her to England. Now she was trying to seduce the poor man. What *did* she think she was doing? Three years ago Juliana Carlotta Ervedosa Colebrook would never have done such a thing. But three years ago she had not yet discovered that a woman alone in the world was a defenceless creature. She had had to learn to stand up for herself when she discovered the full measure of her father's perfidy.

She had always known her father cared not one jot for her. She'd had years of 'If only I'd had a son, Juliana. He would have been my partner in my search for antiquities. Alas, your mother bore only you.' And he would shake his head at the unfairness of life.

In spite of that, she had presumed he would provide for her in some way. Juliana imagined he would leave her a few of his less valuable figurines so she could sell them to a collector, or to one of the universities or museums. That way she would have had an income while she sought a position in Portugal or England. But he had left her nothing at all.

On the day she left Coimbra she vowed that never again would she expect anything from anyone. So, although she longed to be reunited with her family, she was prepared to support herself.

And she would never give her heart to any man the way her poor mother had given hers to Philip Colebrook – generously, extravagantly.

She rolled over onto her stomach, remembering that dreadful trip between Coimbra and Porto. When the sisters at the convent advised her of the desperate need for assistants in the Porto hospitals, she had packed her bags immediately. She'd had no desire to impose on her father's friend one minute longer than necessary. Accompanied by a frightened maid and two decrepit donkeys she had set out for Porto. They had kept to byways, fearful of soldiers on the main highways. It was wartime, and two women on their own were easy targets for marauding males bent on destruction or celebration.

On the wooded slopes outside Porto the maid had deserted her to flee home to Coimbra, which, in a way, had been a blessing. Otherwise the maid, too, would have become a fallen woman like herself. On her own she had been able to keep secret what had happened – the dreadful thing she had done on the wooded slopes outside Porto.

But now they had reached the shores of England. Tomorrow morning she would set foot on England's soil for the first time in eighteen years. She must bury the past. And she must try to behave like a well-bred Englishwoman. She would learn. Dr Barreiro had often praised her ability to assimilate new ideas.

CHAPTER TWELVE

'MISS COLEBROOK, TIME to wake up,' Colly whispered as he stroked her shoulder. It was a shame to wake her. After his appalling behaviour the night before they had both lain awake for hours. She had tried to lie still, but he had heard her unsteady breathing and the occasional rustle of the sheet.

He smiled at the relaxed, tempting body outlined through the transparent shift. The independent Miss Colebrook would hate to know how vulnerable she looked. She might not have the currently popular lush curves, but every single inch of her was delicious.

He frowned as she struggled up from the bunk. She was much thinner than when he had first met her. At first he had presumed her slenderness was caused by the strenuous work she did in the hospital, but during the voyage he noticed that she ate very little. And, after she had eaten, sometimes she sat very still, breathing deeply.

When he left the cabin to give her privacy for her ablutions, he was still in a brown study. Was she ill? Was that why she wanted so desperately to be with her relatives? He chewed his lip. How did he go about finding out if her illness was serious? He had no rights where she was concerned because once they left Portsmouth their marriage charade would be over. They would travel to Trewbridge together but would no longer be 'Mr and Mrs Hetherington.'

He must ensure that Lieutenants Davidson and Harding were not standing close by when he handed his and Juliana's travel documents to the Customs officials. Davidson had already made one or two airy comments about 'How quickly some people get married these days'. Colly was sure the man did not believe they were married. Then again, perhaps his guilt was causing him to be unnecessarily sensitive. The fact that he had saved Davidson's bacon at Douro when Davidson had been too pig-headed to listen to his sergeant should keep the young man's mouth shut. And, of course, Juliana had nursed Davidson at Sao Nazaire. Colly hoped that the lieutenant's sense of obligation would persuade him to keep his suspicions to himself. Anyway, once they left Portsmouth they were unlikely to meet up with their fellow travellers again. Colly had checked the manifest and discovered that Davidson had listed an address near Keynsham, care of his aunt and uncle. It was a long way from Trewbridge but it *was* quite close to Heather Hill. That didn't matter. Colly had no intention of returning to Heather Hill ever again.

They passed through Customs without mishap, and Colly paid a soldier to help him with their baggage as far as the Saracen's Head. Some of the soldiers planned to stay at the Mariners' Rest or one of the cheap inns in the back streets, but most were already making bookings on the stage or hiring horses to escape Portsmouth as soon as possible. Some were desperate to get home, provided they were lucky enough to have a home. Those who did not would head for the thrills of London. When they had run through their pay, they would sign up for another eight years with the army, or sit begging in the streets, displaying their injuries.

'Thank you, Lord, for granting me a decent future,' Colly muttered underneath his breath, as he lugged their belongings into their suite of rooms.

'When do you wish to proceed west, sir?' Juliana asked as they unpacked.

'There are no decent carriages to be had at the moment. Mine host informs me that Portsmouth has been cleaned out of all available transport. But that gives us time to write letters so our people know we are in England.'

He had been eager to start a new life, but now the time was drawing near to their separation, his eagerness had dissipated. He had had Juliana all to himself for two weeks and, in spite of spending most of that fortnight balanced on a knife-edge of sexual frustration, he would give much to have it all over again.

He had had time to study the tilt of her head when she was considering something. Time to watch the chocolate eyes light up with amusement when the captain paid her fulsome compliments. Time to enjoy the rise and fall of her breasts as she brushed her beautiful sable hair each evening. Time to admire her expertise at deflecting Mrs Harding's curiosity about their marriage.

Most of all he had had time simply to enjoy being with her.

And last night, lying awake for hours, he'd had time to speculate if Miss Colebrook had, by any chance, tried to seduce him. Had he wilfully interpreted her whispered 'please' to be an invitation? If so, an invitation to what?

She was innocent, no doubt about it. Her initial startled reaction and her untutored response to his kisses had evoked a protective gentleness he had never felt before. All his previous sexual encounters had been with women who knew how to please a man. It was safer that way. Those women did not expect promises.

But Juliana kept her soft lips closed and her hands tended to wander restlessly. She did not comprehend what sort of invitation she was initiating when those hands roamed.

He grimaced to himself as his groin tightened.

Thank God some remaining shred of decency had pulled him back in time.

He allowed himself a small smile. For once the gods had ceased to thwart his every pleasure. Portsmouth had no transport for them, so he had been granted a little more time with her. The Saracen's Head had given them three adjoining rooms, all perfectly respectable, but they had seen Lieutenant Davidson in the taproom and realized that he, too, was staying here. They had little choice therefore but to continue their charade.

'It might be a good idea to hire a maid,' Colly commented. 'When you meet your relatives it will lend respectability.'

Sipping the coffee he had ordered for her, she pulled a face. 'Is this how the English drink their coffee?' she asked disgustedly.

He laughed. He could afford to. In his hand he held a tankard of English ale. He had longed for this since he'd last set foot on England's soil after the Corunna débâcle, two long, dusty years ago.

'I think, my dear, that you will be obliged to sip glasses of revolting ratafia in the future. And let me assure you that ratafia is worse than our English version of coffee.' He stretched out his long legs in front of him, relaxing in front of the open window. 'God, it's good to be home.' Resting his head on the windowsill he inhaled. 'Fish, seawater, rubbish, hot bread baking, carriages rumbling past....'

She wrinkled her nose. 'Very similar to Portugal. Especially the fish and the rubbish.'

He grinned with unabated good humour. Nothing could burst his bubble today. Later he must face a difficult hurdle. He must apprise his employers of his past. He was sure that John already suspected the circumstances behind Colly's 'choice' to join the army. Fortunately, during his stay at Trewbridge after Corunna, Colly had cemented a strong friendship with the family. Hopefully they would not be as ready as his father to believe ill of him.

He still had all his selling-out money. If the Trewbridges failed him, somehow he would find a way to make a living. He was a very different person from the stunned, unhappy youth who had left England five years ago.

His first responsibility was to repay his redoubtable grandmother – or rather, to try to. He very much looked forward to seeing her again. 'I doubt the army is the best life for you, Colly,' she had said, as she handed him a bank draft to purchase his commission. 'But you need time to stand back and assess what you will do with your life. And you need to do it far away from here. Pray God you don't lose your life while you are finding yourself.'

His grandmother had been right. Killing had not suited him, nor had the vagrant life. Most of all he had found it impossible to bury the mind-pictures of friends he had once laughed and joked with whose lives had been snuffed out like cheap candles. He had mourned over the mangled bodies of so many of his fellows that in the end he had avoided close friendships. Now, at last, he could put down roots and make friends, secure in the knowledge that on the morrow their bodies would not be piled up on top of each other, walling up a breach on the edge of a battlefield far from England.

Lord, the relief at shaking off the shackles of the army!

For many men it was an ideal occupation. But he had never thought that aiming a musket at a man in a different coloured uniform who might well be your cousin, or your neighbour's cousin, was anything less than senseless. Thanks to Juliana and Dr Barreiro he had survived. And done well. He'd been promoted. *So*, he thought, *Father dear, you know what you can do.*

Juliana's voice broke into his musing. Of course he thought of her as Juliana now. How could he do anything else? He had lain beside her and kissed her. He had run his fingers through that dark-as-night hair and had even, for one glorious second, cupped her soft creamy breast in his hand. And he had relished her unmistakable response. It was ridiculous to think of her as Miss Colebrook.

'You are right,' Juliana commented. 'It would be a good idea to hire a maid.'

'I shall ask the proprietor where the receiving office or employment agency is,' Colly promised. 'He'll know.'

The proprietor was most helpful and, though Colly escorted her to the agency, he knew better than to offer to assist. She had seen and done more than any other young woman of his acquaintance. She would quickly adjust to the English way of doing things.

Indeed, barely a half-hour later she joined him at the bootmakers,

where he was contemplating a fine piece of black leather. He was negotiating with the bootmaker to fashion him a neat plain pair of boots.

'No. No ornaments. No tassels,' he said, as Juliana approached.

For some reason she smiled.

'You are finished already?' he enquired in surprise.

'Yes. Mrs Tudbroke is sending two young women to meet me at the
Saracen's Head. One will arrive later today and the other will come
early tomorrow morning.'

He thanked the bootmaker and they retraced their steps to the inn.

He glanced at her. There was a crease between her eyebrows. 'You
seem worried,' he commented. He didn't want her worried, blast it.

There was a short silence as she adjusted her broken pink parasol so
that it shaded her face more.

'It is nothing,' she dismissed. 'I did not expect such high wages, you
see. I had to ask Mrs Tudbroke to send me very young candidates. I
cannot afford the wages of a more experienced maid who would set my
stock up higher with my relatives. A lady's maid in England is paid the
same as a housekeeper in Portugal. However,' she sighed, 'an inexperi-
enced maid is better than no maid at all.'

Damn her feckless father, Colly thought. She should not have to
worry about such things. 'I think it is,' he agreed. 'Let us hope one of the
young women will suit. Your relatives will simply assume she has been
with you all the time.' He paused. 'By the way, I wish you to be easy
about the cost of staying at the Saracen's Head: I shall take care of that.'

When she began to argue he made a slicing movement through the
air with one hand. It was a device he had found worked very well with
subalterns who wished to discuss an order at length, rather than simply
get on with it. 'No,' he said firmly. 'I made the decision to stay here, so
I shall bear the cost. That is all there is to it.'

But he saw the firming of her lips and knew that would not be all. *So
independent*. However, from what he knew of her background, her
independence was understandable.

Then he noticed she was peering around his shoulder at someone
behind them.

'Who is that man, sir?' she asked. 'I saw him watching us when we
arrived at the Saracen's Head. Do you know him?'

Colly turned, but the man had disappeared around a corner. 'What
does he look like?'

'Um … medium height, shabbily dressed. Tanned skin. Possibly a
foreigner. I'm sure I've seen him before.'

Colly smothered a smile. She was already identifying with her

English side. He shook his head. 'I don't remember seeing anyone like that.'

He took her gloved hand and placed it on his arm. They strolled back to the Saracen's Head like any other married couple. Which was just as well, because they met Lieutenant Davidson weaving drunkenly over the uneven cobblestones outside the inn.

He bowed low to Juliana and sketched a careless salute in Colly's general direction. 'Ah, the happy married couple!' Lieutenant Davidson was in his cups. 'What it is to be married, and yet not married. The best of both worlds, eh, Brigade-Major?' He emphasized his comment with a jab at Colly's chest.

Juliana's face blanched.

Colly smiled at her reassuringly and stepped towards the lieutenant, now waving backwards and forwards like a straw in the breeze. 'You seem to be the worse for wear, Lieutenant Davidson. Might I assist you?' As he spoke, Colly got a firm arm-lock on the man.

Davidson stared blearily into his face. 'I'm looking for the Saracen's Head. It's my home away from home, y'know. M'aunt and uncle are sending their carriage, but it won't get here for a couple of days.' He belched with enthusiasm. 'For two whole days I can be free of their whining and man-manipulations. Until then, drink up.' He waved an imaginary tankard in the air.

Colly grinned. 'As a matter of fact you are directly outside the Saracen's Head, Lieutenant. Allow me to help you to your room. I think you need to lie down.'

'Lie down? Lie down? What do I want to lie down for?' Davidson asked indignantly.

'Good Lord,' Colly said, quirking his eyebrows at Juliana. 'He's in prime order. I'll take him to his bedchamber.' He shoved Davidson through the big oak doors and propelled him upstairs by keeping his knuckle fisted in the small of the lieutenant's back.

'All right, all right,' Davidson protested. 'You're like my bloody aunt. Always pushing. Why can't people take life peaceably?' Here, their progress was hampered by Davidson's injured leg, which stuck out stiffly to one side. Colly sighed and persevered.

Ten minutes later, after a nasty interlude involving Davidson casting up his accounts all over his boots and then descending into maudlin self-recriminations, Colly returned to their suite of rooms to find Juliana pacing to and fro.

'What happened?' she demanded, the instant he opened the door.

He struggled out of his greatcoat and checked it for stains before throwing it on a settle. Then he glanced down at his boots. 'He was sick. Everywhere.'

She wrinkled her nose. 'He must be very drunk.'

'Yes. Using up the last of his freedom, I suspect. He seems to have an aunt and uncle who he is reluctant to return home to.'

'Never mind that.' She prowled between the settle and the window like a restless cat. 'What did he say about us?'

'Nothing. He's not capable of stringing two thoughts together.'

She sat down on the settle. 'Thank goodness.'

'Yes. But I must ensure his continuing silence. He's not a bad youth, so I'll appeal to his sense of obligation.'

'Obligation?'

'Well, he owes us both a considerable debt. Me for saving him from the French, and you for nursing him back to health.'

'Oh ... that.'

Obviously saving lives was a minor hiccup in Miss Colebrook's life. She seemed to regard their actions as natural, and under the circumstances, of course they were. But he couldn't envisage any delicately bred Englishwoman taking those things in her stride. God, she was magnificent.

He averted his eyes from Juliana's face lest she detected his ridiculous besottedness. He smoothed down his jacket sleeves, then checked his boots once more.

She sniffed. 'I smell nothing out of the ordinary.'

He grinned. 'Thank goodness. My new boots won't be ready until tomorrow.'

She returned his smile, then hers faded. 'I shall have to interview my applicant soon,' she apologized. 'I am unsure how to explain your presence, however. Are we to be married, or related in some way?'

For a moment he had forgotten. A cold bucketful of water could not have been more punishing. 'Uh ... could I be a friend of your family's?'

She looked doubtful. 'It is still not quite the thing for us to travel together, is it?'

'You are quite right.' He grabbed his coat again. 'I have been too long out of England. I shall go to the stables and admire the horses.'

Juliana smiled. 'I would feel guilty if I didn't know how much you enjoy hobnobbing with grooms and horses. Just the same, it is unkind to make you leave, but I don't know what else to do.'

Colly could see she was unnerved by Davidson's insinuations. Up till now it had been an adventure for both of them. It wasn't that they had ignored the possible ramifications of their behaviour, but they had been far away from England and it hadn't mattered so much. But now ...

He took her hands in his. 'Juliana, do not fret. We shall get through this. I will take care of everything. I am happy to do so.'

Her hands were not soft. They felt work-worn with rough patches here and there. He glanced down. These were not the hands of a gently bred lady. They were honest hands. They had done much work. He traced an upraised scar on her thumb with his own.

He would buy her a present or two – some rosewater and glycerine for her hands and a new parasol. If anyone deserved gifts it was the work-worn young woman he had come to love.

He exhaled sharply. Yes. He could admit it to himself. What did it matter since he'd be the only one to know? He was in for a heap of heartache, but trying to stop himself from falling in love with Juliana Colebrook was as useless as King Canute trying to hold back the tide.

He stood, gazing down into her face. How could he not love her? The memory of her earnest, tender care during his recovery still lingered. Once, as his company had marched through the arid country-side in Spain, he had smelled the fragrance of lemon grass trampled underfoot. Vividly he had been reminded of the citrus tang that wafted from her hospital clothes as she bustled past. And he'd felt homesick, a yearning for home and hearth and a woman with Juliana's face waiting for him.

On nights of small moons he had often stared up at the sky, savouring the memory of those evening visits when they had discussed all manner of things – her cousins, his little sister Felicia, everything except the war. Each day he had waited for evening to come so he might bask in the muted feminine cadences of her voice.

And oh *how* he had relished these past two weeks, listening to the intriguing accent and watching that imperfect little smile, the alabaster skin and the chocolate eyes.

Yes, he loved her all right. And he would do nothing to harm her, such as proposing marriage to her. She did not seem as averse to him as he would have expected, but he would not have her share his shame.

Suddenly he realized he had been holding her hands for far too long and hastily released them. He coughed to hide his embarrassment. 'Um … on my return I will listen at the door before I come in.' He bowed and left – before he said anything he shouldn't.

CHAPTER THIRTEEN

Tonight was their last evening together. Tomorrow they would travel to Trewbridge and then the carriage would take Juliana on to Melksham. They sat in the long summer twilight, watching the comings and goings of people outside the Saracen's Head.

Juliana leaned forward in her chair and Colly followed her gaze. A swarthy well-built fellow melded into the crowd of people on the pavement and Juliana sat back again.

'Did you talk to Lieutenant Davidson?' she asked.

'Yes. I think I managed to convince him that his suspicions were unfounded. I reminded him of the debt he owes us.'

Juliana pulled a face. 'He was a terrible patient.'

Colly laughed. 'That does not surprise me.'

Juliana laughed too and his heart turned over. She looked different. Happy. During the past few days she had blossomed. Her lovely skin had regained its soft bloom and the long, long hair he yearned to drape over his body was shining with health. He would like to think it was because he had taken away her responsibilities for a short while. It was more likely that she was happy to be in England and near to her relatives at long last.

'I wonder what tomorrow will bring,' he murmured.

'Will you visit your parents before you begin work?' Juliana asked.

'No.' He shifted in his chair, hoping she wouldn't question him further.

'Will you tell me what happened?' she asked timidly. 'I – I'd really like to know.'

Ah, hell. In Porto he'd burned to tell her the truth so she could see he was not as black as he was painted, and that she would be safe travelling with him. But now ... what did it matter?

Revealing his past to the Trewbridge family and telling the woman he loved his mean, pathetic tale were two different matters. Especially since he'd already demonstrated his appalling lack of self-control to

Juliana only three nights ago. Fortunately she seemed to bear him no ill-will. But he hated to have her know how stupid he'd been over Amelia Blevin, how very naïve. Lord, he'd been so *young*.

'Tell me,' she coaxed.

He shrugged as if it were of no import and tried not to slouch down in his chair.

'Amelia and her father came one day to speak to my father. After a few minutes my father called me into his study. I thought it was to haul me over the coals about some imagined problem with the stud farm as usual.' Colly pursed up his mouth. 'It was a never-ending battle between us. My brother managed the home farms; I managed the stud. But Father interfered so much it was difficult for either of us to get anything done.' He gazed off into the distance, long-submerged frustration roiling in his blood.

'Fathers!' Juliana said.

He grimaced. 'Well, yours and mine, anyway. John's is a good man.'

With a bit of luck she'd forget about his story and become side-tracked.

But no. 'What did your father say?'

'He yelled at me that I must marry Amelia at once. I didn't know what the devil he was talking about. So Sir Archie, all red and angry, explained that Amelia admitted I was the father of her unborn child. I was flabbergasted. I mean, we'd all been friends forever. But ...' His voice died away. He tried to bury that awful niggling guilt which had whispered to him sometimes: *You knew Amelia Blevin's reputation. Don't deny it. Didn't you think once or twice of joining the queue to try your luck?*

'Do you think her father believed her?' Juliana asked.

'I don't know,' Colly said slowly. 'Things were in such a tumult that I never got a chance to find out anything.'

'Was she a truthful girl?' Juliana asked, wrinkling her brow.

Colly couldn't help grinning. Truthful and sedate Amelia was not. 'Definitely not. She was a handful. I don't think her parents knew what to do with her.'

'Well, I know it's not my business, but it sounds odd to me. You are friends forever, and yet suddenly one day you take it into your head to – no. It sounds as though this Sir Archie grabbed an opportunity to marry her off, but you didn't fall in with their scheme.' She shook her head.

Colly slowly exhaled. That was similar to what his grandmother had said. Why hadn't he challenged Amelia and her father? And his own father, come to think of it. Tripped up by his stupid pride, had he lost the opportunity to find out the truth?

'Perhaps she had a lover she covered up for,' Juliana said cynically.

'Uh … I don't know. I was thrown out of the house and had no time to talk to anyone, not even to say goodbye. I felt utterly betrayed. At the time I did not care *why* she had said those things.'

No. On that awful day he'd been so shattered he couldn't think clearly. Later, he'd begun to wonder what was behind the whole fracas, and by then it had been too late. He was an idiot not to have protested at the time, but truly, he could not have defied his father in front of Sir Archie Blevin. Even though there was something unusual in his father's tone – something he should have investigated – at the time he'd been rocked to the depths of his soul when he'd realized that if his own father didn't believe him, then nobody else would either. So he'd left as he had been ordered to do, and had never returned.

'My father forbade them all to talk to me. My little sister tried. She slipped into my room that day and gave me a locket to remember her by. I lost it when I was injured at Douro,' he explained. 'That was why I was making such a fuss when we met. I wanted to go back and look for it.'

Juliana nodded. 'I remember. You kept saying, "Who took it?" I thought you were delirious.'

He smiled sadly. 'I hope one day I'll see Felicia again.' Then he grinned. 'But my father could not silence my grandmother. She's an indomitable old lady and she has no need of family money. She purchased my commission for me and I was sent to Ireland for training. At first she wrote to me, but I haven't heard from her for many months. I hope my father did not prevail after all.' He sobered. 'Or else she … might have died.' Please God, no.

Juliana eyed him for a moment then offered, 'It's possible that this Amelia was in a corner and used you to get out of it. You felt so betrayed by this Miss – what was it again?'

'Blevin.'

'… Blevin and your father that you decided to show them you could live without them. You joined the army and eschewed all female company.'

'Not all,' Colly put in, grinning in spite of himself.

'Well, all so-called *respectable* women then,' Juliana replied, her lips quirking.

Colly had no doubt that she'd nursed the 'not-so-respectable' types.

It was a relief to be able to talk to a woman who did not take things wrongly, but he would have to watch his step in future.

Then she voiced his main concern. 'Sir, what will you tell your employers?'

Colly sobered. 'Everything. But they can't have heard any adverse rumours about me, or they wouldn't have offered me the stewardship. You've met my future employer. John came to visit me in hospital. He speaks several languages and was one of Wellington's exploring officers.'

She thought for a moment. 'I cannot remember him. I met so many men every week ...' She shrugged.

'Sounds like a debutante's dream,' he commented.

'What does?'

'The fact that you met so many men each week.'

She smiled, then grimaced. 'I doubt that an English debutante would be interested in the unhappy men I nursed. And that is one thing that worries me.'

He raised his eyebrows in a question.

'What will my relatives think of me? Through having to work for my living I have become very independent. I am probably not what they expect.' She sighed. 'I might be very unpopular until I learn to behave correctly.'

He frowned. 'You know my opinion,' he said. 'Relatives are the very devil. Keep away from them. They will disappoint you.'

'For heaven's sake, Brigade-Major! Just because you've had an unfortunate time with your relatives does not mean that mine are cut from the same cloth.'

Colly's heart sank. She was setting great store by a couple of letters written a long time ago. No doubt the hope of reaching England to see her relatives had held her together during the hard times. He could understand a dream like that. But he would hate to see all her anticipatory sparkle and family loyalty quenched by a bunch of disapproving, mealy-mouthed relations.

'They should be honoured to have you come and live with them, Juliana. You are an accomplished and beautiful young woman.'

There was a short silence. Colly felt the heat spreading from his neck up to his face. That would teach him to blurt out what he was thinking. Would he never learn to keep his tongue between his teeth?

'Th-thank you.' She looked shocked, almost disbelieving.

'I meant what I said,' he growled. He felt her trying to examine his averted face, so he said hastily, 'I believe your new maid will be waiting for you.' He hadn't dared say, 'waiting to prepare you for bed,' because beds were a topic that he and Juliana avoided.

He stood up. 'Good evening, Juliana.' And he strode off to his bedchamber.

CHAPTER FOURTEEN

TWO DAYS LATER their hired carriage rumbled through the busy streets of Southampton and swung on to the Bristol road. Juliana sat with her new maid, Tilly, on one side of the carriage, and Colly and his great-coat lounged in solitary splendour on the other.

Juliana eyed him. He looked every inch the man about town now. His uniforms were stuffed into his portmanteau and he was wearing clothes he had purchased in Portsmouth and Southampton. It seemed he intended to set his army days behind him. Portsmouth might not boast such exalted tailors as London, but they had done a very good job with Mr Colwyn Hetherington – very good indeed. He looked delectable enough to eat. Biscuit-coloured pantaloons stretched over muscular thighs; a plain dove-grey waistcoat hugged his chest (she was jealous of it), and the boots – ah, the boots! The new black boots looked magnificent on his long legs. Sigh.

His demeanour now was a far cry from when she had first met him, so long ago. Her gazed fixed on his boots, she remembered how he had been brought to the hospital on a litter by several of his men. Belligerent, his arms flailing in all directions, he had kept demanding, 'Who took it? Where is it?'

She had been unable to get near him to check the sabre wounds on his thigh and chest, so when one of his fists jabbed her in the eye, she had tipped a very large dose of laudanum down his throat.

She smiled to herself and stroked her new parasol. He had replaced her broken one with a beautifully crafted lightweight parasol with trailing yellow ribbons on the handle. Ribbons? She always thought of herself as a practical woman, but Colly must see her in a different light. She leaned forward.

'Thank you for the parasol,' she said. 'I do not think, in the haste of the moment, that I thanked you. And for the' – she glanced at Tilly – 'other things.' Including those three dark-eyed little pansies, now nestling inside her hatbox.

'Not at all. When you stopped stammering, you thanked me very prettily,' he said, grinning.

'I'm sorry. I was quite overcome. I've not received any presents for some time, you see.'

He cleared his throat and looked out the window. 'The weather is fine and we should make good time, Miss Colebrook.'

She nodded her understanding. She wasn't nodding because she trusted his estimate of the road conditions. She was nodding because she understood she had become 'Miss Colebrook' again.

'Is this mode of travel to your liking? It was the best available,' he explained.

She laughed. 'Sir, it is luxurious. Far, far better than the donkeys we used between Coimbra and Porto. They were so old and slow we walked faster than they did. Of course with a war on, "no horses could be spared for a fool woman and her maid travelling through countryside occupied by opposing forces".' She pulled a face. Then she stopped as she remembered how correct that prediction had been.

'Is that what everyone said?'

She straightened her back. 'Not everyone. Some people were most kind. My father's friend said that when I told him I wanted to offer my nursing services in Porto.'

Colly's gloved hand, lying carelessly on the seat beside him, curled and uncurled.

'Did he not offer to house you after your father died?'

'No.'

Colly surveyed Juliana's face. That single word told him a lot about her father's crony. Philip Colebrook and his friend must have had similar natures.

'Would you have stayed if he'd offered?' he enquired.

'No. I might have stayed if he'd been kind. But he didn't like me and I didn't like him. I could not have borne being an obligation in his household.'

Colly reflected that she might well be stepping into that same situation here in England. He must find a way to keep in contact with her. It was a pity the new maid, Tilly, was a naïve country girl. She would be unable to write, so he could not ask her to send him word if Juliana needed him.

Then he sneered at himself. Huh! Just what did he, an accused rapist, think he could do if she needed his help anyway? Beg his employers for time off and come riding like a knight to his lady's rescue? Not bloody likely. Even if he did that, he'd be sure to do the wrong thing.

He hunched a shoulder and stared out the window.

When they arrived at Trewbridge, Juliana expected to take the carriage straight on to Melksham. However, as they drew up in front of the most impressive house she had ever seen, servants came running and she and Colly were escorted inside by an insistent butler who exclaimed, 'Sir! Brigade-Major Hetherington, may I say how very pleasant it is to see you again?' The man beamed from ear to ear and his bow was so low it was almost obsequious, if such a stately character could be obsequious.

'Hello, Twoomey. The bad penny returns, you see.'

'Not at all, sir. We have been awaiting your arrival with much anticipation.'

Juliana smothered a giggle. The pompous butler spoke as if he were the hospitable master of the house. Struggling to contain her laughter, she caught Colly's eye. His lips twitched.

'Colly! At last!'

Colly spun around and held out his hand. 'John! Or do I call you Brechin now?' he enquired mischievously.

'That's enough from you, thanks.' John pumped his arm.

Juliana realized that she did indeed remember John, Lord Brechin. He was the quiet man with the sabre slash down the side of his neck. She tended to recall her patients' wounds and illnesses rather than their names.

The two men laughed and slapped each other's backs and for a moment she felt left out. *How* she wished she had friends like that.

Then John Trewbridge recollected his manners. He bowed. '*Bom dia, Señorita Colebrook*. I apologize for our rudeness.'

'Not at all,' she murmured. She hoped Colly appreciated what a good friend he had. No doubt Lord John would have Colly enmeshed in the goings-on at Trewbridge in no time at all and Colly would soon forget the nurse he had befriended for a short time.

She swallowed and raised her chin. She would carve out a good life for herself with her uncle's family and be content. Most of the time, anyway.

CHAPTER FIFTEEN

DINNER AT TREWBRIDGE was like nothing Juliana had experienced. After the first dinner bell everyone assembled in the large drawing room, a well-appointed salon with solid oak furniture and intricately embroidered wall hangings. She had thought her own bedchamber was beautiful – indeed, she mentally echoed Tilly's awed 'Ooh, miss!' – but it paled into insignificance beside this quiet elegance.

Lord Brechin's new wife was not at all what Juliana had expected. Many of the sick officers she nursed had told her about the strictness of English society. They'd explained how a young woman of unblemished character could overnight become a target for the gossipmongers because her father had been found cheating at cards, or her sister had eloped to marry a man 'beyond the pale'. Juliana was mindful that her background might not pass muster.

Marguerite Trewbridge was a forthright young woman with a lush figure and a slight limp. When Colly introduced them Marguerite inclined her head politely, then abandoned all pretence of formality. She stepped forward, smiling, and said, 'I have been most anxious to meet you, Miss Colebrook. My husband tells me you've been nursing soldiers on the Peninsula. You must be very brave. How did you begin such a thing?'

Juliana relaxed. This was no formal, chilly aristocrat. 'My grandparents sent me to a convent school. The sisters did not believe in idleness and trained us all according to our abilities,' she answered shyly. She could feel Colly eavesdropping from across the room. Although he appeared to be listening to a discussion between the marquess and Lord Brechin, Juliana knew from his attentively cocked head that he had overhead Lady Brechin's question.

'Oh dear, that would dish me,' Lady Brechin exclaimed. 'I have no particular talent for anything.'

'I'm sure that's not true, Lady Brechin.'

'Please call me Marguerite. We've only recently acquired the title and when someone says Lady Brechin it takes me a minute or two to realize they're talking to *me*.'

Juliana grinned. Marguerite was a very down-to-earth young woman. She had about her an air of industry, of wanting to get on with the task at hand.

And the Marchioness of Trewbridge was another such. Threading her arm through Juliana's, the imperious little lady drew both young women aside and murmured, 'We will have a comfortable coze after dinner, ladies.' Then she bustled off to her husband's side to hear what Colly was saying.

Well, if all English people were as delightful as this, Juliana thought, she would have no difficulty making friends. She hoped her uncle's family was the same.

Lord Brechin's Portuguese was fluent. He had winkled the history of the Ervedosa family out of her and expressed his sympathy that she did not know where in Brazil her relatives lived. As she sipped the excellent sherry the butler had handed her, the anxious knot in Juliana's stomach eased.

Closing her eyes for a moment in blissful enjoyment of the excellent sherry, she opened them to find the marquess standing at her side, regarding her with amusement. 'Miss Colebrook, we have not yet been introduced. I am Trewbridge.'

She bobbed a curtsy. 'My lord,' she murmured, taking the proffered hand. For a bad moment the sherry glass was in peril, but she managed to swap it to her left hand without mishap. Thank goodness she had dressed in her best Italian crepe. She knew the restrained jade-green colour suited her, and although her gloves had seen better days, she hoped the marquess would not notice. However, she had an idea that this man noticed everything. Shrewd, sharp grey eyes travelled over her swiftly and returned to her face.

'I am pleased you find our sherry palatable, Miss Colebrook.' He smiled. 'I regard you as a connoisseur since Colly tells me you have spent much of your life in Portugal.'

'My mother was Portuguese, my lord.'

He inclined his head. 'So John told me. I believe you have lost touch with your Portuguese family, Miss Colebrook. That is unfortunate because family is very important.'

Juliana speared a triumphant glance at Colly, who was hovering nearby.

'I have been telling Mr Hetherington that for some time,' she said.

Colly came to stand beside her. 'On the other hand, my lord, family can be the most destructive force in one's life,' he interposed.

The marquess flicked him a glance. 'I would have to agree with that too, Colly. The most important, but sometimes the most destructive influence in one's life, Miss Colebrook. I stand corrected.'

Juliana's jaw dropped. That was the *last* thing she had expected the marquess to say. For a moment even Colly looked shocked, then he rallied. 'I'm glad you agree, my lord. Miss Colebrook has a yearning for family, you see.'

Juliana bristled.

Then the second dinner gong sounded. Colly exhaled carefully and the marquess threw back his head and laughed. He leaned towards Colly and murmured, 'Saved by the bell, Colly.' Then he moved forward to take his wife's arm. 'I believe dinner is served,' he said, still chuckling to himself.

Colly proffered his arm to Juliana. As they followed the Trewbridges in to dinner, Juliana barely allowed her gloved fingers to touch Colly's sleeve. She was still seething at his uncalled for comment about relatives. Couldn't he understand that the closer she got to her English relatives, the more apprehensive she became?

Once seated, she stared at the array of silverware in front of her and hoped she could find the correct knives and forks for each course. At least the soup spoon was easy enough.

'Ah ... Miss Colebrook?' The marchioness was trying to attract her attention. 'We should love to have you stay on at Trewbridge for a few days, my dear.'

Leaving her soup untouched, Juliana stared at the vivacious little lady in concern. 'Oh! That is very kind of you, your ladyship, but ah ... I believe my aunt and uncle are expecting me.' Well, she'd written to them as soon as they'd landed at Portsmouth so she *hoped* they expected her.

The marchioness waved a careless hand, narrowly missing a footman as he took away her soup plate. 'Notes can be written,' she said. 'Marguerite and I are desperate for female company and you are the sort of person we admire. You have *done* something with your life, Miss Colebrook.' The Marchioness of Trewbridge nodded her head approvingly, and the circlet of pearls adorning her hair twinkled and bobbed in the bright candlelight.

It was the pearls that decided it. 'Thank you, my lady, but I must not,' Juliana said. She was wearing her only evening dress. Tilly had done her best with it, but it did not measure up to the glorious dresses of the two other ladies at the table. Nor had she any pearls, or indeed jewellery of any sort, merely her mother's hair combs and rings. She simply did not belong here.

And, thanks to Colly's continued pessimism, she was beginning to worry about the reception she would receive from Uncle Sholto and his family. Seventeen years ago she had seen Uncle Sholto as a kindlier version of her father. Being twins, the two had looked much alike. But thanks to Colly's continual harping, she had to acknowledge that she knew very little about her uncle and dared not run the risk of displeasing him.

Of course she'd rather stay at Trewbridge. Anyone would. And although she was cross with Colly at the moment she still wanted to see that all went well for him. The Trewbridges obviously liked him, but employing a man who had been accused of rape by his own father was a different matter.

'Oh, for heaven's sake,' she told herself under her breath. '*What do you think you can do if they change their minds about Colly?*'

No, she must not stay here any longer, no matter how hard the marchioness pressed her. It was no business of Juliana's what Brigade-Major Hetherington did with his life. He had made it plain that he found her resistible. Not the sort of thing a woman needed to know.

'It is a shame you cannot stay, but I understand,' the marchioness said with a sweet smile. And she probably did understand, Juliana reflected. The marchioness, like her husband, had shrewd eyes. Juliana was not at all surprised when the marchioness waylaid her outside the dining room when the ladies rose to leave the gentlemen to their port.

'Now, my dear. Come into the drawing room and tell me about these relatives of yours.'

Lady Brechin tossed Juliana an apologetic glance and walked over to the piano to sort through the sheet music inside the piano stool.

'I do not know much about them, my lady,' Juliana explained. 'All I know is that my uncle – he is my father's twin brother – kindly offered me a home some time ago. When I sent them news of Papa's death, I mentioned that I very much wished to return to England. I didn't hear from them for months and then they wrote and offered me a home. But I had begun work at Sao Nazaire by then, and Dr Barreiro was not prepared to release me. Later, I discovered that finding a way to return to England was very difficult. Thank goodness for Brigade-Major Hetherington,' she added a trifle incoherently. 'Of course, I will find an occupation straight away. I must not be a charge on my family.'

Her stomach began its familiar after-dinner churning and she pressed a hand over it protectively. Perhaps she could escape to her room before the pains got too bad. She should not have eaten so much, but after two weeks of ship's fare, the food had been remarkably good.

'Hmm.'

What did that 'hmm' mean, Juliana wondered?

'Would your uncle be Sholto Colebrook, by any chance?' the marchioness enquired.

Something in the lady's demeanour puzzled Juliana and made her cautious. 'Why, yes. Do you know him?'

'I know of him. After all, he is more or less a neighbour. You will be able to visit us whenever you wish, Miss Colebrook.' The marchioness laid her hand over Juliana's. 'And if you are ever in any trouble, please come straight to us. Promise me.'

The little lady was so insistent that Juliana stammered, 'Yes, ma'am. You are very kind.'

'Just pragmatic, my dear. You are almost alone in the world. Sometimes we need friends more than relatives.'

Juliana's heart drooped. For many months she had looked forward to arriving on the Colebrooks' doorstep and being hailed as their long-lost niece. She had thought no further than that. But she had not missed the marchioness's differentiation between knowing someone and knowing *of* someone. What did the Marchioness of Trewbridge know about the Colebrooks?

'If I find employment, it might be difficult for me to visit,' she said. 'I know nothing about working conditions in England.'

She glanced up in time to see the marchioness open her mouth and shut it again. Puzzled, she glanced across at Lady Brechin. But Marguerite's head was bowed as she fingered a page of manuscript before placing it on the music stand.

'Tell me, Juliana – may I call you Juliana? – what is wrong with Colly? When he came to us before he was a trifle bitter, but at least he was relaxed. He seems very tense and worried this time. Has something happened?'

'I couldn't say, your ladyship, uh ...'

The marchioness smiled. 'What you mean is that you know, but you will not break a confidence. Never mind. We will sort it out.' The lady nodded as if it were all settled. 'Since we cannot persuade you to stay any longer, I will arrange for the carriage to take you to Melksham tomorrow morning.'

Thank goodness. Juliana had been cudgelling her brains over how she was to get to Uncle Colebrook's house.

'Ah, here are the gentlemen,' the marchioness said.

Juliana examined Colly's face. He *did* look strained. He needed to make a clean breast of the accusation against him as soon as possible.

'Miss Colebrook is to leave us tomorrow,' the marchioness announced.

Juliana swallowed.

The marquess raised his eyebrows. 'Does Trewbridge not meet with your approval, Miss Colebrook?'

'My lord, hardly! Trewbridge is very beautiful,' she replied. 'It is not that, but from now on I am reliant upon my uncle's hospitality. I cannot afford to upset him by starting out on the wrong foot. No doubt he expected me to arrive today.'

'You must say that we detained you, Miss Colebrook. That should suffice,' the marquess replied in a cool, cynical tone.

Juliana was taken aback to discover that the marquess and marchioness plainly disliked her family. However, she understood that in the country small misunderstandings between neighbours sometimes grew out of all proportion. Perhaps her uncle had done or said something of which the Trewbridges did not approve. Heavens, she hoped her uncle was not like her father. He had forever been at outs with someone.

'Anyway, Marguerite and I are determined to call upon you,' the marchioness said, smiling. 'We shall be interested to see how you are going on.'

Marguerite nodded her agreement. 'Do not think you are without friends, Miss Colebrook.'

Lord Brechin strolled over to the piano and twirled one of Lady Brechin's loose curls around his finger. Marguerite sparkled up at him as he bent over her and she reached up a hand to trace the scar on the side of his neck with two fingers. Juliana stared enviously. Lucky Marguerite.

She looked across the room at Colly and surprised a despondent, brooding look on his face as he watched the couple. But the second he felt her glance, he altered his expression to a polite smile.

Dearest Colly, let it go, she thought. *You could be happy like that too.* Not with Juliana, of course. She was not a suitable bride for Brigade-Major Colwyn Hetherington.

The Hetheringtons were fools to have hurt him so badly. She understood his pride but she hoped he would not carry the bitterness forever. It was not good for him, and if ever a man deserved happiness and good fortune, it was Brigade-Major Hetherington. Somewhere, if he managed to slough off the shame eating away at his pride, a lucky woman waited for him. If he showed willing, there would be a bevy of giggling young ladies anxious to secure his hand in marriage, damn them. And whoever was lucky enough to take his eye – well, she would have a considerate lover and a charming companion who would always see she was safe and comfortable. Closing her eyes for a moment Juliana remembered the warm fire of Colly's lovemaking. Yes, his bride would be *very* lucky.

Then at her husband's behest Marguerite began to play, and Juliana dragged herself out of her introspection. To her surprise, Colly crossed the room to sit beside her. Under cover of Marguerite's very spirited rendering of a Scarlatti sonata he murmured, 'Is your stomach hurting you, Miss Colebrook? I've noticed you often have some pain after eating.'

Good heavens! This was not the sort of thing a man and woman should discuss. As a nurse she had naturally discussed all sorts of things with her patients, but she was no longer a nurse, nor was he a patient. Knowing he was as stubborn as she was and that he would wait all evening for a reply, she muttered, 'It is nothing. I have had it for years. I over ate.' She attempted a dismissive smile, but a particularly vicious twinge of pain jerked her back in her seat.

He reached out. 'Miss Colebrook … Juliana …'

'Don't,' was all she said, and he pulled his hand back as if bitten.

'I fail to see how four mouthfuls of food can be called over-eating,' he hissed. Then he slid to the far end of the settle and pretended to concentrate on Scarlatti.

Oh dear. Did the man watch her every move? He even counted her mouthfuls. She sat very still, willing the pain to subside.

Then she realized what she had done. He had reached out to her and she had repulsed him. Under her reticule, the hand rubbing her stomach stilled. She should have handled Colly's concern with better grace. He had given her an opening, the only one she might ever have. She could have pretended to be distraught, to need his help. She might even have used it as an excuse to speak to Colly about—

About what? There wasn't anything left to say. Nothing at all.

She stopped fiddling with her reticule and concentrated on Lady Brechin's talented recital. It was easy to do. Marguerite's playing style was not the usual vapid, mechanical rendering. On the contrary, she was an extraordinarily accomplished performer. Juliana joined everyone else in demanding more from the pianist. Marguerite smiled shyly and began a stately, dreamy pavane that Juliana had often heard played by mandolinists in Porto. She leaned back against the settle, swallowing the stone in her throat as she remembered the music and sun and loneliness of Portugal.

*

As she took her candle from the table at the bottom of the stairs, she ventured one last try. Turning to Colly where he stood in the shadows she asked, 'Shall I see you again before I leave, Mr Hetherington?'

He shook his head. 'Lord Brechin and I mean to ride out after breakfast so I can familiarize myself with the estate. I expect you will have left by the time we return.'

She could feel her lips trembling and bent her head so he could not see. Over Lord Brechin's protest that it was not necessary to set out too early, she dipped a curtsy in the men's general direction. She held out her hand. 'Then I shall thank you now, Brigade-Major Hetherington, for your escort from Portugal. I could not have been in safer hands.' She had been rehearsing the last sentence for several minutes, willing him to understand that his presence had offered security and protection from harm, and that she had felt safe with him in spite of the charges against him.

He was no rapist. His father had it all wrong.

Because she could not say what she really felt, she tried to show it in her eyes.

He took her outstretched hand and bent over it. 'Goodnight, Miss Colebrook. I hope we shall ... we shall ...' – his voice faltered 'see more of you in the future.'

She did not look up at him, but her bruised heart eased a little. He had not said goodbye, and he had left the door open a little. A very little. Firming her lips, she steadied the candleholder and with a ramrod straight back ascended the stairs in the wake of the marchioness. As she turned the corner she squeezed a glance out the corner of her eye and saw him standing still, watching her leave.

CHAPTER SIXTEEN

FEELING EMPTY, RATHER as if he was on retreat and had not eaten for several days, Colly rode out with John across the upper fields. A sense of anticlimax enveloped him. He had put all his efforts into escorting Juliana to England and now that the task was done, he was bereft. She was leaving. And once she became ensconced in her uncle's household, she would not visit Trewbridge often. She would have all she wanted – her family – and she would not need him any more.

'John,' he asked, ranging his horse alongside his friend's mount, 'what is it that your parents have against Miss Colebrook's relatives? It's obvious they've had dealings with them in the past.'

'No idea, Colly. I've never heard them mention the Colebrooks before.'

'Oh.' He would have to ask the marchioness directly. That is if she would still talk to him once he told the Trewbridges about his past.

Restlessly he fidgeted in the saddle. He should tell them now and get it over with. He took the bull by the horns. 'John, when we return to the house, I must talk to your family. It is a serious matter. I shall understand if you do not wish me to take up the stewardship.'

John glanced at him, obviously ready with a funning quip, then his face changed when he saw Colly's expression.

'Ah … this is the Big Announcement, is it not? My parents had the feeling there was something preying on your mind. I thought it related to Miss Colebrook, but Mama said she didn't think so.'

Colly flinched. There was a good side and a bad side to living in a big household. Everyone knew what went on in your life. But although curiosity could be uncomfortable, he knew it had its roots in the concern of the household members for one another. After living alone for so many years, he had forgotten that. Not that he had been *alone* in the army precisely, but nobody there had cared whether he was happy or unhappy.

'John, I …'

His friend smiled, and they wheeled their horses and headed back to Trewbridge.

As they approached the house, the smaller of the Trewbridge carriages turned out of the gate. John nodded towards it. 'Will you be seeing her again?' he asked.

'I can't. When I explain, you'll see why.'

John glanced at him, but said nothing further. That was like John. He had never been one for unnecessary gabbling. But would he still be a friend when he had heard Colly's despicable story?

Life could be very strange. He'd kept his history a secret for nearly five years, and then in the space of a week he'd had to tell the tale twice. He shook his head as he dismounted. He rather thought Juliana believed him, but he wasn't entirely sure. Sometimes she cast him speculative looks he didn't understand.

He desperately hoped the Trewbridges believed him.

'So, of course, I had to tell you this, in case you should uh ... decide to change your minds about employing me,' he finished weakly, a half-hour later. Everyone was in the small drawing room and Colly suddenly found it claustrophobic. The elegant furnishings closed in on him as he sat alone on one side of the room facing the Trewbridge family.

'Right. Now we have heard what you were accused of, we need to hear your side of the story, Colly,' the marquess said.

'Sir?' At least the marquess was going to give him a hearing. Which was more than his father had done. Sometimes his father had puzzled him. On the surface Ambrose Hetherington was all bluster and indignation, but Colly had often wondered if his manner cloaked deeper emotions.

Colly had left Heather Hill on an autumn afternoon of gentle rain. For years he had not allowed himself to remember the details of that day. But now he recalled the soft scurry of raindrops on the window as he had stuffed a few clothes and books into a valise, snivelling all the while like a baby. He had been twenty-two, yet he had felt like a desolate child of six or seven, crying hopelessly against a parental edict.

As he snapped shut his portmanteau, his little sister had sidled into his bedchamber and shoved a roll of banknotes and a small locket at him. 'Remember me,' she whispered. 'God be with you.'

'How did you—?' he had begun, but she had scurried out and closed the door in his face.

And as he lay injured after the Battle of the Douro, the locket had been torn off him by one of the despised carrion who plucked keepsakes from their dying brethren.

How could he explain all this to the Marquess of Trewbridge? The gentleman was a proud, authoritative man with a respected name who would brook no lies or subterfuges. And he would certainly not house a criminal under his roof. But at least he'd asked Colly for his side of the story.

'I don't have much of an explanation to make, my lord. Sir Archie Blevin was a neighbour. All our lives, Amelia, my brother William and myself had been companions. My sister is considerably younger so we did not see much of her. Our family spent most of the year at Heather Hill and we children were thrown together a great deal.' Colly looked down at his feet. 'Then Amelia went to London for her first Season, and after she came home, this happened. She was much changed when she returned from London. Miss Colebrook thinks she was covering up for—'

'Miss Colebrook knows of this?' Incredulity sharpened the marquess's tone.

Colly soldiered on. 'Yes, my lord. She persisted in asking me to accompany her from Porto to England. In the end I had to admit why I was not an appropriate escort for her.'

'I see.' The marquess sounded amused. 'She is a very determined, independent young lady, isn't she, Colly?'

'Yes.' Colly's reply was heartfelt.

The marquess seemed to be smothering a grin. 'Does she believe in your innocence?'

'I'm not sure. I hope so.'

'I cannot see her allowing you to escort her if she had doubts about your innocence.'

I can, Colly thought. *She was so desperate to get to England she thought the risk was worth it.*

'Colly, you are not the first young man to be falsely accused thus,' the marquess continued. 'Since you stayed with us after Corunna, we have followed your career with interest. From what I know of you, I do not think you would abandon a young woman. I think it is more likely you would marry the young woman and smother her with kindness. But … do you have any idea who the father of Miss Blevin's child might be?'

Colly felt an appalling constriction in his throat and prayed the others did not notice. The marquess believed him! 'No,' he croaked. 'Perhaps somebody from London.'

'Hmm.' The marquess thought for a moment while Colly chewed over his words. He needed to get to his feet and pace, but as the marquess was seated, he could not.

'You know, Colly, this whole thing needs to be cleared up. I cannot understand why you have let it colour your whole life. Why not pay a visit to Heather Hill to find out the lie of the land?'

'I cannot. My father banned me from the property. Besides, I have no wish to go back there.'

'Ah – pride, Colly, pride,' the marquess mused.

Colly thought that was rich, coming from the Marquess of Trewbridge. In the same circumstances the Marquess of Trewbridge would be a dashed sight more prideful than Colwyn Hetherington.

'Colly,' the marchioness burst out, obviously unable to keep silent any longer, 'why don't you write to your mama? I am sure she is longing to hear from you.'

Colly shook his head. 'I should very much like to see my mother and sister again, my lady. But my father ...' He shrugged. 'However, I shall visit my grandmother as soon as convenient. My father has no jurisdiction over her, and she was very supportive when I needed it most.'

Apparently his father had been furious when he discovered she had bankrolled Colly into the army. He had forbidden the old lady to have anything more to do with him. But nobody could bully Grandmama. She was wealthy and independent and made no bones about her dislike of her pompous son whom she had dubbed 'His Highness'. However, since Colly had not heard from her in months, it *was* possible that Father had intercepted letters between Colly and his grandmother.

'As for my mother and sister, my father and brother will block me from seeing them,' he finished.

'Your brother too?' John enquired.

'Yes. My brother tends to follow prevailing opinion,' Colly said drily. 'When I was first accused he was nonplussed, but then he changed and refused to speak to me. Things had not been right between the two of us for some time, you see.'

Colly looked down at his feet again. This was devilishly awkward to explain. 'Even though William was not very interested in Heather Hill, Father insisted he should spend more time there. He wanted William to be ready to take over the reins.'

Here Colly paused, feeling embarrassed. 'Father was forever going on about how he expected to die soon. Every little twinge brought on – well, never mind.' He cleared his throat. 'Unfortunately William has never been a good judge of horseflesh and the arguments between them reached epic proportions during my last year in England. They would both apply to me for my opinion, then they'd disagree with it. Things became very awkward.'

'Dash it all, Colly! You are the best judge of horseflesh I know,' John protested.

Colly felt even more embarrassed. 'I don't know about that, but my interest in horses seemed to irritate Father. He kept saying it wasn't fair, or some such thing. I was never sure what he meant.' Unable to remain seated any longer he sprang to his feet and began to pace. To hang with politeness. Because his legs were longer than most, four paces brought him up short by the door. He swivelled and prowled back to the window. 'As we grew further apart, I learned to keep my own counsel.' He shrugged. He'd bared his soul enough. There wasn't anything else to say.

The Trewbridges exchanged glances. Colly eyed them nervously.

The marquess stood up and held out his hand. 'Well, Colly, you had best put it all behind you. Welcome to Trewbridge.'

Colly, throat burning, clasped it thankfully, like a drowning man grabbing a lifeline.

He hoped Miss Colebrook was receiving a similar welcome from her family. *Good luck, my love*, he thought as he accepted a celebratory glass of claret from John.

CHAPTER SEVENTEEN

JULIANA, TO HER dismay, received no more than a tepid greeting from her aunt and uncle. The Trewbridge carriage bowled up to a small, run-down house set well back off the Melksham road. There were no flowerbeds, just an ill-kempt patchy lawn. The groom ran to the horses' heads and, as the front door of the house remained shut, Juliana and Tilly had to jump down from the carriage without assistance.

'Sorry, miss,' the groom apologized. 'There's nowhere for me to put 'em at the moment.'

Tilly dragged their valises down from the carriage while Juliana trod up the steps and looked around. Nobody had opened the door, so she tapped as best she could with the broken doorknocker. One tap and the gargoyle on the knocker came apart. Tilly stifled a giggle and Juliana muttered out the corner of her mouth, 'Not a very good omen.'

There was a scramble of movement inside, then a maid wearing an over-sized cap cracked open the door and peered cautiously through the narrow slit.

'I'm Miss Colebrook,' Juliana said. Who had the housemaid been expecting?

'Sorry, Miss. Do come in. James!' the young woman yelled in the general direction of the interior. Juliana flinched and Tilly looked shocked. James pelted towards the door, pulling on a jacket. As he rushed past, Juliana said, 'Please see that the groom receives some refreshments before he returns to Trewbridge.'

James stopped dead in his tracks. 'Refreshments?' he asked, as if this were an unusual request.

Juliana blinked. 'Yes, please. The Marquess of Trewbridge was kind enough to lend me his carriage.'

'What's this?' a voice boomed. 'Trewbridge's carriage, is it? Then hop to it, James.'

Juliana turned to greet her uncle. And got the shock of her life.

Sholto Colebrook was the spitting image of her father.

'*Déjà vu* is it, my dear?' Sholto Colebrook's voice sounded amused. 'But you must have expected it?'

Juliana wasn't sure if that was a question or not. She settled for a vacant smile.

He extended a careless hand, barely touching the ends of her gloved fingers. 'Young lady, we expected you yesterday. When you wrote to us from Portsmouth you said we were to expect you on Wednesday. I have the note here,' he added, as if she were about to argue the point. 'You inconvenienced us.'

Oh, no. Her heart sank. She *knew* she should have come straight on instead of staying the night at Trewbridge. How she wished she had not listened to the marchioness.

'I'm very sorry, sir,' she apologized, anxious to placate this man who held her future in his hands. 'The Trewbridges were most pressing. Indeed, had you not been awaiting me, they would have kept me even longer.'

'You stayed at Trewbridge last evening?'

'Yes. They—'

He interrupted. It seemed he had no interest in explanations. 'Why did you not say so?' Then he turned on his heel and strode away, leaving Juliana and Tilly standing in the hall.

Juliana was stunned. What should she do?

At that moment a thin, middle-aged lady fluttered in their direction, trailing wisps of clothing that had seen better days. This must be her aunt. Stretching out a languid, lace-mittened hand towards Juliana she intoned, 'My dear Juliana, we expected you yesterday. Sholto was much put out.'

Juliana bobbed a curtsy. 'Good day, ma'am. I have already explained my lateness to my uncle.' She did not wish her relatives to think her inconsiderate or rude, but anyone would imagine her late arrival was a national disaster.

A short silence ensued. Her aunt peered around the hall as if she could not quite remember why she had come there.

As the woman showed no disposition to welcome her, Juliana thought it best to retire to her room to unpack.

'Aunt, would you be so kind as to find someone to direct me to my room?' she asked.

Her aunt looked puzzled for a moment then wafted from the room calling out 'Annie!' in dieaway tones.

'Not very welcoming, miss, are they?' Tilly said, as she shook out Juliana's clothes.

'No. It's my fault for arriving a day late.'

'All the same,' Tilly muttered, 'you'd think they'd be right glad to see you. There you are, miss. If you need me for anything, just call out. I'm next door.' She nodded further along the narrow hallway.

Well, that showed where Juliana stood in the household: with the servants.

Perhaps she should make immediate enquiries about available work. She had been sure her relatives would advise her to have a small holiday first, but from their unwelcoming attitude that no longer seemed likely. So much for her visions of open arms and cheerful faces. She had imagined the smell of biscuits cooking and beeswax on the furniture and gentle questions.

Hah! More fool her.

However, in some ways it was fortunate they showed no interest in her. If they'd enquired who had accompanied her from Portugal, she would have had to prevaricate so they did not discover that she and Colly had posed as husband and wife. She could not yet warm to her aunt and uncle, but even so, she did not wish to lie to them. Perhaps with time they would find their way around one another. That was it. She must give it more time.

She could not agree with Colly's jaundiced outlook on family, but deep down she knew her rosy expectations had been ... well, unrealistic. But they had buoyed her up at times when her work was particularly distressing. This cool reception might be disheartening, but she would manage.

By dinnertime she knew the whole thing was a terrible mistake. She forced down a few mouthfuls of fatty mutton broth followed by chunks of a boiled joint of tough meat dressed with cauliflower sauce. For the past hour the smell of boiling cauliflower had permeated the hallways. Judging from the taste, the broth was made from the water the mutton had been boiled in. Her portion boasted a tiny piece of carrot and a shred of onion. She thought longingly of last evening's meal at Trewbridge.

'So, my dear,' her uncle said as he crammed as much meat into his mouth as possible, 'tell us about Trewbridge.'

Not about her parents. Not about Portugal. About Trewbridge.

'Are the private chambers elegant?' he enquired.

'Very. But I saw only the guest wing, withdrawing room and family dining room, sir. I cannot tell you much. It is a very well-run household.'

Sholto Colebrook snorted. 'So it should be with the number of servants they have running about. Lucky they can afford to feed them all.'

She persevered. 'The marquess and marchioness are very kind. If you permit it, it is possible that the marchioness and Lady Brechin might call upon me ... er ... us.'

'*Here?* They might come *here?*' Aunt Colebrook interpolated. 'Fancy that, Sholto!'

Sholto Colebrook grunted into his food.

Juliana stared down at her plate and realized that an uncomfortable night lay ahead of her. Undercooked meat and rich sauces were the very things that most offended her tender stomach. She hoped this meal was not representative of many to come. She had seen only two servants about as yet, so perhaps the cook had her day off today. She could not imagine her uncle employing a male French chef, such as they had at Trewbridge. Sholto was just too ... too English for that.

Sholto Colebrook clattered his knife and fork onto his platter. 'Well, young Juliana,' he mumbled, around a mouthful. He chewed enthusiastically for a moment.

Placing her utensils on her plate, Juliana waited.

'I think we might have hit upon the very occupation for you. I made some enquiries on your behalf.'

She wished he hadn't. She didn't know why, but she wished he hadn't. If he was as like her father as he seemed, then she rather thought any occupation Uncle Sholto found, might not be to her liking. But he had not offered to house her as befitted a daughter of the house. It seemed she was to be a poor relation. Their cross to bear. So she must find employment quickly.

She looked enquiringly at him.

He nodded. 'The very place. The poorhouse in Hungerford is in dire need of good workers at its infirmary. They were pleased to employ you when I told them about your extensive nursing experience. There now, you cannot say your uncle has done nothing for you, can you, my dear?'

Concerned, Juliana stared at him. She knew nothing about poorhouses, but they did not sound like very nice places. She had rather hoped for a genteel occupation as a companion to an ailing lady, or something of that sort. Inwardly she sighed. She had no choice. She could end up in the poorhouse herself if she did not take this opportunity.

'Thank you, Uncle. I shall abide by your advice and see the person in charge. How will I get to Hungerford?'

'All arranged, m'dear. Each morning the carter's dray comes past our gate at six-thirty. In the evenings the superintendent will bring you home in his carriage. You are to start tomorrow,' her uncle said, as if he had accomplished a great feat.

Tomorrow! Was she not even to familiarize herself with Hungerford and Melksham first?

Bitter disappointment seeped into her bones as her dreams of a happy, loving family faded even further. From now on, not only would she earn her keep, she would make a large contribution to household funds, if the furnishings were anything to go by. The whole place suggested a faded dowdiness and none of the rooms she had seen thus far had been cleaned very well either. She could only conclude that Uncle Sholto was of the same mind as her father had been – that a penny spent on anything apart from himself was wasted money. Would she ever see her earnings, or had the superintendent and her uncle arranged for her wages to go straight to Uncle Sholto? She surveyed her uncle's smug face. She was sure he would milk her for everything he could.

But maybe she was being uncharitable and Uncle Sholto had very little money. Perhaps her aunt and uncle were living in genteel poverty.

Later, as she lay in her narrow bed in the attic – no furnished bedchamber for the poor relation – she wondered if Lieutenant Davidson was faring any better with his aunt and uncle. Now she understood why he had got himself drunk during his last hours of freedom. To be obligated to heinous relatives was the most helpless feeling in the world.

Juliana pulled the thin coverlet up over her shoulders and allowed herself a small admission. 'You were right, Colly,' she whispered.

She was sure Colly would have a good life with the Trewbridge family. And if he could manage to swallow his pride and contact his family, he might be able to make Amelia Blevin admit that nobody had ever coerced her. Or if they had, then that person had not been Colly.

Once he was freed from the shadow of guilt, no doubt his straitlaced father would see to it that he wed a proper English miss. She would be mealy-mouthed and would keep him away from all likelihood of scandal. He would forget an independent half-English, half-Portuguese woman with a very tenuous claim to being a lady.

A tear rolled down her cheek and she wiped it away. Obviously she had been alone for too long. If her family had not turned out the way she had expected, that was too bad. She must make the best of it.

She got out of bed and scrabbled in her hatbox. Gently lifting out the three pansies Colly had given her, she saw in the faint moonlight that the edges of the petals were already brown. She would press them. That way she would have them forever.

'Colly,' she whispered into the darkness.

CHAPTER EIGHTEEN

S HIVERING IN THE clammy morning mist, Juliana and Tilly clung to the side of the dray as it lurched along the lanes towards Hungerford. Beneath her cloak, Juliana wrapped her arms around herself and wondered how long it would take to get used to the chilly beginnings of England's early autumn days.

Today was her second day of work. She hoped it would not be as bad as her first. During her years at Sao Nazaire she had endured some dreadful sights and sounds, but the workhouse infirmary at Hungerford took the prize for sheer misery.

It comprised three blocks of faceless red-brick buildings in the shape of an open square. There was not a plant or flower to be seen in the big, dusty courtyard. Her work was in the women's section of the infirmary. Although she had never been inside a prison, she was sure the Hungerford Charity Homes for the Indigent were as near to a prison as made no odds.

In Porto the stench had been of hot, unwashed bodies, vomit and excrement. At the infirmary the stench of despair overrode everything. It was equally distressing. She had swapped one unwholesome environment for another.

Clambering down from the dray she held out two pennies to the carter. Just as he had yesterday, he curled his lip at the meagre offering.

'It is all I can spare. I'm very sorry.'

As he jogged his big carthorses to a trot, she took from her reticule the huge key to unlock the iron gates. Yesterday, with due ceremony, the superintendent had handed it to her as if he had been entrusting her with the keys of Heaven.

'Because of my friendship with your uncle I know I can trust you, Miss Colebrook. Remember, once you are inside, lock the gates behind you.'

Clang! As she and Tilly dragged the heavy gates together they resounded like the knell of doom. And, for many of the people inside, that's what it was, Juliana thought. After enduring the superintendent's lecture yesterday, she had nothing but sympathy for the inmates. The stringent policies and procedures of the Hungerford Charity Homes were enough to depress even the most sanguine inmate.

Trudging up the unkempt driveway Juliana and Tilly smiled at a group of small children crouched on their haunches in the dust. They were not playing. Childhood had already been knocked out of them. Aimlessly they scrawled patterns in the dust.

'Good morning,' Juliana said brightly.

'Morning, miss,' a curly-headed tot replied.

She smiled. Such a nice boy. Yesterday he had held a basin of water for her while she bathed his mother's face and hands. Juliana had found the woman huddled in a dark corner, moaning in pain.

And the poor boy had been punished for his helpfulness. Mr Sourface Superintendent Pettigrew, her uncle's friend, had appeared behind them suddenly and cuffed the boy about the head, roaring at him, 'Put that down at once, boy. How dare you steal that basin?'

Juliana had been appalled at such a ridiculous assertion. 'Sir, please. Stop it!'

She had dragged Pettigrew's arm away as he continued aiming blows at the child. Fortunately the boy's agility enabled him to duck around the corner out of harm's way.

'No ... no.' Juliana's patient had moaned in distress. The woman was very ill. Juliana had seen that look before when fever took a hold.

'Damn you, sir! Go away.' Juliana had not cared how uncivil she sounded. Mr Pettigrew had no place in the women's part of the hospital, and he had no right to upset the sick mothers and children.

'How dare you, madam!' he had hissed at her, his self-importance cut to the quick.

Juliana had stood up. She was taller than Mr Pettigrew by a full inch and a half. 'I dare, sir, because this woman is very ill and needs my help. That is the job I am here to do. Her son offered to hold the bowl for me. I obtained the water from the pump as you instructed this morning.' She had glared at the superintendent. 'And I fail to see why a ... man should be in this particular part of the infirmary.'

Frankly, she thought designating him 'a man' was raising him from the gutter where he belonged. Comparing this worm to real men like Colly Hetherington and John Trewbridge was ridiculous. She did not like or trust Mr Superintendent Pettigrew and she let her contempt drip into her tone. It made no odds to her. She did not intend to stay at the infirmary very long. Red-faced, bristling with anger, he had spun on his heel and left.

'He's always here, miss. He likes watching the children.' The speaker was a scrofulous-looking woman whose meaning was all too clear. She nodded her head towards Juliana's little helper and winked surreptitiously, screwing her face up into a mask of revulsion.

'Not while I'm here,' Juliana had retorted.

And when Mr Pettigrew came to convey her home in his carriage that evening, she had scurried to the door to meet him to prevent him from entering the infirmary. He'd folded his lips tightly but said nothing. There was nothing he *could* say and they both knew it. She had been employed to manage the women's section as she saw fit. Those had been the board's instructions. When Pettigrew had told her that, his lip had curled. He must have resented her before he even met her. Her experience with the sick undermined his authority.

Today, however, he left her alone. She did not see him as she went about persuading some of the more able-bodied women to help her scrub the walls with lye soap. No doubt Superintendent Pettigrew rationalized that, not being familiar with how things were done, she would soon find herself at *point-non-plus* and need his assistance. Then she would have to beg him for it. He was that sort of person.

Huh. She smiled to herself as she rinsed out a rag. Mr Pettigrew had reckoned without her experience of difficult situations and difficult people. And to make matters easier, the women in her care were very knowledgeable. They had been tending themselves for many months with only a midwife available for serious cases.

And Juliana had Tilly. Dear Tilly had rolled up her sleeves and taken the scrubbing brush from Juliana. 'Let me do it, miss. I'm used to this.'

Juliana smiled her thanks and washed her hands. Then she began to dig around in her bag of medical supplies.

'You done a lot o' nursing then?' An unkempt young woman with a piratical appearance nudged her elbow. Her wild black hair and one sightless eye were not pretty, but she worked diligently at scrubbing down the walls, and Juliana didn't care one whit about the woman's appearance. She was good-hearted and helpful, and that counted most in here.

Juliana smiled. 'Well, I've nursed a lot of soldiers, but not many women – only a few Portuguese ladies who needed assistance with birthing and well … medical problems.' She thought of the prostitutes who had crept around to the back door of Sao Nazaire to get help. What would become of them now?

'Coo. Wasn't you scared of them men?'

'No. They were far too sick to bother me.'

The pirate sniggered. 'But what abaht when they got better?'

Juliana laughed. 'Well, then I sent them to the convalescent hospital.'

'What's a con...?'

'Convalescent hospital? That's where they recovered. Then they were sent back to the war.' She bit the words out. She had always struggled with the concept of tending injured men who were then nurtured until they could return to fight and become injured all over again. Or die.

'Poor buggers,' said the pirate.

'Yes.'

'What's your funny accent then?'

'My mother was Portuguese and my father was English.'

'Was?'

'Yes.'

The pirate did not proffer her sympathies. Juliana understood that where the pirate came from, death was common and not a thing to be exclaimed over or examined.

'So why did you come here?' the woman demanded.

Juliana did not answer. She knelt to sponge the face of her little friend's mother. The woman's condition had worsened.

The pirate followed and knelt down too. 'The lass is done for,' she whispered.

Juliana could not help but agree. The woman was wringing wet with sweat, and her skin was blue-white and dried like parchment. Her head swung constantly from side to side as she tried to suppress her moans of pain.

'When did she have her baby?' Juliana asked the pirate.

'Two weeks past.'

'Poor lady. I've seen this before. It is a fever that sometimes comes on after childbirth. The baby?'

The pirate shook her head.

Distressed, Juliana swallowed the lump in her throat. 'She was left far too long without help. I realized yesterday that I could do nothing, but—'

Suddenly the woman opened her eyes and stared straight at Juliana. 'Help him. Help the boy. Go to Sir Alexander Mortimer. He will help.' She spoke in a cultured voice, but then, as if the effort of speaking had exhausted her, closed her eyes again and slumped sideways against the wall.

'Fetch me some ... no, I'd best go myself.'

'If it's water yer want, I can get it.' Juliana's self-appointed assistant hauled herself to her feet. 'Old Pitiless Pettigrew won't bother us now you've put him in his place. Gutless, that's wot 'e is. You did a good job yesterday.' The pirate chuckled, snatched the basin from Juliana and lurched out of the room leaving Juliana with the dying woman.

It was not the first time she had held the hand of the dying. And it would not be the last. Her stomach began its familiar rolling. Reaching inside her pinafore pocket with her free hand, she pulled out a precious bottle of laudanum. The superintendent had been very niggardly with medical provisions. Too bad. This lady did not deserve to die in agony. Nobody did. The woman's lips were so cracked and dry that Juliana would have to moisten the parched lips and mouth first, otherwise the poor thing would never be able to swallow the laudanum mix.

''Ere.' The pirate slopped water as she staggered across the room.

Juliana took out a fresh rag from her apron bib and soaked it with water. Then she pressed it gently against the chapped lips of the dying woman. A cracked cup was all she had to hold the water. Yesterday, when she'd seen the primitive tools available to her, she had scoured that cup most thoroughly. This morning she had again scrubbed the basin and cup. Tonight she would take home her rags and wash them out. No ladies' hands for her. She thought longingly of the pretty container of glycerine and rosewater that Colly had given her.

Conditions at Sao Nazaire had not been pleasant, but the wealthy people of Porto had made sure that Dr Barreiro had good equipment. Even when the French stole some of it, the British Army and the Portians had replaced everything. Of course, that had been an important military hospital. This infirmary was merely a holding pen for the indigent.

As she held the cup to the dying woman's lips, a shudder shook the woman's body and she fell back against Juliana. Juliana sat still for a moment, quietly saying a prayer for the dead. Then, placing the body on the floor, she blinked to clear her vision. No matter how many deaths she attended, she could never get used to the desolate feeling of helplessness.

'Sorry,' she whispered. 'I'll try to help the boy.'

''Ere,' said the pirate. 'You don't want to go making promises you can't keep, miss. Ain't no chance of getting out of here once you're in.'

Juliana turned to her in surprise. 'What do you mean? Surely there is work for the men and schooling for the children?'

'Sometimes,' the woman agreed. 'But her young feller is too young for work or school. He'll go to the foundling hospital.'

'Well, that's better than nothing.'

'If you say so, miss.'

Juliana kept silent. It wasn't for her to enquire into the administration of the Hungerford Charity Homes. It was her business to succour the sick women and children as best she could. And she had a huge job ahead of her.

All the same, she planned to find out where Sir Alexander Mortimer lived.

CHAPTER NINETEEN

That evening when Mr Pettigrew signalled he was ready to convey her home, Juliana decided to approach him on the matter of wages. It was all very well to say that he and Uncle Sholto had arranged things between them; she needed to know if she could purchase some aprons and perhaps a new dress. She was heartily tired of her old, worn clothes.

It was just as well she was thin, for with Tilly jam-packed between Mr Pettigrew and herself, there was very little room on the narrow carriage seat.

'Mr Pettigrew,' Juliana began, when Mr Pettigrew had fussed and organized the reins to his liking. He was proud of his bone-shaking carriage. Juliana thought their journey might be faster and smoother if he spent more time feeding his weary, undernourished horse rather than dusting the seats of the cheap, seen-better-days old carriage.

She understood his reasoning. He had a carriage; therefore he was a gentleman. However, it would take a lot more than a carriage to make Mr Pettigrew a gentleman.

'Yes, Miss Colebrook?'

It could not, by any stretch of the imagination, be said that his tone held more than mild civility.

'I understand that you and Uncle Sholto organized my work at the infirmary, for which I thank you. But I need to know how much I am to be paid, and when. You see, I—' She got no further.

'Excuse me, Miss Colebrook,' Pettigrew interrupted, his face as red as a beet. 'You must allow *me* to know best when it comes to financial matters. Really, your upbringing must have been sadly lacking.' His voice rose. 'You have constantly undermined—'

Tilly stared wide-eyed at the spittle on the man's chin.

'Mr Pettigrew!' Juliana had to shout to be heard. 'If you are referring to yesterday, then I stand by my actions. You had no right at all to enter the women's quarters without warning us first.'

'You ...' He gobbled, unable in his anger to get the words out.

She hastened to placate him. 'I understand that you are the overall superintendent of the Hungerford Charities and I respect that. Of *course* you must inspect all the premises periodically. But in future you must let me know when you wish to examine the women's infirmary. As an experienced superintendent you will understand I have no wish to be summoned before the board of governors to explain away any errors in propriety.'

She gazed earnestly at him, peering past Tilly's pert little chin, willing him to calm down. To her relief he settled back in his seat, staring straight ahead between the horse's ears. Juliana exhaled carefully. Thank goodness she had considerable experience in dealing with recalcitrant males.

'Hmm. Well, it is true you will have to attend the board's monthly meetings with me.'

Really? How interesting. Trying to sound like the dithering, helpless women he plainly admired, she whispered, 'Oh dear. I hate meetings.'

Gracious! She had acted too well. For one second Mr Pettigrew's hand drifted from the reins and reached across Tilly to pat Juliana's knee. 'Never fear, Miss Colebrook. I shall tell you what to expect and how to go about things.'

No doubt. Juliana struggled not to cringe away from him. Poor Tilly had drawn herself up as thin as a straw in an effort not to be touched by the man.

'About my wages, sir—'

'You will have to ask your uncle. I have arranged for him to receive your wages on quarter day as he requested. I'm sure he will see that you get your pin money,' he finished condescendingly.

Only by compressing her lips was Juliana able to bite her tongue. Her fingers curled and away went her intransigent stomach again. She would never see a penny of that money unless she went down on bended knee to her uncle. Her father had been like that. If her mother had needed money for any small thing, she had had to cajole and plead, even if what she wanted was intended for *his* comfort and even though the Ervedosas had supplied most of the income. Like his brother, Uncle Sholto did not begrudge spending money on himself. No, indeed. She had noticed his clothing was of the finest quality, likewise the appointments in his study. Yet her aunt was garbed in out-of-date, unbecoming dresses that even Juliana, with her ignorance of current fashion, could see were not at all the thing. And as for the household furniture – she had seldom seen such battered chairs in desperate need of covering.

Well, whatever Sholto Colebrook and Mr Pettigrew had decided, it was *her* money. She sighed. So much for having a responsible relative she could trust. *Colly, how right you were.*

'Here.' The rattly carriage drew to a halt at the gates of the Colebrook residence. Mr Pettigrew did not bother to drive them to the door. She hoped he would be more accommodating in inclement weather.

'Thank you, Mr Pettigrew. Until tomorrow.'

He grunted in reply and she scrambled down, bunching her skirts in one hand. Yesterday Tilly barely had time to clear her skirts away from the carriage wheels before he had taken off.

They trudged upstairs, Tilly trotting behind Juliana, divesting her of her cloak and bonnet as they went. They must hurry. Their dinners were being kept for them in the kitchen and they were anxious not to upset Cook for it was well after six o'clock.

Juliana pushed open her door and tossed her reticule on to the bed. Then stopped dead. Someone had been in her room. Things were not where she had left them. Uncle Sholto had made it clear that she and Tilly would clean their own rooms. Therefore she knew exactly where everything should be. But several items on the rickety dresser had been changed around. The armoire door swung on its hinges in the draught from the open window. The cheval mirror had been angled to reflect the floor, and someone had seen fit to prise up a loose floorboard and then replace it.

She thumped down on her bed, shattered. What was going on? Had her uncle or aunt been sifting through her things out of sheer curiosity, or had they been searching for something specific? Her eyes travelled to the open casement window. The attic rooms were very hot at this time of year so she had left her window open.

But not *that* far open.

Perhaps it had not been her aunt or uncle, but a common housebreaker. She leaned out the window and peered downwards to see if it was possible for anyone to climb up to the third storey.

It was. And very easy it would be. The stout branches of an oak tree brushed against the side of the house, and an experienced housebreaker could have gained easy access. In fact, with a little ingenuity she could manage it herself.

Easing back down on to the bed she discovered she was shaking. How odd. She had survived many worse situations, yet for some reason this frightened her more than anything else. This was different. This time she did not know *who* the enemy was. How could she fight if she didn't know who her enemy was? Did he come from within? If not, why would a common housebreaker ransack her room?

She must wait and see if anyone else in the household complained about having their room turned over. It would be wise to say nothing in the meantime, especially if her uncle had perpetrated the crime. What could Uncle Sholto possibly hope to unearth in her room? She had no secrets. Perhaps it was just morbid curiosity. Or perhaps he had done it to prove he held the upper hand.

In which case she would pretend sublime indifference. She set her bonnet on the shelf. She would eat in the kitchen, then she and Tilly would wash out their rags and aprons as usual.

But when she went downstairs, Tilly wasn't in the kitchen. That was odd. Tilly was normally most attentive and eager to prove herself as a lady's maid. Juliana chuckled to herself. She had a maid, yet she ate in the kitchen, lived in an attic and worked for her living.

'Cook, have you seen Tilly?'

'The master came looking for her, Miss Colebrook. She's with him.'

Juliana dropped the spoon into her soup with a hot splash and, scraping back her chair, rushed upstairs to her uncle's study. Barely pausing to knock, she thrust open the door.

Her uncle was seated behind his impressive desk and Tilly stood on the rug in front of him. Her gamine face was distressed and her hands nervously twisted the ends of her apron. Sholto Colebrook's round face expressed smugness and superiority that slid like melting wax into an avuncular expression when he spied Juliana. 'Ah, Juliana. I have just advised Tilly that now our household has expanded, the existing staff need some help. I have decided that once you become better established in your work, Tilly will spend her days helping Annie and James.'

'But, Uncle, I must have a chaperon, particularly when coming home with your friend each evening.' Juliana tried to sound placatory, but he was probably left in no doubt what she thought of his friend. 'Also, I understand there are times when I'll need a chaperon at the workhouse. And Tilly is invaluable at the infirmary.' She nodded to Tilly. 'Thank you, Tilly. Have your meal now.'

Tilly scuttled out the door gratefully, casting an apologetic glance at Juliana.

The gloves were off. Juliana faced her uncle. 'Please do not try to manipulate my maid, Uncle Sholto. It is not gentlemanly of you.' There, that should give him at least two things to think about.

A dark flush rose beneath his skin. 'How dare you, young woman!'

'No, sir. How dare you? Do you think I am some silly ninny to be used as you see fit? And while we are about it, I want to know how much I am being paid by the board of the Hungerford Charity Homes.

I am short of funds with which to pay Tilly and the carter and I need to purchase a few items for myself.'

Sholto Colebrook glared at his niece. 'You, madam, have far too much to say for yourself. Mr Pettigrew will hand your wages to *me* each quarter day.'

'So he told me. However, what neither of you has seen fit to inform me is how much I am to be paid.'

He tried to change tack. 'Ah, you'd best let me handle all monetary transactions, my dear.'

'Uncle Sholto, I handled all such transactions for myself when I worked in Porto. And prior to that, in Alexandria and Coimbra I handled all our money matters. Papa was sadly inept at that side of things, as well as a lot of other things,' she added.

'Alexandria! Coimbra!' he spat. 'Those heathenish places! I am not surprised Philip found the people there difficult to deal with. But you, with your mother's foreign blood in you, no doubt you are incapable of understanding—'

He got no further.

Juliana launched herself across the room and slapped her hands hard on his desk. Leaning forward, she came within two very uncivil inches of her uncle's face. 'Uncle Sholto,' she hissed from between gritted teeth, 'I may not seem like the ideal niece to you, but you are not my ideal uncle. And if you say one more word against my mother, her country, or her family, I shall know how to act.' She didn't have the slightest idea what she was talking about, but the effect of her words was instantaneous. Sholto Colebrook shrank back from her and seemed to shrivel inside his skin.

He waved a hand vaguely. 'No need to get testy, my dear.'

A coward, she thought contemptuously. 'The Ervedosa family supported us for years. They even stood by us when some of my father's *discoveries* turned out to be fakes. I'm sure my father understood that applying to you for funds would have been pointless.'

He ignored her allusion to his brother's questionable dealings. 'Oh, very willing to share, y'know. But I don't have the funds to give. Never did have.'

Juliana laughed. 'You are *so* very like him.'

He took this as a compliment at first, then realized she did not mean it in a complimentary manner. 'You've a waspish tongue, Juliana. It is no surprise you are unmarried.'

'You will catch cold at that one, Uncle. I have had offers, but none to tempt me.' Not strictly true, but her uncle didn't need to know the truth.

'No doubt you seek a paragon.'

Juliana thought longingly of Colly. 'Oh no, not a paragon. I couldn't bear to live with a paragon.' She switched topics. 'So, how much do I earn?'

He snickered. 'You won't catch me out, Juliana. I've been pursued by the best debt collectors in the land.'

Good heavens! 'I'm sure you have. I thought as much when we were kept standing on the doorstep the day we arrived. I suppose most callers are tradesmen dunning you for unpaid bills. However, I am your niece and I do not expect to be treated like a creditor,' she said acidly. 'May I assure you, being the daughter of your brother, I am well used to debt collectors. It took me six months to pay back his outstanding debts after he died.'

'Good Lord, child!' Her uncle looked shocked. 'Never tell me you paid his debts even though he was dead! No need to do that.'

'Oh,' she said drily. 'I did not care what people thought about *him*, but the Ervedosa family is an honourable one, much renowned in Portugal. In spite of your dislike of *foreigners*, in Portugal it is the English who are the foreigners. The Ervedosas are infinitely better born than the Colebrooks.'

He stared at her. 'You sound proud of your lineage.'

'I am. In Portugal we were respected. Believe me, Uncle Sholto, Papa was regarded with disgust when it became known he had not provided for me. When my mother's friends discovered I intended to work in a hospital, they were horrified. Young Portuguese women are kept cloistered.'

Sholto Colebrook stared at his niece as if she were a changeling. 'You are the very antithesis of what I expected,' he said at last. 'Nothing at all like your father. You appear to have the temperament of a merchant. However, while you are under my roof, you will do as I say.'

Juliana smiled at him ironically. 'Of course, Uncle.' She turned to go, then said as an afterthought, 'By the way, may I have the key to the room I'm occupying?'

'Got something to hide?' he came back, quick as a wink.

'No, not really.' She shrugged. 'After living in lodgings for so long, I value my privacy.'

'As you wish.'

He fiddled in one of the drawers in his desk and produced a bunch of keys. With his stubby fingers he flicked through them. 'I think this is the one.'

Would he have handed it over so easily if he wanted to search her room again? Was there a duplicate key? Perhaps now he had searched her room he was no longer interested, but that bunch of keys had possibilities.

Her mind seething with ideas, she accepted the key and left.

No doubt he thought he had won. He had avoided telling her about her wages. But it didn't matter any more because while they'd been talking, she had had an idea.

At the next meeting with the board of governors she would make enquiries about her wages. That would be the sensible solution. After all, the board members would not be interested in playing the silly games that Sholto Colebrook and Mr Pettigrew were so fond of.

CHAPTER TWENTY

COLLY STRETCHED OUT on his bed, his arms propped behind his head, and rubbed the scar on his chest. For at least the fifth time today, he wondered about Juliana. Lord, he missed her.

How was she faring with her relatives?

He had finally inveigled out of the marchioness the reason for her dislike of the Colebrook family.

'Good gracious, Colly! I don't know what to tell you. But my heart sinks when I think of that lovely young woman in the clutches of that awful man.'

Alarm had zigzagged through Colly. 'Please, your ladyship, in what way is he awful?'

'Nothing has ever been proven against him, Jeanne,' the marquess had intervened. 'Don't put ideas into Colly's head.'

Colly's head had snapped back and forth between the marchioness and marquess like a marionette on strings. His dinner had gone untouched as he tried to fathom why the marchioness mistrusted Juliana's uncle.

'He – well, he's such a slimy character,' the marchioness said at last.

Colly couldn't help grinning. Her ladyship's bluntness was startling. He caught John's eye across the table. Marguerite giggled.

'There's more to it than that,' the marquess said, with a pained glance at his outspoken wife. 'He's renowned for never paying his bills. He's been dunned by every tradesman in the district. On top of that, on our open days he arrives exuding bonhomie as if we were bosom friends.' The marquess's aristocratic nose twitched. 'The strange thing is that he is garbed respectably, yet his wife looks as though her garments come from the rag-bag.'

A fleeting image of Juliana's father flitted through Colly's mind. 'Perhaps he is like his brother,' he opined.

John raised his eyebrows.

Colly explained. 'From what Miss Colebrook let slip, her father was the same. Very conscious of his own comfort but no interest at all in the well-being of others.'

'Toad!' the marchioness exclaimed. 'We have to get Juliana out of there.'

'My dear.' The marquess sounded perturbed. 'It is none of our business.'

'So you would leave Juliana there, would you?' the lady demanded. The marquess flinched.

'Let her be, Father. Last time she interfered in another family you ended up with a very nice daughter-in-law,' John said, laughing. Marguerite blushed and dimpled at John.

Colly felt a sharp jab of jealousy at their blatant happiness, then felt ashamed. Lord, he was a paltry fellow to be envious of his best friend.

'There is something specious about your reasoning, John,' the marquess mused.

John just grinned and shrugged.

Colly gazed down at his dinner and wondered what he could do to help Juliana. He loathed the helpless feeling that assailed him. If only he had the right to … He shifted his fork from his right hand to his left and back again. Then he glanced up and saw that all eyes were on him.

There was a short silence.

'Ma'am, why don't we go and visit Juliana soon?' Marguerite suggested in the hiatus. 'I know we said we'd call in a week or two, but why not visit tomorrow? That way we can see if everything goes well with her.'

'Excellent idea.'

'And what do you propose to do if all is not well?' the marquess enquired politely.

'Bring her back here of course,' his loving wife responded. 'What else is there to do?'

'I – I'm not sure that's a good idea, ma'am,' Colly said.

'Why not, Colly?'

'If she burns her bridges at her uncle's, she has nowhere else to go, unless she can trace her mother's relatives in Brazil. She might feel it is better to stay with the Colebrooks, even if she is unhappy.' Colly knew he sounded unsure. Damn it, he didn't want her being unhappy and he certainly didn't want her to go to South America. He would never see her again. Her relatives would marry her off to some dapper, aristocratic Portuguese fellow and she would never return to England.

'Hmm. I think the most sensible idea is the one Marguerite suggested,' the marquess said. 'You could visit her and see how she is faring. After all, she may be living in the lap of luxury and have no desire to change her circumstances.'

The marchioness snorted.

'No, Jeanne, I agree. I do not think it is likely. But we must be sure. Then ... well, I do not know what we can do. Perhaps she could stay here until she finds work as a companion to an invalid, or something of that nature.'

'That would be ideal,' Colly struck in eagerly.

'Then we shall visit her tomorrow,' Lady Trewbridge decided.

CHAPTER TWENTY-ONE

SHOLTO COLEBROOK BOLTED from his study and erupted into the foyer. Surely that wasn't...? It was.

'I am very sorry to keep you waiting, your ladyship, madam.' He bobbed in the ladies' direction, feeling like an apple in a bobbing barrel.

'Strange welcome,' the marchioness said brightly, 'but a very enlightening one.'

Colebrook wondered what the old bat was talking about.

'We have come to call upon your niece, Juliana.'

Sholto Colebrook felt his mouth droop in consternation. Damn. 'What a shame! Juliana is from home at present. She has employment in Hungerford, your ladyship.'

Why on earth was the marchioness looking like that?

'*Really?* The young woman has only been with you a few days and already she has been put to work?'

He flinched. He might need the old dragon's goodwill if one of his schemes went awry, but on no account did he want the Trewbridges nosing around his affairs.

'No, no, my lady. You mistake the matter. When Juliana wrote to us she said she would seek work rather than be a charge on us. So before she arrived I found her—'

'*You* found her work? What sort of work?' The words snapped through the air, and he could feel them descending like arrows on his skin. The lady had a nasty tongue.

'At the infirmary, my lady.'

'Infirmary?'

The younger woman explained. 'At the workhouse, I imagine. Is that so?' she asked Sholto.

He did not get a chance to answer.

'The *workhouse*?' The marchioness sounded as though the workhouse was one step from Tyburn Tree.

Sholto struggled to placate her. 'It is good employment, your ladyship. The workhouse and infirmary are government-owned with an approved board of governors,' he hastened to assure her. 'It is guaranteed employment.'

'You, I trust, are not a member of this board?'

'Oh, good gracious no, my lady. That would not be ethical.' He tried to sound as virtuous as possible, but the marchioness pinned him with a look akin to a man of science regarding an unusual species of insect.

'It is to be hoped the income is generous. Heaven knows the poor girl will earn every penny of it. No doubt she is exposed to every rampant disease and to some of the most scrofulous people on this earth.'

'No, no. She deals only with the women and babes, your ladyship.' Sholto Colebrook was becoming anxious. Many doors would shut in his face if he displeased the Marchioness of Trewbridge. Not that he had ever heard she used her influence unfairly, but for some reason she had a bee in her bonnet about his niece.

He cursed the day he had replied to Juliana's letter. She was more trouble than she was worth, and at the moment she could be worth a great deal to him. 'Ah … her day off is Sunday, my lady. Perhaps—'

'Oh, she gets a day off, does she? In that case I shall send my carriage to collect Miss Colebrook next Sunday morning at ten o'clock. Is that clear?'

Colebrook gritted his teeth. The damned woman talked to him as if were a half-wit. Then, without a farewell, the marchioness trotted out the door, trailed by the younger woman who had a noticeable limp. Not much to look at either. That must be the new Lady Brechin. He watched a solicitous groom assist them into their carriage emblazoned with the Trewbridge coat of arms. Before he could collect himself the carriage took off and bowled briskly around the curve in the driveway. Blast it! He'd had the most valuable woman in the county here and he hadn't offered her any refreshment. If he had done that, they might have sat down and discussed many more useful things than his difficult niece. Well, he would make damned sure Juliana carried no tales to the Trewbridge household.

CHAPTER TWENTY-TWO

S EATED ASTRIDE HIS horse on the hill above Trewbridge, Colly watched the smaller of the two Trewbridge carriages approach the gates. He glanced at the sky. Just past noon. Why was the marchioness returning so soon?

His heart clutched in his chest. Had they not found Juliana? What had happened?

He could not go back to the house yet to find out. He must check on the two tied cottages nearest the road. The marquess had decided that Colly's first task would be the assessment of all the buildings on the estate, since that work had been delayed while a new steward was appointed.

From habit he rubbed the scar on his thigh. No doubt he would learn in due course what had happened at the Colebrook house. He could tell himself it was no business of his, that all he felt was a certain responsibility, but God, he missed her so much – that imperfect little half-smile and those chocolate eyes. 'Anyway, Hetherington,' he told himself. 'She's not for you. Get on with your work.' With the familiar feeling of having put himself in his place, he rode down the slope towards the cottages. He scrambled through his inspection of the head shepherd's cottage, hoping to get back to the main house as soon as possible.

'A bit distracted-like today, are you, sir?' Mrs Battersby enquired.

He saw the gleam in her eye. How much did the Battersbys know about what went on in the big house? Everything, probably. Battersbys had served Trewbridge for three generations.

He mumbled something indistinguishable.

Mrs Battersby smiled kindly, giving him the impression she was humouring the village idiot, and pressed him to try some of her home-made plum brandy.

'Next time,' Colly extemporized, and fled. He was sure he heard her laughing as he unhitched his horse and headed for the tied cottage nearest Trewbridge itself.

He'd been told that the second tied cottage was unoccupied. To his surprise he found signs that someone was living there. Although kindling was laid in the grate, no fires had been lit, which, to an experienced campaigner from the Peninsula, meant someone did not want to be seen. Dust lay undisturbed in the two rooms upstairs, but there were large muddy footprints going back and forth across the main room. A blanket lay folded in one corner.

Colly went outside and quartered the ground. It looked as though a man wearing heavy boots had walked back and forth several times. The footprints always led in the same direction – behind the main house. He would check to see if this cottage could be seen from the big house. He doubted it. The contour of the ground rose between the two buildings and besides, the wall of the Lady's Garden both sheltered the cottage and hid it from view.

Pondering, he rode back to Trewbridge. He didn't know if it was the normal thing for Trewbridge to shelter vagrants. Perhaps the family was aware that travellers occasionally used their empty buildings. Perhaps. An anxious disquiet nagged at him.

Normally he rubbed his own horse down. He enjoyed the equine whickers and quiet busyness of the stables. But today he could not spare the time to linger so he left his horse to be tended by an under-groom and strode to the study where he knew he'd find John and the marquess.

He found the marchioness and Lady Brechin as well. A family conclave was taking place. He backed out, but John called, 'Colly, come in. We need your help.'

'Yes?'

'Mama is thinking of kidnapping Miss Colebrook.'

Startled, Colly stuttered, '*K-kidnapping* her?'

Marguerite laughed. 'More or less. She was not home when we called.' Then she sobered. 'It is not good, Colly. Already they have set her to work. At the workhouse.'

'The *workhouse?*' He did not understand.

'The infirmary connected to the workhouse,' the marquess explained.

'Ah.' For one awful moment he had envisaged Juliana imprisoned forever with all the broken, penniless wretches who had nobody to intercede on their behalf, nobody to aid them. 'But how could she have started work so soon?'

'Her loving uncle had already organized it for her,' the marchioness said drily. 'Sholto Colebrook's reputation for eking the very last groat out of a situation is legend. That is why I was concerned. He has surpassed himself this time. I doubt whether Juliana rested for even one day before plunging into work.'

Colly's lips tightened. 'I warned her. I cautioned her to be careful of relatives she hadn't met for years. But she wouldn't listen because—'

'Because she was alone in the world,' the marchioness broke in. 'Don't judge her harshly, Colly.'

Colly swallowed hard. The rock in his throat threatened to choke him. The marchioness was quite right, and he hadn't meant a word he'd said. He was just so damned *worried*. His hands curled into fists. He needed to punch something – or someone.

'Anyway,' Marguerite said, 'we decided to send the carriage for her on Sunday which is her day off.'

Colly breathed deeply to force himself to relax. On Sunday they would get to the truth of the matter. If Juliana was in trouble, the Trewbridges would offer her a temporary home. Knowing Juliana, she'd be searching for work before the sun had set on her first day at Trewbridge. In his mind's eye he saw Juliana tenderly tucking a rug around a little old lady. She was a wonderful nurse. He should know. And how he remembered those hands – those soothing, firm, callused hands. He might not be able to marry her, but he'd damned well make sure her future was secure.

Then he caught himself up. There were other problems at hand. 'Could I discuss the tied cottages with you?' He didn't want to alarm the ladies, so although he spoke to the marquess, he looked hard at John.

'Of course. Let's spread the estate map over these tables,' John said. He smiled at Marguerite. 'I shall see you at dinner, my love.'

Marguerite cast him a curious glance, but said nothing.

'For heaven's sake! Tied cottages. We are discussing Juliana here. Much more important than tied cottages,' the marchioness objected. Her husband grinned and set his hands on her shoulders. Then he walked her to the door.

'I shall see you soon,' he murmured, tickling her cheek with his finger. And then he shut the door.

'What is it, Colly?' The marquess sounded intrigued.

Colly told them what he'd discovered and his lordship frowned. 'That's very close to the house. Do you think someone is spying on us? For what purpose?'

'The footprints lead from the cottage around to the door at the back of the kitchens. I checked.'

'I see.' The marquess nodded to John. 'John, would you and Colly question the kitchen and gardening staff about any strangers seen around here? I cannot go snooping around or it'll raise all sorts of speculation.'

And after Colly and John had heard the full story of the stranger from the kitchen gardener, they knew their problem was not about a prospective thief or vagabond passing through.

On the previous day an under-gardener had been startled by the sudden appearance of a stranger in the herb garden directly outside the kitchen door. The stranger must have studied the household for some time, because it was the time of day when only a few staff were on duty. At first the man said he was looking for work. However he must have seen the scepticism on the young gardener's face, for who would question an under-gardener about a job? So he changed tack and asked after Miss Colebrook. At that point the head gardener had come along and escorted the man from the premises. As the head gardener had said, 'Everyone knows that employment at Trewbridge is by word of mouth. He should have applied to Mr Hetherington. As for asking after Miss Colebrook ...' Here, the head gardener had shaken his head, 'Too smoky by half.'

Colly's stomach clenched. Trewbridge was not the target of the interloper. Juliana was. 'I think I have been very remiss,' he said.

The marquess raised his eyebrows and signalled John to take a glass of claret to Colly, brooding in a corner of the study.

'How so?' he asked.

'Well, when we were in Portsmouth, Miss Colebrook mentioned something about a man who seemed to be following us. I'm afraid I dismissed it as female imagination. Er ...'

Both the marquess and John Trewbridge nodded. They understood.

'Now I'm not so sure. What if this vagrant and that stranger are one and the same person?'

John tossed back his own glass of claret and got to his feet. 'We'll investigate further,' he said.

Colly and John walked around the cottage to see if they could find any more clues. It hadn't rained for several days and the visitor's footprints between the cottage and the kitchen gardens were easy to see. He had made no attempt to erase the muddy marks.

'Not an army man,' Colly commented.

'No, nor a Runner,' John added. 'So that leaves—'

'Someone up to no good,' Colly finished.

'Well?' the marquess enquired as soon as they returned to the study.

John shook his head. 'The person seems to have moved on, but ... I don't know. He left his blanket at the cottage. He may intend to return.

Surely he must have expected the cottage to be inspected at regular intervals?'

'Perhaps he isn't from the country,' suggested Colly. 'He mightn't be aware that an empty cottage is not necessarily an abandoned one. But it's frightening that he mentioned Miss Colebrook. Juliana must be warned. Perhaps he asked other people about her. Could we question the villagers, my lord?'

Colly seethed with overwhelming frustration. He could not interview anyone without the family's authority, and his instincts told him there was no time to lose.

'Rest easy, Colly. We'll make urgent enquiries both within the household and around the farms. John, would you ride into the village? The villagers don't know Colly yet, and they might not answer his questions. After that ...'

The marquess and John walked away, heads together, planning their course of action.

Within hours they had their answer. Two days previously a friendly stranger had accosted one of the grooms as he took a shortcut across the fields. The traveller had asked if the young lady was still at Trewbridge. On hearing that she had gone he'd become agitated, so the groom explained that she'd only gone to visit her uncle. Relieved, the stranger had thanked him and walked away in the direction of Melksham.

'Did I do something wrong?' Jack asked the head groom anxiously.

The head groom was wise enough to treat the incident casually. 'Not at all, lad. Thank you for your help. However, next time a stranger asks about anything at Trewbridge, it would be best to direct them to me.'

One thing the gardener and groom agreed upon was that the stranger was not from Dorset or Wiltshire. His tanned face and sing-song tones hinted that he might once have been a Cornishman, yet his clothes, though threadbare, suggested London.

Colly kicked himself for not being more observant. When Juliana had fancied they were being followed, he should have taken more notice. But he hadn't. Fool that he was, he had failed her – he who prided himself on his powers of observation that had kept him alive during his years on the Peninsula. His famous powers of observation weren't doing Juliana much good. Even now she might be— He drew a deep breath and said, as if it were a mantra, 'Sunday.'

'The day after tomorrow,' John said helpfully.

Colly prayed that Juliana would be all right until then.

CHAPTER TWENTY-THREE

JULIANA SAT ALONE at the scrubbed kitchen table as she did every evening. Tilly perched on a stool in the corner. Even though her mistress had been relegated to the status of a servant, Tilly refused to eat with her. She had been scandalized when Juliana suggested it. The kitchen was friendly and warm, and Juliana preferred to eat there anyway. Even if she'd been encouraged to eat in the dining room, she doubted she would have done so. The dirty gloom in there was not conducive to a healthy appetite. Cook, on the other hand, kept her kitchen spotless.

As usual, Cook barely gave Juliana time to wash her hands before she cheerfully banged dinner down on the big table where they kneaded the dough for bread. Juliana lolled in her chair. She was exhausted. It wasn't her work she found tiring – it was the endless unhappiness she encountered every day. And no matter how she helped them, the women still regarded her as an outsider. Sometimes she heard them muttering among themselves but all conversation ceased the moment she approached.

She was used to nursing men who had often poured into her ears the frustrations of a lifetime. Most of them would never admit they were in appalling pain but she had found their openness on other matters easier to deal with than the reticence of these women. Even Tilly came in for her share of wary looks. The Pirate had tried to help. More than once Juliana heard her say, 'She's all right. That Miss Colebrook.'

But still the women kept their own counsel.

And she did not understand why the women admitted to the infirmary did not bring their young children with them. It was a kindness that the board allowed the babies and little ones in leading strings to stay with their mothers unless, of course, the mother was infectious. Yet since Juliana had arrived she'd seen only newborn babies and very few toddlers. Kit was the only child over four she'd met.

As she cleaned and bound a festering wound on one young woman, she had asked about the woman's children.

'Their father has 'em in the workhouse, miss.'

'The workhouse! Surely that is no place for little children. What happens to them while their father works?'

'They are looked after. Whoever has no work for the day minds 'em,' the young woman explained. 'Some of the old codgers don't mind. Makes 'em feel useful. And when the tykes are old enough, they go to the Ragged School.'

'But … I don't understand. There's plenty of room here, and the board approves—'

'Board? That there board don't know what goes on in here, does it?' The woman had pulled her arm away as if Juliana were a leper.

Juliana had shrugged helplessly. Sometimes the English were a mystery to her. The Portuguese were far more practical and easier to understand. There must be some tradition here she had not heard about.

'Eat up, miss, before you fall asleep in your dinner,' Cook admonished her, and Juliana snapped out of her reverie. She and Cook had come to an understanding. When Cook saw Juliana wince and clutch her stomach after eating, she had been angry. 'It ain't my fault. The master is that mean, it's impossible to make good meals out of what he allows me to buy.'

Juliana had been forced to explain her stomach ailment. Since then Cook had been most kind, creating nourishing soups and setting aside for Juliana some of the tender cuts of meat destined for Sholto's dinner plate. Cook seemed to think that having a sensitive stomach was the preserve of self-indulgent gentlemen. 'What's a nice young lady like you doing with an old man's illness?' she had demanded.

Of course Cook's kindness came at a price. A few coins changed hands, and Juliana now had precious few coins left. When she'd tried to give Tilly her last shilling the young woman had said staunchly, 'When you get your quarter's income, Miss Colebrook, then you can pay me. I am suited. Mother togged me out before I came into service. I need nothing.'

'Dear Tilly.' Juliana blinked back tears, astounded that her maid had such faith in her. 'If you have the chance of a job elsewhere, please take it. I am very willing to give you a good reference. I don't know where I will go, but I intend to leave the workhouse as soon as I receive my first quarter's wages. It is not just the job. It is disheartening, but it's not the worst job in the world.'

Tilly shuddered and Juliana smiled. 'I've been in worse circumstances, Tilly. But I must get away from this house. I'm sure you understand. I'm going to ask the Marchioness of Trewbridge to recommend me for a position.'

Tilly startled Juliana with the fervency of her loyalty. 'I'll not leave you, miss. With all the goings-on around here you need someone on your side.'

Juliana smiled weakly. 'It seems silly for a working woman to need a chaperon, but the parish board would have had to supply one anyway. Mr Pettigrew tells me that when epidemics arise in the workhouse, I shall have to nurse the men as well as the women and children.'

Tilly was appalled. 'But they can't do that, miss!'

'Apparently they can. Believe me, if I'd known in Portugal what awaited me here, I would have stayed in Porto. At least Dr Barreiro did not expose his nurses to infectious diseases. He preferred to use medical students to attend those with infections, saying they must become hardened to disease.'

Tilly's jaw hung open. 'Are you saying those savages in Portugal treated you better than...?' She trailed off, realizing in the nick of time that her employer was one of those 'savages'. She gulped. 'Anyway, Miss Colebrook, you need me when that awful Mr Pettigrew comes creeping around.'

'Yes, I do. Not that Pettigrew is really interested in me, but I wouldn't put it past my uncle to box me into a corner and demand I make an honest man of Pettigrew or some such rubbish. They might feel a lot happier if I were under their thumbs, or they may have a different fate planned for me, which is even more frightening. Anyway, that's not for you to wonder about, Tilly,' she ended quickly. She had been rattling on as if Tilly were her best friend. Heaven only knew, she could do with a friend.

But Tilly nodded sagely. 'I reckon that Mr Pettigrew and your uncle are in a few shady dealings together.'

Juliana stared hard at Tilly. 'What have you heard, Tilly?'

'Nothing much,' Tilly said airily. But it was obvious she kept her ear to the ground. 'On Annie's half-day off last month she saw Mr Colebrook and Mr Pettigrew coming out of Prior's Bank in Hungerford together. They looked very pleased with themselves, laughing and talking.'

Juliana thought it was probable the two men had an illegal scheme going and that they'd been banking the proceeds. 'Tilly,' she mumbled, around a mouthful of deliciously tender beef, 'I know my room is very small, but would you mind...?'

'Yes, miss. I'll move my things into your room. Annie or James will help me shift the bed. Don't you worry none, Miss Colebrook.'

Anyone would think that of the two of them, Tilly was twenty-three and Juliana was sixteen. But a dose of country common sense stood Tilly in good stead.

They both started when Sholto Colebrook oiled his way into the kitchen. Juliana surreptitiously stuffed a succulent slice of meat beneath the inevitable boiled cabbage on her plate.

'Ah, my dear. I was searching for you,' he said, as if he had expected to find her anywhere but the kitchen. 'You had some callers today.'

Her heart soared and she looked up expectantly.

'Lady Brechin and the Marchioness of Trewbridge called. Was that not kind of them?'

Her heart settled back into its usual place. For one moment ... but of course Colly wouldn't call to see her. Ever. Unless his name was cleared. And it wouldn't make a blind bit of difference anyway because of her past.

'Yes. Very kind of them.'

'They have invited you to visit Trewbridge on Sunday.'

'Oh?'

'The marchioness is sending her carriage.'

Juliana stared at her uncle. He sounded pleased and yet, not so pleased. She was unsure of his mood.

'Why you, and not I and my wife should receive this invitation I have no idea. You are but recently come to England, yet she invites you as if you were bosom friends.' His mouth twisted in petulance.

Ah. Sholto Colebrook had been looking forward to toadying up to the Marquess and Marchioness of Trewbridge. He either did not know, or did not care, that the Trewbridges held him in aversion.

It was a pity she had not heeded the Trewbridges in the first place, but she had been hell bent on finding her relatives. Well, she had found her relatives and they were not what she'd expected, not at all. She suspected her uncle was a fine hair short of a criminal.

Her aunt drifted about the house like a ghost and assumed a cloak of vagueness to cover her unhappiness. Juliana rarely saw the woman. At the hospital, when soldiers had shown depressive tendencies like that, Dr Barreiro had found them an occupation. Sometimes he would set them to work sorting out clean rags. If they were convalescent, he sent them to outlying farms to help provide the food that was in such short supply.

But Aunt Colebrook could not be put to work.

Well, the Colebrooks might see Juliana as a poor relation, but she was much better off than they were. Certainly she was more fortunate than poor Aunt Colebrook. She had self-respect and, as long as she had two hands, she could work. Thank the Lord for the good sisters at the convent in Coimbra who had trained all their young ladies in useful occupations.

None of her thoughts showed on her face. Over the years she had had much experience in concealing her emotions. 'Thank you, Uncle. I shall not keep the carriage waiting.'

He glared at her. 'And see you carry no tales to the Trewbridge household, miss.'

'Tales?' Juliana made the word sound as incredulous as she dared.

'Yes. The Trewbridges are to be informed that we have treated you with great kindness.'

'Of course, Uncle.'

'And don't behave too familiarly, my girl. You might consider them friends, but you work for a living. There's a gulf that can never be breached between them and you.'

Tilly lingered in the shadows watching and listening. With the instincts of a hunter, Sholto Colebrook stiffened and spun around.

'You!' He pointed.

Tilly shuffled forward. 'There's no need to accompany your mistress on Sunday. You can make yourself useful around here.'

Juliana opened her mouth to argue, then thought better of it. If Tilly stayed here, she could report anything untoward that happened in Juliana's absence.

Taking her cue from her mistress, Tilly bobbed a curtsy that Juliana could not fault. In its brevity it was supremely insulting. Sholto hesitated, then swung on his heel and left.

They both exhaled with relief and Cook, who had been lurking in the scullery, waddled in and stood beside Juliana. 'You mark my words, miss. He's after your blood. You watch yer back.'

No need for that advice. Since the moment they'd arrived, Juliana had sensed the venom lurking beneath the avuncular veneer. She had shown her hand when she'd defended her mother's family and he could not *wait* to get even with her. Just like his brother. Her father had never let common sense get in the way of paying back a slight either. She must tread carefully. She shivered and Tilly scolded, 'You're cold, miss. You go on up and I'll bring your washing water.'

'Perhaps you'd like a bath, miss?' Cook enquired.

'Oh *yes*, I would, Cook, very much,' Juliana said in heartfelt tones. She always arrived home from the poorhouse feeling grubby. Many of her patients were admitted to the institution straight off the streets, and they were filthy. Worse, however, were the ones who had been sent down from Bridewell and Bethlem; they were crawling with lice and fleas. The last time she'd felt truly clean was the day she left Trewbridge.

'It is only a hip bath, but it's better than nothing. I'll put it in the scullery so *he* won't know about it. That will save Tilly trotting up and downstairs with jugs of water, too. You might like to wash your hair as well.'

Juliana wondered if that was Cook's inimitable way of telling her she smelled rank.

'We'd best be quiet, though, miss,' Cook explained. 'The master's quite firm about only one bath a week. Uses up a lot of fuel you see, heating the water.'

Juliana's lips twisted. 'How many baths does the master have, Cook?'

'He bathes every day, miss.'

They stared at each other.

The man was a self-centred nuisance like her father had been. But unlike her father, Uncle Sholto might possibly be a dangerous, self-centred nuisance.

CHAPTER TWENTY-FOUR

NEXT MORNING THEY arrived at the infirmary to find the Pirate stamping around in a fury.

'Where is he? Where's the boy?' she was demanding.

'What boy?' Juliana asked.

'You know. Kit Mortimer.' The Pirate twitched with anxiety. A tuft of midnight-black hair dabbled over her bad eye and her fingers were tightly clenched.

'The one whose ma just died?' Tilly enquired.

'Yes. I just *knew* Pettigrew would take him away. All the little ones disappear as soon as their mothers die. His ma asked me to protect him, but I failed. I shouldn't have brought them here in the first place. Oh, hell.' The Pirate hunched herself into a ball on the floor and rocked to and fro.

One of the other inmates dragged herself off her pallet and knelt down beside her. 'We never saw anything,' she murmured.

Distress tumbled through Juliana. Sweet little Kit, the helpful boy whose mother had begged her to 'go to Sir Alexander Mortimer. He will help.' She'd meant to ask Pettigrew where she could find Sir Alexander Mortimer, but it had slipped her mind. And now Kit had disappeared. If anything happened to him, it was her fault. Then the Pirate's distressed words sank into Juliana's consciousness. 'Pirate, stop cursing and talk to me. What do you mean Pettigrew takes the little ones when their mothers die?' She shook the woman's shoulder.

'Me name's not Pirate.'

Juliana blushed. 'Sorry. It is how I think of you.'

The slitted mouth turned up at one corner. 'Afore my accident I used to work for the Mortimers, you know. That's why I've kept me eye on young Kit. His ma was old Mortimer's daughter-in-law. Kit be his grandson.'

Juliana swallowed. Things were getting complicated. 'But who *is* this Sir Alexander Mortimer?'

'Local gentry. He's on the board of this 'ere place.'

'What?'

Several heads turned as Juliana's voice rose.

The Pirate fluttered her grimy fingers in front of Juliana. 'Hush! Don't let Pettigrew know, miss. He has no idea. To him, Mrs Mortimer was just another dying woman. We planned to see Sir Alexander, her and me. But the babe came too soon and—'

Juliana crouched down beside the Pirate whilst Tilly hovered beside them. 'You need to explain a few things to me, Pirate er … what *is* your name?'

'Minna. But since the accident most folks bin calling me Pirate.' She grinned half-heartedly.

'Minna, explain it to me. Why is Sir Alexander's grandson in here?'

'Usual story.' Minna's expression was grim. 'His son married a young lady Sir Alexander disapproved of. Well, 'tweren't that he disapproved of her exactly. But Sir Alexander already had a young woman picked out for his son. And he's a stubborn ol' coot. He threatened to disinherit the boy, so the young couple ran away. The master's valet and I went with them. We were the only witnesses to the marriage. There was no problem there. They were both of age. Just as well we went with them. Young Mr Mortimer and my lady had no more idea of how to set up house than a cat.' For a second she smirked at some reminiscence. 'But Mr Christopher's friends rallied round and gave him little commissions and the mistress took in sewing. We survived. And young Kit was born. Then last winter there was a carriage accident.' Minna pointed to her eye. 'It were nobody's fault; just a nasty accident on a wet, slippery day. A job-carriage taking a corner too fast slithered into ours. The young master bore the brunt of it.'

'What a ghastly thing, Minna!' Juliana thought of the multitude of injuries that such an accident could cause – the broken bones, the dislocations and abrasions and most of all, the debilitating shock that would slow down the healing.

'What about *your* injuries?'

'I weren't as bad as the master, Miss Colebrook. We couldn't afford a real surgeon, so a country doctor set the bones in his leg. But infection set in and—' She shrugged helplessly. 'It were heart-rending. He lingered for weeks in terrible pain and she – well, she was already expecting their second.' Her one eye glared at Juliana. 'When she got real sick I brung her 'ere. You saw the end of the story.'

'Oh, *Deus*. Both of them dead and Sir Alexander doesn't even know he has a grandson!' Juliana wrung her hands. 'What happened to the valet?'

Minna stared at the floor. 'No idea. The mongrel left us after the accident.'

'You must all have suffered dreadfully.' And no doubt poor Minna had borne the brunt of the work and anguish.

'What's done is done,' Minna said. ''Twas all some months ago.' A lifetime of hard knocks lay implicit in her words. 'When I brought the missus here after the birth she were mortal bad. I *must* find Kit. I'm all he's got.'

'*Sim.*' Juliana's distress grew as she envisaged Kit's confusion and despair. 'Minna, what did you mean when you said Pettigrew took the others?'

'Bless you, ma'am. You're a real innocent, aren't yer?' The Pirate gazed pityingly at Juliana. 'Where d'yer think the little tots get taken when they've no relatives to tend them?'

Juliana shrugged. 'To the foundling hospital, I suppose.'

Minna nodded. 'Yep. Some do. They're the lucky ones. Some don't. They get sent to Lunnon.'

'London? Whatever for?'

Minna's shoulders squirmed in embarrassment. 'What d'yer think, lady? What d'yer think? There's not many options for little tykes in Lunnon.'

Juliana ticked off what she knew of London. 'Climbing boys? Crossing sweeps? But who would take Kit to London?'

The Pirate squinted at her. Then she looked away. 'Pettigrew,' was all she said.

A black chasm opened at Juliana's feet. Urgent warnings crept up her spine. She crouched down next to the Pirate. 'Now see here, Minna. You'd better be very sure about these allegations of Pettigrew selling children into illegal apprenticeships, because if it's true, then I'll ... well, I'm not sure what I'll do but I'll work out *something*.' Her stomach roiled. That sweet little boy. He was no more than four years old. She shuddered to think of some bad-tempered employer lighting a fire in a grate to make him shin up the inside of a dark chimney.

Leaning her back against the wall, she hunched her head over her knees. Minna knelt beside her, patting her hand awkwardly. 'There, there, miss. Umm ... I take it you ain't never been to Lunnon?'

Juliana shook her head. 'But I've heard plenty about it.' She felt sick, sick, sick. Damn Pettigrew. He must not win.

She pushed herself to her feet and began pacing. 'It's Saturday today, isn't it, Tilly?'

'I think so, miss.'

'Tomorrow I can get help, but not today. And one day might make all the difference for Kit.' She swung around. 'Minna, when did you first notice his disappearance?'

''Bout an hour ago, Miss Colebrook.'

'Then he might still be somewhere close by!' She turned to Tilly. 'Tilly, you must pretend to go into Hungerford on an errand. Let me see ...' Juliana racked her brains to think of an errand that would sound viable to Pettigrew. She scrabbled in the bib of her apron and brought out her last four pennies. 'Here, Tilly. Take these and pretend I've asked you to procure me some – ah, some lavender water from the apothecary. You must search everywhere possible, but take care not to draw attention to yourself.'

Tilly nodded, her bubbly curls bobbing. 'I understand, Miss Colebrook. If they try any funny business with me it will be a different kettle of fish. I'm not a scared four-year-old who's just lost 'is ma.' She stomped off, the back of her neck bristling with anger.

Juliana immersed herself in work. Closing her mind to the suppurating sores prevalent among the women, she spread spermaceti ointment and bandaged where she could. Because the beds were straw palliasses dumped on the floor, she spent a considerable amount of time on her knees. Every day she wished for raised wooden cots such as they had at Sao Nazaire. She was sure she smelt permanently of eau de arnica because she rubbed so much liniment on her aching knees they were always slippery.

The gloomy day sent fingers of dusk into the corners of the room and she did not realize how time had flown until awareness slammed through her. It was well past noon, probably nigh on two o'clock. Where was Tilly? Juliana prayed that nothing bad had happened to dear, generous Tilly.

'Has anyone seen Tilly?' she called out.

Nobody answered. Blank faces turned away from her.

Their stubborn silence irritated her. 'Well then, does anyone know what happened to Kit Mortimer?'

Still no answer.

'Damn you!' She stamped her foot. 'Why won't you tell me? If one of *your* children were missing you'd expect me to help. Why won't you help me find Kit?' she demanded, her voice rising.

'It's not the same; he ain't yours,' a voice from the far end of the room sniped.

'He may as well be. I promised his mama I'd send him to his grandfather.' She loathed the way her voice was quavering but she couldn't seem to stop the pain seeping into her words.

'Ah, miss.' The Pirate approached her and laid a hand on her arm. 'They're sorry. But you see, until this morning they suspected you were one of them.'

'Them?'

'Pettigrew and the others who sell children for prostitution.'

Juliana could feel her mouth hanging open. She grabbed a desperate breath and clung to the windowsill. 'Sell them for...? Ohhh.' Facts were falling into place with the discordant clang of errant church bells. Pettigrew was admirably placed to sell children into lives of misery. Most of them, no doubt, died early deaths from disease and injuries. She could only begin to imagine the appalling agonies the children endured in the hands of the revolting scum who could afford to pay for their 'services'. Now she understood what the Pirate meant. And why the other women refused to deal with her. Juliana stared at the circle of faces around her. She found her voice at last.

'How could you?' she demanded. 'How could you think I would be a party to something so ... dastardly?' She struggled to find the English to communicate her abhorrence.

'Well, ain't you related to one of 'em? That bouncy little feller who's always visiting Pettigrew?' someone asked.

Her heart sank. If her uncle was in league with Pettigrew as she suspected, then she *was* related to 'one of 'em'. Oh yes. She could well imagine oily Uncle Sholto embroiled in a scheme where he and Pettigrew sold helpless orphans to anyone who could afford the fee. Both men were cold moneygrubbers, oblivious to morality or the feelings of others. She sprang to her feet. 'They shan't get away with it! I won't let them.'

The expressions on the women's faces ran the gamut from disinterest to scorn. One woman sniggered. No doubt they thought she stood no chance against a syndicate of criminals. They were wrong. Tomorrow she would seek help from the marchioness. She remembered Lady Trewbridge's words. 'If you are ever in any trouble, please come straight to us.'

But it was unlikely the Marquess of Trewbridge would allow his wife to interfere in the affairs of a government-run group of charities unless there was incontrovertible proof that crimes had been committed. Unlike a private charity, evidence of criminal activities would have to be explained to a hierarchy of persons; therefore that proof must be irrefutable.

She would worry about that tomorrow. At the moment, Tilly was her most pressing problem. Had she followed a trail that had ended in disaster?

'We will wait to see if Tilly returns with any news. I can do nothing more today, but tomorrow I am visiting some people who will help,' she told the circle of women. She was not as confident as she sounded, but she wanted to show these poor women they could trust her, even if she did speak with a foreign accent and had an uncle who was a shameful creature.

She peered out the window again. It was barely mid-afternoon. Plenty of time yet for Tilly to return. There was still hope.

She signalled to her assigned helper to begin checking the ambulatory patients.

The westering sun, struggling out from behind the clouds, poked weak shafts of sallow sunlight through the window. Juliana leaned her head against the window and prayed for Tilly and Kit. Something terrible must have happened to both of them. Juliana tried to stamp down on the helpless feeling welling inside of her. Lord, she needed a shoulder to lean on. She had got far too used to having Colly around.

'Have any of you actually *seen* any children being abducted?' she asked the group huddled around her.

'Well, I seen a little girl being shoved into Pettigrew's carriage once't, but that was afore your time, miss.'

'My man says as how it's been common knowledge around these parts for more than a twelvemonth,' another said.

That wasn't much help. She needed facts. The board might think that inmates' opinions were prompted by spite or disgruntlement. However the authorities might listen to her, Juliana Colebrook, a nurse employed by them – unless, of course, they thought she was attempting to incriminate her uncle due to some family squabble. She rubbed her arms, trying to warm herself up. This whole thing was such a tangle.

'There's only one thing I can do right now,' she told the assembled women. 'I shall have to ask Pettigrew if he has seen Tilly. I'll tell him the tale we concocted, that I sent her out to buy a bottle of lavender water early this morning and she has not yet come back.'

'Ooh, d'you think that's safe, miss? Bet he's got Tilly. He might take you away too.'

Wonderful. Juliana swallowed. 'I – I don't *think* so. The board knows I'm here, and Pettigrew is answerable to the board.' She was not at all sanguine about that because obviously Pettigrew was expert at pulling the wool over the eyes of the board members. Unless, of course, the board members were in on the ... no. Her imagination was taking flight.

She must *do* something. All her life she had done things, not agonized or talked about them. Her instincts nagged that time was running out for Kit and Tilly. To murmurs of 'You be careful, miss' she left the infirmary and crossed the quadrangle to the superintendent's office.

Pettigrew oozed unctuous concern. 'What's this, Miss Colebrook? Sent her out with some money? Good heavens, dear lady! Surely you don't expect her to come back whilst she has fourpence to pay for drink?' He laughed derisively.

Her heart sank. She had given Tilly exactly fourpence. That revolting creature had answered her question. It was too much of a coincidence for him to mention the precise amount. But she dare not challenge him without having someone to back her up. Stomach roiling she retraced her steps to the infirmary.

'What happened?' The group crowded around.

She shook her head. 'He has her. I know it.'

There was a collective gasp of horror. 'What will you do, miss?'

'Somehow I shall have to search the whole place to see if she's being held prisoner here.'

'What if Pettigrew catches you?' Minna asked.

'Then I shall tell him the truth, that I'm looking for Tilly. He won't know I suspect him of having anything to do with her disappearance.' Juliana would not stand around doing nothing while Tilly was in danger. Tilly had been wonderfully loyal to her, and if she were missing, she knew Tilly would move heaven and earth to find her.

'I'll come with you,' the Pirate said. 'You can search for Tilly and I'll look for Kit. I'll show you how to find your way around the workhouse and the men's infirmary.'

Juliana raised her eyebrows. 'Minna, I don't even know how to get past Pettigrew's office to get into the main building.'

Minna smirked. 'That's easy. Follow me.'

And off she trotted as Juliana struggled to untie her apron. She caught up with Minna outside the door and Minna raised a grimy finger to her lips. Pettigrew was crossing the square from his office to the men's infirmary.

'Excellent,' Minna beamed. 'Now we can go past the front of the building instead of creeping around the back.'

Juliana followed the Pirate's every move. Obviously Minna had *lots* of experience coming and going in places where she had no right to be.

Her serge-clad form disappeared behind a small building set back on its own behind Pettigrew's office. Juliana had never noticed it before.

'What is this place?' she whispered.

'Dunno. Storehouse mebbe.' The Pirate was more concerned with peering in the back window of Pettigrew's office. 'Well, they ain't in there,' she announced, after she had clapped a hand over her bad eye and peered hard with her good one for a few minutes. 'His office looks the same as usual.'

It was on the tip of Juliana's tongue to ask Minna how she knew what Pettigrew's office looked like, but she decided she didn't need to know what Minna got up to. It was more important to find Tilly and Kit than worry about Minna's illegal excursions.

Treading cautiously through the dried grass she edged along the side of the small outbuilding and around the corner. The building had no windows at all, but the padlocked door held possibilities. There was a large crack where the door hinges joined onto the jamb, but all was darkness within and she couldn't see anything. Now this was interesting. It was the sort of place where people could be hidden.

'Tilly?' she whispered as loudly as she dared. 'Kit?'

No answer.

'Look out! 'E's coming back.' The Pirate's shocked whisper stopped her in her tracks.

'*Deus*!' She scuttled back to Minna and they rushed alongside Pettigrew's office then set off at an angle behind the men's infirmary.

'If we go around here, we can get back to the women's infirmary by going in a circle,' Minna explained.

'Can't we carry on looking for Tilly?' Juliana asked, dismayed. 'We've hardly started searching.'

'I can, but you can't. 'E'll be coming to fetch you shortly. Time you went 'ome,' the Pirate explained.

'Oh! Yes, of course it is. I must hurry.' Juliana turned to Minna. 'Minna, don't get locked out tonight searching for Kit and Tilly. Remember the watchman locks all the doors at six o'clock.'

'Oh, I remember all right,' Minna said with a grin. From which Juliana deduced that Minna's nightly excursions were a regular occurrence.

They scurried back to the women's infirmary.

'Did you see anything?' a couple of women asked.

'No. No sign of them at all, and Pettigrew is prowling about,' Juliana said. 'There's nothing else I can do tonight. I will tell the marchioness everything tomorrow,' she said.

'Marchioness?' Minna asked in surprise.

'Yes. I'm going to see the Marchioness of Trewbridge,' Juliana explained. 'She's a very helpful lady. She'll know what to do.'

'Oooh, you be careful, miss. You're a nice lady, but you're not … well, if bad things happen, them nobs stick together like glue.' Minna worried her bottom lip with her teeth and a couple of the other women's faces looked doubtful. Obviously their experiences of the nobility had not been good ones. Juliana understood that. She had had similar experiences in Portugal. It seemed that often those with the most, were dab hands at ignoring the needs of those who had the least.

But the inmates were wrong about the Trewbridges. And, of course, Colly would help. He might not be influential, but he wouldn't sit by and let Kit and Tilly become absorbed into the black underbelly of London. She knew that as sure as she knew her own name. He might not see himself as honourable because of his father's indictment, but Colly was everything that was honourable, and more. She could rely on him.

She snapped herself out of her daydream. Pettigrew would be coming in a minute and she must have her wits about her to deal with him on the way home.

CHAPTER TWENTY-FIVE

HOLLOW-EYED AND exhausted, Juliana lay back against the cushions in the luxurious Trewbridge carriage praying that Tilly had escaped her captors and was on her way home this very moment. 'Keep safe, Tilly. Keep safe,' she muttered under her breath.

She wondered how on earth she could introduce the topic of child prostitution into the elegant atmosphere of Trewbridge. She could not imagine any social discourse that would lend itself to: 'By the way, did you know that child selling is rife in Melksham and Hungerford?'

But when the moment came, she found it quite easy after all.

As the carriage drew up at the bottom of the steps, she prepared to alight. The great oak doors flew open and instead of Twoomey, Colly strode out. He took the steps from the groom and extended an arm to Juliana.

'Good morning.' She placed her gloved hand on his muscled forearm and cast him a half-smile. Oh, it was *so* good to see him again.

'I have been out of my mind with worry,' he muttered, his face creased with a frown. 'Are you all right, Miss Colebrook?'

Puzzled, she struggled to understand. How could they possibly have heard about the troubles at Hungerford? 'I'm well, thank you.'

'We've all been concerned about you. Come inside. Everyone is waiting.'

He took her to the small withdrawing room where the entire Trewbridge family was assembled. Still clinging to Colly's arm, she stopped on the threshold and blinked. She felt rather like an actress at centre stage playing a role only the audience knew.

The marchioness surged forward. 'Dear Juliana, come and sit down. We have much to discuss.'

If Juliana was puzzled by Colly's behaviour, she was warmed by the marchioness's greeting. Marguerite, too, smiled a welcome and patted a space on the settle beside her.

'We are pleased to see you, Miss Colebrook. We've all been anxious about you,' the marquess said.

Juliana stared at the elegant, suave figure of the Marquess of Trewbridge and wondered why such an exalted person should be concerned about her.

Twoomey entered with a tray laden with decanters and biscuits. Colly, sizzling with impatience, prowled from one end of the room to the other whilst Twoomey dispensed glasses of Madeira and ratafia. Unlike the other ladies, Juliana gratefully selected the Madeira. Twoomey had scarcely left the room when Colly burst into speech.

'Juliana—'

Only Juliana saw the grin on John's face. She reddened and raised her chin. Colly didn't notice.

'Have you had any problems at your uncle's place?'

'Yes, but how did you know?'

'Just after you left, we discovered that somebody had been asking questions about you at Trewbridge and in the village.'

'Before I even arrived at my uncle's house? That doesn't make sense.'

'What do you mean, it doesn't make sense?' Colly demanded. There may as well have been only the two of them in the room. The Trewbridge family sat still and silent as Colly and Juliana stared at each other.

'I wasn't any threat to them until I found out what was happening at the Hungerford Charities. And I hadn't even *heard* of the Hungerford Charities until I arrived at Uncle Sholto's.'

'What the hell have Hungerford Charities got to do with the prowler?' Colly demanded in exasperation.

Juliana stared at him. 'What prowler? Are you not referring to the child selling at the Hungerford Charity Homes?'

Colly goggled. '*Child* selling?' He subsided on to a leather chair.

'Child selling!' Marguerite echoed. 'Juliana!'

'Do you have proof of this, my dear?' the marquess asked.

Juliana smiled wryly. 'I knew that would be the first thing you'd ask. I'm afraid I only have the word of several inmates and my own experiences.'

'And your own experiences are?'

So Juliana told them the tale of Kit Mortimer and about Tilly's disappearance. She also admitted that her uncle might be involved. There was a short silence.

The marchioness spoke first. 'You may leave Sir Alexander to us. We are acquainted with him.'

The relief to have that off her shoulders! 'I'd be very grateful, your ladyship. I had no idea how to find him. If he sees you are acquainted with me he might be disposed to trust me. After all, Pettigrew *is* the government-appointed superintendent and they trust him.' Then she added, 'Of course, it is even possible that Sir Alexander, too, is involved.'

The marchioness regarded her with respect. 'You have thought this out well, Juliana.'

She shrugged. 'I had nothing else to do all night. I was determined to stay awake in case my uncle … well, I don't know. And I hoped against hope that Tilly might manage to find her way home. I was too anxious to fall asleep.'

Colly jumped up again. 'There's something else you should know. And after that, perhaps you should …' He turned to Marguerite.

'Yes.' Marguerite nodded to Colly. 'Juliana, after we have discussed everything you must lie down and rest.'

Heavens, she must look terrible. 'No, no. I might oversleep,' she demurred.

'It won't be a case of oversleeping, Juliana, because you are not going anywhere. You will stay here,' Colly said firmly. Then he backtracked. 'Sorry, my lord. Uh …' He cast an anxious glance at the marquess, whose lips twitched.

'Of course she will stay here,' interrupted the marchioness. 'On no account will you return to that dreadful place, Juliana. And be assured we will do our best to help you find Kit Mortimer and Tilly.'

'Provided the reason for their going missing is the result of foul play,' her husband struck in.

The marchioness lifted a shoulder as if to say, *well, of course, foul play is involved.*

Juliana was amused to see the Marquess of Trewbridge lean over his wife and flip one of the artful curls arranged to hang near her earlobes. 'Let us not blunder in, my dear,' he murmured.

From which Juliana deduced that the marquess had occasionally suffered from the marchioness's impetuousness. Juliana smiled at Lady Trewbridge, admiring her impulsive loyalty and quicksilver reactions.

'However, we have not addressed the other problem,' Colly said, frowning.

'Other problem?' Juliana asked. Now what?

'The prowler that Colly mentioned,' the marquess explained. 'A stranger has been asking questions about you, Miss Colebrook.'

Juliana sagged back in her seat.

Colly rose to go to her, then sat down.

'Oh, no. I did not mean to bring trouble to Trewbridge,' Juliana apologized. 'Truly, I have no idea who – oh!' She turned to Colly. 'Could it be that man I told you about at Portsmouth?'

'I think it might be.'

'I racked my brains trying to work out what was familiar about him,' Juliana said, 'and yesterday I remembered. He did not seem to be English or Portuguese. He reminded me of some Spanish soldiers I nursed once.'

'Spain?' the marquess queried. 'Well, that enlarges the field. The people he spoke to did not mention a foreign accent, just that some of his English was difficult to understand.'

'Looks Spanish … difficult to understand,' John said. 'Probably Cornish.'

Colly nodded.

Juliana felt more puzzled than ever.

'Why would a Cornishman follow you around?' Colly asked.

'How should I know? Heavens, I don't *know* any Cornishmen,' Juliana said pettishly. Every limb was heavy and she longed to lay her head on a soft pillow and sleep for hours. She rubbed her forehead.

'Bed,' the marchioness said decisively.

Juliana stood up. 'Thank you, but I cannot stay here. It would be rude of me to leave my uncle's house without … I think some of this is my fault. I realize I am not the sort of niece he expected. Perhaps I should have tried harder to—'

'Tosh. Come with me,' Marguerite said and dragged her out of the drawing room.

Colly wondered by what peculiar peregrination Miss Colebrook had arrived at the idea that she was to blame for her uncle's behaviour. After longing for a family for years, even when faced with evidence of their perfidy, she could not quite bring herself to admit that the much-wanted family was beyond the pale. Instead, she had decided the fault lay not only with her family, but also with herself.

'If she tries any harder she will explode,' prophesied the irreverent marchioness. 'How ridiculous! She is the sort of young woman anyone would be proud to call family, yet that greedy Sholto Colebrook can only see her earning potential.'

Colly rose and began his usual pacing from one end of the room to the other. 'But what connection does Miss Colebrook have with a Cornishman?' he muttered to nobody in particular. 'She has no family connections in Cornwall.'

'Would her uncle have sent the man to keep an eye on her, d'you think?' John asked.

'But the fellow was in Portsmouth,' Colly objected. 'At that time her uncle wouldn't have known she was in the country.' He thought for a moment. 'Well, he might have. We wrote our letters as soon as we landed, and Juliana saw the fellow a couple of afternoons later. However, it's not likely. Why on earth would Sholto Colebrook send someone to spy on his niece? She was coming to stay with him anyway.'

'Perhaps the Cornish fellow was in Portsmouth carrying out other business for her uncle,' John surmised, 'and realized that Juliana was the niece of his employer. After all, Juliana mentioned child-stealing so I imagine every ship that comes in is surveyed for prospects.'

'You think her uncle might be that deeply involved?' Colly asked, appalled.

'It's possible.' This came from the marchioness. 'I hate to say it, but *nothing* would surprise me about Sholto Colebrook.'

'Now, Jeanne. We don't know anything for certain or we would not have let Juliana go there,' the marquess interrupted.

'Hmmph!' the marchioness muttered, *sotto voce*.

And when Juliana had slept for several hours and awoken refreshed, she said that nothing would keep her from returning to her uncle's house. 'I *have* to go back,' she explained. 'How else will I find Tilly and Kit?'

'You did your best to find Tilly, Miss Colebrook,' the marquess said gently. 'I suggest you leave any further investigating to us. I've already sent a messenger to London. However, I agree that you should return to your uncle's house so as not to raise suspicions.'

Indignant and startled, Colly raised his voice above the others' protests. 'My lord! What if something should happen to J— Miss Colebrook?'

'Now that I've visited here, my uncle and Mr Pettigrew would be reluctant to harm me, surely?' Juliana couldn't stop her voice from wavering.

'Yes; they will not risk any enquiries from this quarter,' the marquess said in an uncompromising tone. 'While you were resting I sent a note to Sir Alexander Mortimer asking him to come to Trewbridge as soon as possible.'

'Oh!' was all Juliana could say. She imagined Sir Alexander had been startled to receive the summons.

'I referred to the Hungerford charity homes. No doubt he will be very curious.'

'But what about the intruder?' Marguerite struck in. '*He* might be dangerous. And even though your uncle and this Pettigrew person might not harm you, they might keep you away from the infirmary so they can cover up their wrongdoing. That way we will never learn what is going on.'

Juliana grimaced. 'Our only recourse is to rely on Sir Alexander's co-operation. I hope he does not disbelieve me. But he'll know I'm not lying about his grandson because the Pirate can prove it.'

'Who?' five voices demanded.

Juliana blushed as all eyes were riveted on her. 'That's her nickname. Her correct name is Minna. She used to be employed by Sir Alexander and left to work for his son and daughter-in-law.'

'Excellent,' the marquess said. 'But you'd better make sure this Pirate doesn't go missing too.'

'No. Minna is safe. You see, Mr Pettigrew doesn't realize Sir Alexander's grandson has been in the infirmary. He takes no interest in the patients at all – never speaks to them.'

From across the room she felt Colly watching her. 'You won't try any more investigating on your own, will you?' he asked.

'Oh.' Juliana blushed. 'I was just thinking—'

'No!' said five voices in unison.

'Very well.' She subsided. It was immensely comforting to know she did not have to tackle this problem on her own. Almost as good as having family.

That evening when the Trewbridge carriage brought her home, she greeted her uncle with a serene countenance. 'Good evening, Uncle Sholto. The marquess and marchioness send their regards. I have a few preserves here from the kitchens at Trewbridge to give to Cook.' She showed him the basket supplied by Marguerite. It was a masterly touch, designed to let her uncle assume a friendship that did not exist.

'Well!' He smirked. 'That was very kind of them indeed, very kind.' He peered into her face and she edged back a step. 'What did they ask you about the infirmary?'

'Nothing. I could not describe the things I see every day in front of the marchioness or Lady Brechin. They are not used to such things,' Juliana said virtuously.

'Of course not.' He nodded, satisfied. 'Of course not.'

Breathing a sigh of relief Juliana went to her room, hoping she had thrown him off the track.

CHAPTER TWENTY-SIX

BUT HER NEWFOUND confidence did not last. Being in the lion's den was frightening. The following morning she hurried into the infirmary, almost twitching her skirt out of Mr Pettigrew's way as she passed. Trying to quell the cold shudders rippling down her spine from his gaze on her back, she scurried across the square and slammed the door behind her.

'You came back then,' was the Pirate's welcoming salvo.

Juliana nodded and said nothing. Should she tell Minna about the plan to talk to Sir Alexander Mortimer? Minna had every right to know about the rescue plans for young Kit. But it would be best if the investigation into Pettigrew was kept a secret. Loathing Pettigrew as she did, the Pirate might start prattling to the inmates about the plan. And with Pettigrew so cunning and unscrupulous, that would never do. He might well lay all the blame for their enterprise squarely on her uncle and, although Uncle Sholto was a nasty piece of goods, he *was* her uncle. Pettigrew must be caught red-handed with no chance of wriggling out of his share of the blame. Most important of all, they had to find Tilly and Kit before they disappeared into the London underworld and they could not do that without a certain amount of co-operation from Pettigrew.

So all Juliana said when she drew Minna aside was, 'Those people I told you about are helping us. They are meeting Sir Alexander.'

Minna's one eye lit up like a tallow candle. 'Miss! However did you do that?'

'Hush. Pure luck. It turns out he is a neighbour of theirs and they know him quite well. Please, *please* be quiet about this, Minna. And remember, we will need you for questioning.'

The Pirate grinned. 'I'm not going anywhere. I wouldn't mind seeing stubborn old Mortimer again. Bet he wishes he'd never driven his only son away.'

Juliana tiptoed through the day praying that the inmates would not question Minna's sudden high spirits. Her lugubrious stoicism had been replaced with a rollicking cheer rarely found in the infirmary, and Juliana gritted her teeth when Minna said loudly, 'Hey! Give Miss Colebrook a hand here. She shouldn't be carrying buckets o' water.'

Juliana had carried buckets containing a lot worse than water, but suddenly she was a heroine to the Pirate. However she needn't have worried. The other inmates were sunk in their usual apathy. They had already forgotten what had happened two days ago.

How she wished she knew what was going on at Trewbridge! If only she were there, in the thick of things. It had been *so* good to be with Colly again. In her uncle's house she felt alone, as if half of her was torn away. But as soon as she'd laid her hand on Colly's arm, she'd felt the loneliness recede. Best of all, she had seen how much the Trewbridges trusted Colly and relied on him. He was thriving in their household.

And he must have missed her too. He'd helped her into the carriage and his face had been taut with anxiety as he whispered, 'Please stay alert, Juliana. I don't like this at all. God be with you.' And when she'd gazed back at Trewbridge as the carriage turned to exit the gates, she had seen him standing beside Twoomey on the driveway.

She paced over to the infirmary window and peered out, trying to guess what hour it was. By now, Kit and Tilly could be in London. And the dread was steadily growing that Pettigrew and Sholto Colebrook might have sampled the goods first. It was not an unreasonable assumption. Neither man had any sense of honour or self-discipline. They would take what they wanted and someone else would pay for it.

By the time the summons came, her stomach was burning and biting.

At the knock on the door, her head jerked up from where she was spooning soup into the mouth of a young, vacant-faced woman sent recently from Bethlem. Some inept doctor had decided that this wretched bundle of misery had been 'cured' enough to work. So when Pettigrew's bang on the door frightened the woman into a trembling huddle, Juliana's simmering fury erupted. 'Yes?' she snarled, yanking open the door.

Pettigrew stepped back looking startled. 'Good heavens, Miss Colebrook! You had better show a pleasanter face than that. We are summoned to meet the board of governors this very minute.'

She stared at him, her thoughts tumbling end over end. 'Now? Is this the usual time for a meeting?'

'I fail to see what business of yours that is. I daresay they wish to meet you.'

Hah! Which meant he didn't know what the meeting was about. Good. It was too soon for the Trewbridges to have set any wheels in motion, but she might get to meet Sir Alexander Mortimer at last.

'One moment please,' she said to Pettigrew. She rushed to untie her stained apron and wash her hands.

Pettigrew grabbed her arm in an iron grip as they stepped out across the quadrangle and for one awful moment she wondered if, in fact, they were not going to a meeting at all. Then from the corner of her eye she saw two well-dressed gentlemen heading toward the big double doors of the workhouse and she relaxed. It was all right. A genuine meeting *was* taking place.

They walked into a hall set up with a long refectory table and chairs. As soon as the board, consisting of four gentlemen and a lady were seated, Pettigrew dragged her forward to introduce her.

There was something very strange about Pettigrew's attitude. He seemed hell bent on giving the impression that she was a close friend of his, *very* close indeed. Puzzled, she turned to stare at him and surprised a ferocious, almost desperate gleam in his eyes. It was as though he looked to her to lend him respectability. She tugged her arm away. She had no intention of letting these people think there was any sort of association between herself and Pettigrew.

One of the gentlemen stood up. 'I am Sir Alexander Mortimer, my dear,' he said.

She was not sure about the paternalistic 'my dear' but he looked to be a most respectable gentleman, just the sort of grandfather she would have chosen for Kit. He was a trifle portly with an air of pomposity, but he seemed kind. She smiled, and he smiled back conspiratorially. 'Later, you and I will have a chat, Miss Colebrook. The Trewbridges speak most highly of you.'

She bobbed a curtsy and he sat down.

Then a young man at the end of the table nodded to her. 'Very pleased to meet you, Miss Colebrook. I'm Easton. Hetherington and I spoke this morning and he told me about your war nursing. We are grateful to have such an experienced nurse at Hungerford.' He moved around the table and shook her hand.

Colly and the Trewbridges *had* been busy! They must have been up at dawn.

The other two gentlemen introduced themselves, then Sir Alexander introduced her to the lady. 'Lady Richelda, this is Miss Colebrook.'

Lady Richelda Stonehouse looked to be a rather starched-up young woman, but she nodded civilly and said in die-away tones, 'I don't know how you did it, Miss Colebrook, how a delicately brought up young lady could work amongst the wounded as you did ...' She trailed off.

Juliana reflected that 'delicately bred' did not describe her at all. For which she was thankful. If she had been 'delicately bred' she would not have survived the first day at Sao Nazaire.

'It is a pity other delicately bred women could not alter their principles and tend to the sick and dying,' Captain Easton said drily. Juliana smothered a grin when Lady Richelda cast him a venomous glance.

'Yes, well.' Sir Alexander cleared his throat. 'Now that the introductions are complete, I shall declare the reason for this special meeting.'

Juliana could hear the capital letters in his tones. He was a puffed-up old fellow. No doubt he often irritated the other members of the board, but all that mattered was that he would help her find his grandson.

'There have been some unusual allegations made about the disappearance of people from the women's infirmary,' he began, but got no further.

'Disappearance? Disappearance?' Pettigrew demanded like a wound-up parrot. 'How can people disappear?' He rounded on Juliana. 'Do you know anything about this, Miss Colebrook?'

'Miss Colebrook has nothing to do with it,' Captain Easton interpolated. 'These disappearances occurred before Miss Colebrook arrived.'

Everybody watched Pettigrew. Behind the wary eyes Juliana could see his brain racing. She could almost hear him sorting through ideas, discarding some, adopting others.

'Then it must be something to do with the midwife, Mrs Bunnythorpe,' he said at last.

'Mrs Bunnythorpe left the infirmary six months ago, Pettigrew.' Everyone in the room knew that Sir Alexander had purposely omitted the 'Mr' in front of Pettigrew's name. 'Some of these disappearances occurred within the last four months. Can you explain it?'

'I don't know what you mean. It sounds ridiculous. How can people just disappear?' Pettigrew blustered.

'Children, actually. It is children who have disappeared, Pettigrew.' The expression on Sir Alexander's face was that of a tenacious dog with his teeth into a tasty bone. He turned to his colleagues. 'I propose that we repair to Pettigrew's house to discuss the matter. It's not fair to ask him such questions in front of Miss Colebrook.'

This last comment appeared to be by way of a sop to Pettigrew's feelings. Juliana was not sure what it really meant.

Then Sir Alexander stood up and bowed in Juliana's direction. 'Miss Colebrook, we will meet later. But first we must resolve these complaints. The good name of the Hungerford Charities is at stake.' He turned to the other board members sitting at the table. 'Who is free to come with me to interview Pettigrew?'

Only Lady Richelda declined. Juliana realized the decision had been made earlier. This was not the first meeting the board had convened today. They wanted to see inside Pettigrew's house, otherwise they would simply have asked her to leave the room.

'You had best leave your carriage here, Pettigrew. You will travel with me,' Captain Easton said. He reminded Juliana of Colly. He had the same whipcord strength and calm certainty. He was the sort of man she trusted.

Lady Richelda beckoned to her. Oh dear. Now what?

'Miss Colebrook, I should like you to escort me through the women's infirmary if you please.'

Juliana stared at her, aghast. The lady had the right to see the infirmary, but did she have the courage? Some of the sights there were not for ladies such as she.

'Uh—'

'I usually organize the supplies for the women's infirmary. Captain Easton insists it is time I saw what my task er … involves.' Lady Richelda appeared to be speaking through her teeth. 'I shall rely on you to help me make a list of what is needed, Miss Colebrook.'

Amused at Easton's efforts to prod his dilettante colleague into doing more than dabbling her toe in the murky waters of 'charity', Juliana hurried the lady across the square. It would be best if she raced through the procedure because she did not expect Lady Richelda Stonehouse to last more than a few minutes. Meeting the Pirate should do for Lady Richelda nicely.

But Juliana had misjudged her woman. As, no doubt, had Captain Easton. Lady Richelda followed Juliana through the big room, nodding to the inmates and noting the supplies that Juliana required. When they settled in the corner allotted to Juliana for office work, Lady Richelda produced a small square of paper from her reticule and stared at it ruefully.

'I doubt this will be much good,' she said. 'And we have no ink. Can we raid Pettigrew's office?'

'Why not?'

Giggling like schoolgirls, they pattered back across the square and entered Pettigrew's sanctum.

Then stopped in the doorway. There was a stranger there, dressed in a bright red waistcoat. He was rifling through hundreds of papers stacked high on Pettigrew's desk.

'Ah, excuse me. Who are you?' Juliana enquired.

Lady Richelda elbowed her. 'He's a Runner,' she whispered.

'*Runner?*' Juliana eyed the stout individual doubtfully.

Lady Richelda giggled and the feather on her bonnet danced a little jig. 'A Bow Street Runner,' she explained.

'Oh, I see.' When she was younger, Juliana's father had mentioned the Runners and the work they did in the London area. She wondered what a Bow Street Runner was doing so far west of London. Her father had likened the Bow Street Runners to robin redbreasts. This rotund gentleman did not look as though he could investigate his way out of a blind alley.

But he knew about paperwork. He shuffled through papers as if dealing cards. The speed of his chubby, dexterous fingers was fascinating. 'May I help you, ladies?' he enquired, as if he were the owner of the premises.

'We need some paper and ink please,' Lady Richelda said.

'Help yourselves from the drawers. Just don't touch anything on the desk.' He gestured towards Pettigrew's impressive piece of furniture.

'Will we interrupt you if we stay here?' Juliana asked.

'No.'

Lady Richelda blinked and raised her eyebrows, but Juliana respected his forthrightness. He was busy, searching for something specific. His attitude indicated that he would not allow two silly women to prevent him from doing his job thoroughly. The Runners must already have uncovered Pettigrew's enterprise from the London end, which struck a chill into Juliana's heart. She could not see how her uncle could escape the law. On the other hand, Tilly and Kit stood a much better chance of being saved if the law was involved.

When the provisions list was complete, Lady Richelda stared at it. 'It is much larger than usual.'

'I'm sorry,' Juliana responded. 'But I've had to supply my own rags, lye soap and salve since I began working here. Laudanum is in short supply too, and Pettigrew only allowed me one basin. I need more.'

'B-but just last month the apothecary sent him two big bottles of laudanum on my behalf! I spoke to the man this morning and he commented that the infirmaries use a lot of laudanum. And I distinctly remember the Ladies' Guild from St Clement's sent two score earthenware bowls for gruel earlier this year to the women's infirmary.'

Juliana said nothing.

Lady Richelda was naïve but not stupid. 'I see,' she said. 'Pettigrew. He's made a profit while he denied the inmates what they needed. That man has a lot to answer for.' Tugging on her gloves, she got to her feet. 'Miss Colebrook, by tomorrow afternoon you will have all the supplies you require.' Her face very flushed, she continued, 'Captain Easton was right. I am guilty of not executing my duties satisfactorily. It is just as much my fault as Pettigrew's. I made it easy for him to withhold medicine from those poor women because I never checked to see how the supplies were used. You have my assurance that from now on I will carry out my duties more efficiently. Good day to you.'

She held out a gloved hand to Juliana, then, head held high, hurried through the big gates. Juliana could see a glossy carriage waiting. A groom stood at the heads of a pair of anxious blacks decorated with ostrich plumes, and a bowing manservant held the carriage door open.

Lucky Lady Richelda. Although at the moment the lady was embarrassed, she would come about. She had the strength of character to do so. Juliana shut the gates behind her.

Meanwhile, everyone had forgotten Juliana. How was she to get home? She walked around the rear of the main building. Only Pettigrew's horse and carriage were left. Everyone must have assumed that Lady Richelda would convey her home.

Perhaps she would have to stay here tonight. Then again, if Pettigrew implicated her uncle in his nefarious dealings, what would become of her aunt? Aunt Colebrook was ill equipped to deal with such a catastrophe.

No. She would have to go home, such as it was. She might be needed. And it seemed the only way to get home was to walk. It was a pity the board had not discussed payment of her wages before they left, otherwise she might have walked to the inn at Hungerford and hired a driver and carriage.

She turned Pettigrew's unhappy horse out on to the enclosed greensward at the back of the workhouse and said goodbye to her charges. Then she began the long trudge back home.

CHAPTER TWENTY-SEVEN

WEARY, SHE DID not relish a seven-mile walk after such a tumultuous day. In fact, she would give much to settle down beneath one of the hedgerows and curl up to sleep. Fortunately her sturdy, unfashionable half-boots were made for hard work and would stand her in good stead.

Tilly and Kit. Tilly and Kit. The refrain dogged her every step and hammered at her mind. It was all very well knowing Pettigrew was being questioned, but would the creature give up any useful information? God knew what was happening to those poor children – because Tilly, for all her sensible ways was still a child.

That slimy Pettigrew. Her hands tightened on her reticule. By heavens, if *she* questioned Pettigrew, she'd … well, she'd yank the information out of him in a trice. No gentlemanly rules for her.

She stumbled over a stone. *Concentrate*, she told herself. *Put one foot in front of the other as fast as you can and hurry home to find out what is happening.* Lord, she was tired, so tired. Her wretched stomach was burning again.

In order to skirt Marlborough she would have to take the Pewsey road, the same as the carter's dray did each morning. When she glanced up at the signposts, she realized the sun was beginning to set. It might not be a good idea to walk down the road alone at dusk. She hadn't heard any bad things about the area, but then she had heard nothing at all about this part of England. How could she? She worked six days a week and during that time met only disheartened women who cared nothing about the outside world.

A twig cracked behind her and she spun around. In the distance she could see a horseman descending the hill, but there was nobody close by. Behind her she heard a scurry of feet and relaxed. Just a rabbit, or perhaps a fox.

Then two sinewy arms wrapped around her and she screeched. *Deus*!

'Miss …' husked a voice in her ear. It was a long, drawn-out syllable that sounded oddly unlike English. Oh, God. She froze in fear, unable to escape those imprisoning arms. Her heart raced wildly, but she forced herself to calm down and think. That unusual accent – it must be the man who had been lurking around Trewbridge, asking questions about her. She was sure of it.

How could she escape? She heard his exclamation of annoyance as the feather on her bonnet tickled his nose. He was not very tall. She squirmed then sagged, a dead weight, hoping to surprise him. But he knew all the tricks and although he was short, he was very strong. As his fingers bit cruelly into the soft skin on her arms, she could feel the muscles in his forearms and chest flex. The pulse in her head thundered. It was happening all over again, that thing outside Porto. How many of them were there this time?

Unable to move her arms, she could at least call out. 'Help! Help! *Assaltante*!'

'Ssh!' Her assailant's hands smothered her mouth and she bit down ferociously on the soft skin of his palm. Then she recoiled and shuddered. His hands stank.

'*Aiyee*!' he yelled and uncovered her mouth to shake his sore hand.

Teeth gritted, heart threatening to break out of her chest, Juliana wriggled and elbowed, desperate to escape. Then she heard the most welcome sound she had ever heard – the thud of hoofs. A voice called, 'Coming, Juliana!' and Colly Hetherington thundered towards them on a huge black hunter the size of a giant mill wheel.

Her attacker's grip released abruptly and she whipped around to see Colly lying alongside his horse's flank. He dropped to the ground as his mount slowed, then launched himself at her attacker.

She stood aside. She was independent, but she was not stupid.

Her attacker put up no fight at all. Not surprising. Colly was six feet four inches and every inch meant business. Parlaying was not his style, action was. The attacker obviously recognized that fact and gave in.

Colly pulled the man to his feet and removed his jacket, then reversed it. He stuffed the captive into it and tied the man's hands together with his scarf.

'Juliana?'

His anxious voice soothed her heart. She swallowed the fear and said sedately, 'I'm fine, thank you.'

Colly quirked an eyebrow. 'Really?'

She had the grace to blush. She felt fine *now*. Now that he was here. Trying to look calm, she brushed down her gown and took off her bonnet to straighten the strings.

Colly cast a quick glance up and down the road, probably checking to see if their captive had any accomplices. Then he addressed the man in a conversational tone as if the past few minutes had never occurred. 'Now, fellow, tell us what this is all about.'

The captive looked dazed. Exactly the way Juliana felt. She shut her mouth. She knew it had been hanging open. When she had ever-so-casually enquired from his fellow officers about Colly's army career, they had been full of praise for his courage. They had mentioned his willingness to make decisions and bear the consequences of those decisions. They had been amused at the way his men cheerfully cursed him then followed his every order. But nobody had mentioned the speed at which he operated. *Now* she understood why he had been promoted. She had always assumed his courage alone had gained him that promotion, but the sheer speed with which he had reacted just now enlightened her.

She remembered Lieutenant Davidson. He had lingered where he shouldn't have, and Colly had raced in and grabbed him back to safety. Speed. Yes. She smiled to herself.

'You're looking much better,' Colly said, no doubt wondering why she was grinning like a Cheshire cat only two minutes after being rescued from a dangerous criminal.

'He's the man from Portsmouth,' she said.

'Hmm,' was all her rescuer vouchsafed. He walked over to his horse, standing quietly ('yes, of course it *would* be,' Juliana thought to herself, remembering the trouble she'd had in guiding Pettigrew's old bonebag into the meadow). Looping the reins, he tied them to the saddle. He rummaged in the saddle-bag and pulled out a canteen. Then, shocking both Juliana and her attacker, he slapped the thoroughbred's rump and said to the riderless horse, 'Home!'

'B-but ...' Juliana began.

'Horse!' Her assailant stared open-mouthed at the horse fast disappearing down the Pewsey road.

'Yes,' Colly said. 'He's one of John's best. He'll go straight home. They'll send someone to search for me.'

Juliana raised her eyebrows sceptically. He had a lot of faith in a mere horse. She'd had very little contact with horses, but her limited experience with Pettigrew's unco-operative mare and her time with the two donkeys between Coimbra and Porto had left her with no complimentary impression of the equine fraternity. Now the three of them were stuck here on a country road, awaiting the pleasure of the Trewbridge grooms, always supposing the damned horse *did* go home.

*

'It will be all right, you'll see,' Colly said confidently.

Well, he was not *totally* certain that Brigand would head straight home. Brigand adored milk thistles and there were hundreds of milk thistles between the Pewsey road and Trewbridge. But Colly had no alternative. He could not manage Juliana, a prisoner and a horse all at once. And he owed it to the Trewbridges to take the assailant directly to them. They needed to find out if the man had been loitering around Trewbridge for reasons other than his interest in Juliana. If so, what had he learned about Trewbridge and what did he plan to do with that knowledge?

Colly lowered his captive on to a patch of clover beside the road. Whipping his own cravat from around his neck, he hobbled the prisoner with it.

'Thank goodness you were on this road,' Juliana said.

He nodded towards the crossroads. 'I was at a farm on the Upavon–Pewsey road negotiating the purchase of some livestock.' He didn't tell her that he could have arranged for the purchase any day this week, but when Captain Easton told him their plan for unmasking Pettigrew, Colly had decided to work as near as possible to Hungerford in case Juliana needed him.

And she had. Thank God he had come upon them at just that moment. Otherwise the fellow might have dragged her off the road and he would not have found them so easily.

Juliana eyed her erstwhile captor. The man had been sleeping rough for some time and needed a bath. Colly was amused to see her reach into her reticule and pull out a handkerchief to wipe her mouth. She scrubbed it over her teeth.

He grinned. 'Bit him, did you? Tsk, tsk.'

'What did you expect me to do?' she asked, raising her chin.

'Exactly what you did. Behave like a sensible woman and not swoon or do anything silly like that.' He grinned again and she smiled back. He felt his heart lift.

He tramped the high grasses flat for her at a suitable distance from her grubby captor, then reached out and took her hand. 'Sit down, Juliana. We might have a long wait.'

The sun had set and gabbling waves of sparrows and rooks were settling in a line of poplar trees further down the Pewsey road. In the soft twilight the two of them sat down to wait.

'Here.' Colly handed her the canteen of water.

She drank, obviously washing away the awful flavour of whatever it was that had her curling her lips. Colly did not offer the canteen to his prisoner, although the man eyed it longingly.

'I'll leave it to the marquess to question him,' Colly murmured. He had to bend closer to her so the Cornishman couldn't hear. At the same time Juliana turned her head to face him. Two inches apart they stilled, remembering ...

Colly contemplated the smudge of dirt on her neck and the flushed, damp skin that told of fear rigidly suppressed, and forgot everything – all his long-held resolution, his past, her future. She needed reassurance. He could give it. He was the only one who could.

'Juliana,' he breathed, fingering a loose tendril of hair curling on her shoulder. Of their own volition his hands slid down and curled protectively over the fragile feminine bones. He pushed off her bonnet and tugged her closer. She leaned into him and rested her head against his chest trustingly. Colly's heart contracted. He actually felt it tighten and quiver. Then he closed his eyes. His other arm came up to enfold her.

Mine. This was his woman; the one he wanted forever; the one he couldn't have. But on a country road in England on a late summer evening, he was making a memory he would always cherish. For a while she was his.

CHAPTER TWENTY-EIGHT

THAT WAS HOW John found them, more than an hour later. He rode up, following the smaller Trewbridge carriage. When Brigand had come home without Colly, John's first thought was that Colly had been thrown. However, as soon as the groom told him about the looped, carefully tied reins he knew that Colly was sending him a message. It was a trick they'd used on the Peninsula. If the rider had looped the reins around the pommel then set the horse free, he was probably injured and unable to ride any further.

So John was not unduly worried when the head groom informed him that Brigand had trotted home, a milk thistle protruding from his teeth, rather blown and very pleased with himself. John had requested the under-groom to take the small carriage as far as the Upavon–Pewsey road and followed along on horseback. Colly had gone in that direction earlier. He should be easy to trace provided he had kept to the main road.

Sure enough, John came upon his friend in the moonlight, Miss Colebrook in his lap, his head resting on hers. Colly's long body was twisted like a corkscrew to accommodate Miss Colebrook's frame, and the lady was asleep. Her lips were parted, and as John dismounted he heard a distinct whuffle when she exhaled.

He hobbled his horse and strode over to them.

'Thanks, John,' Colly murmured quietly. He nodded towards a disconsolate figure huddled on the grass. 'There's our visitor.'

'Vis—? Oh, you mean the person who's been lurking around Trewbridge?'

'Mmm.' As Colly replied, Miss Colebrook stirred. She wriggled on his lap and burrowed closer, her face nuzzling his throat.

John smothered a laugh. His poor friend must be *very* uncomfortable. He knew from experience that when Marguerite wriggled on his lap like that, his only recourse was to rush her upstairs to the privacy of their bedroom. However, poor Colly could not do that with Juliana.

'Ah ... Juliana?' he heard Colly whisper.

John looked at the prisoner who stared back, chin raised, saying nothing. This criminal might be a hard nut to crack but that would change, John thought grimly. He had no hesitation in leaning on a man who'd not only attacked Juliana, but who had used Trewbridge as a means to an end.

There was a gasp from Juliana as she surfaced.

'S-sorry,' John heard her mutter as she struggled out of Colly's lap. He strolled over and stretched a hand down to her.

'Here you go, Miss Colebrook.' He grinned to himself. Would he have fun teasing Colly later! Miss Colebrook clearly didn't care a jot about Colly's so-called bad reputation. She seemed to be very content there in his friend's arms.

As for Colly, John had never seen such a wistful expression on his friend's face. Defiantly Colly stared John down, and John turned away to gaze reflectively at Venus in the heavens. He heard a rustle as Miss Colebrook rearranged her skirts and then some stamping from Colly as he restored the circulation in his long legs.

We must keep these two together, he thought. They are made for each other. What was keeping them apart? Only Colly's pride, surely? Or was there something else?

Then John shook his head. He had things to do. There would be time enough to worry about his friends later.

CHAPTER TWENTY-NINE

JULIANA WANTED TO go to her aunt at once, but John and Colly overrode her protestations.

'You are coming home with me ... er ... us,' Colly said.

Her heart gave a hopeful little flip. He wanted her with him. Also, she noticed how he had said 'home'. He now looked upon Trewbridge as his home. That was good, very good.

But she did not feel at all happy when she interpreted what their prisoner had to say. The scruffy fellow sat in the kitchens, gulping down a large mug of water. They had thought it prudent to question him there rather than above stairs where he could run his eye over the household appointments.

Twoomey shooed all the kitchen staff off to their quarters. They'd been pleased to have an early night, but had all been *very* curious to know what was going on. Juliana heard Twoomey making them a vague explanation that actually said nothing at all. In spite of his nosy, finicky ways, he was a great asset to Trewbridge.

The prisoner was not forthcoming. He leaned away when Colly brushed past him but treated John to another of his hard-edged stares that contained a certain amount of contempt.

Until John stood up and strolled towards him.

Colly and John both had experience in questioning prisoners of war and John was the more experienced. He stood behind the prisoner and pressed his hands on the man's shoulders. The prisoner jumped and screwed around, trying to see John's face.

'Sit still,' John growled. His wife and parents looked on in surprise.

'Wh-what are you doing?' the prisoner asked.

'Nothing. Absolutely nothing.'

'I don't believe you!' Again, the scruffy fellow tried to move and John pressed down hard.

'I said to keep still.'

Their captive licked his lips and tried another tack. 'Here.' He held out his empty cup, probably hoping that John would release him and take the cup.

Colly stalked across the room to join them. 'I'll take that,' he said.

And now the wretched man was sandwiched between two uncompromising, seasoned campaigners whose stance had subtly altered. There was a short silence, then the prisoner babbled, 'I'm not to blame. Just acting under orders.'

He worked for Mr Sholto Colebrook, he said. John grunted and cast a meaningful glance at his father.

But that was the simplest part of his story. Juliana found his words very difficult to translate because of his broad accent. And she was desperate to know what he was saying because the man might possess vital knowledge about Tilly and Kit.

Sitting near the dying embers of two big ovens, they tried to sort out the stumbling explanation from the prisoner. It seemed that Sholto Colebrook had long ago expanded his employment business beyond the gates of the Hungerford Charity Homes. He employed several scouts, one of whom was their captive, to search out suitable children and young women. They concentrated on those who were orphans or friendless.

'If they'se come from outside Lunnon, they often be cleaner and fresher, if y'know what I mean,' the scruffy man explained. 'There be a good market for new blood.' The cadences of his sing-song voice failed to hide the horror implicit in those words.

Juliana swallowed. *Please* God, keep Tilly and Kit safe. 'Why did you follow us?' she asked the man. 'I saw you at Portsmouth and then you came here, searching for me. Why?'

'You wasn't supposed to notice me at Portsmouth, miss. I got too close. Didn't expect you to see me.'

'Why?' she demanded.

'Mr Colebrook reads all the shipping news, he does, and since you wrote to him a year ago, we all been primed to keep an eye out for ships from Portugal. When you come, you was to be a feather in 'is cap, you was.' The creature nodded at Juliana. 'We need a nurse 'cos some of the children get awful sick. Plenty more where they came from o'course, but sometimes they're favourites. Men ask for 'em specifically.'

Juliana shuddered, and the marchioness pulled her skirts tightly around her ankles as if to avoid all contact with the miserable creature in front of them.

He didn't notice, intent on his story. 'Your uncle thought you'd be a real hasset to the business.' Then he shook his head in sorrow. 'But when you arrived, you wasn't what we expected. Not a real Colebrook 'tall, Mr Colebrook says.' Here, the prisoner lapsed into gloomy reflection, no doubt ruminating upon the waywardness of females.

Juliana stared into the fireplace. She did not dare look at anyone. What must they think of her appalling family? Nauseated, she pressed a hand to her stomach.

'Miss Colebrook?'

Twoomey was holding out a glass of sherry. 'Th-thank you, Twoomey,' she murmured, flicking a quick look at the marquess. The marquess was not looking at her in horror, however. Instead, he was looking thoughtful.

'Tell me, my man,' he said to the prisoner, 'is there someone in London who runs the business from that end? Someone else apart from Mr Colebrook, that is.'

The prisoner's entire demeanour changed. He shrank within himself and muttered, 'No, no. You don't want to tangle with 'im, my lord. No. He's evil. Please, sir—'

'His name?'

'Dunno,' whispered the wretched creature. 'Doan't want to know. Please—'

'Where does he live?'

'Doan't know. Whitechapel mebbe?'

'No doubt,' the marquess said drily. 'Unfortunately, Colly, that has probably put paid to the idea of keeping the whole thing quiet. We can't control an unknown individual whom we have no jurisdiction over.' He turned to Juliana. 'I'm sorry, my dear. We will do what we can, but I fear your name will no longer be a reputable one.'

Had it ever been, she wondered? She stared at the marquess, struggling not to cry as a ball of tears burned her throat. Oh God. Could the Colebrooks sink any lower? At this rate she and her aunt would find themselves in Newgate. 'Why did you search my room?' she asked her attacker.

The fellow blanched and shuffled his feet. 'It were 'im from Lunnon sent word I was to do that. Colebrook wasn't to know. The Lunnon man wanted to know all about you.'

'What did you tell him?' Colly asked.

'Sent word you was just what you said. Colebrook's niece. A nurse.' The fellow shrugged.

Colly looked at him in silence, an unpleasant expression curling his lips.

'What are you going to do with me?' Juliana's attacker asked fearfully.

'Give you back to the evil man in London,' John said, carelessly.

The man folded up like a set of bellows in summer. 'No! Please, sir. I'll do anything ... anything ...'

'In that case,' Colly said acidly, 'be quiet and let us think.'

Eventually it was decided to feed the man and send him on his way – south, back to where he'd come from.

'If we hear you are back in these parts, I shall have you in Newgate before you can say Cornwall,' the Marquess of Trewbridge warned him.

'It were a job, my lord, just a job. No jobs to be had in Cornwall.'

'Try the tin mines. Now get out,' his lordship replied bitingly.

Twoomey grabbed the man's arm and dragged him out of the kitchen.

Everyone looked at Juliana. She could feel the pressure of unshed tears sitting on her chest and couldn't prevent a small sob escaping.

Colly reached for her, but the marchioness got there first. She tucked her arm around Juliana. 'Come, my dear. You need to sleep.'

Sleep? Juliana lay in the beautiful bedchamber allotted to her and wondered how the Marchioness of Trewbridge could possibly imagine that having an uncle who had committed such heinous crimes would be conducive to peace of mind. Dear Lord, she came from a despicable family. Her father had certainly not been lily-white. He'd been involved in the most awful scandal in Egypt over some artifacts that had turned out to be replicas. And now her uncle ... What on earth had made the two brothers like that? Mãe had been honest and true, and Juliana could not imagine what she had seen in Philip Colebrook to invoke such blind love.

She rolled over in the big soft bed. It wouldn't be long before the marquess decided to wash his hands of the whole débâcle. A man in his position could not afford to be connected to people like the Colebrooks.

She wondered if the Runners had arrested Pettigrew. If they had, he would incriminate her uncle to save his own skin. Colly had whispered as he handed her down from the carriage earlier that her uncle seemed to have disappeared.

What was going to happen to her? The Hungerford Charity Homes would not want her as an employee now that her uncle was implicated along with Pettigrew.

A tear slid down her cheek. All that bright promise of a new life had sloughed away. She was alone again.

Hours later she slid into an exhausted sleep wherein she was chased by strange creatures. She seemed to be running towards something or someone but she wasn't sure where she was going.

CHAPTER THIRTY

S HE JOLTED AWAKE when a maid eased back the heavy velvet curtains. 'Sorry, miss. They said to wake you. There's a gentleman downstairs waiting for you. I brought your hot water.' She bobbed a curtsy.

She had also brought a cup of hot chocolate. Such luxury! Juliana wriggled her toes and stretched before realizing what Dora had said. 'Dora! It *is* Dora, isn't it?'

'That's right, miss. Now don't you worry about your dress. I've pressed it right and tight and Lady Brechin sent along brushes and combs for your hair.'

Juliana finally managed to shake off the cobwebs of sleep. 'Someone is waiting for me, you said?'

'Yes, miss. Sir Alexander Mortimer, his name is.'

'Oh! Dora, please send word that I shall be ten minutes only.'

'Ten minutes?' Dora asked doubtfully.

But Juliana had already bounced out of bed. She glanced down and saw she was wearing an embroidered night rail, not a flannel one as usual, but a fine lawn one, delicate enough to crush and hold in one hand. Marguerite again. Juliana had been so exhausted last night she hadn't noticed what Dora had slipped over her head. Dear Marguerite was a good friend. Juliana would miss her.

'Ten minutes is all I need,' she assured Dora.

And she was true to her word, although gulping down hot chocolate first thing in the morning was not the best thing for her digestion. As she hurried along the hallway, Dora trailed behind her, pinning up loose tendrils of hair.

Sir Alexander Mortimer sat in the small withdrawing room reading the *Observer*. He flung the paper aside and sprang to his feet when she entered. 'My dear Miss Colebrook, I believe you had a dreadful time of it yesterday. It wasn't that we forgot you, but our business took longer than we expected.'

'Sir,' she broke in, 'have you found Kit?'

Sir Alexander shook his head. 'It took us a long while to wring any useful information out of Pettigrew. And although we now know which part of the London rookery the children are sent to, there is one glaring problem that only you can rectify.'

'I?' Juliana asked. Was he going to question her about her uncle's involvement? She knew nothing that would help. And she shrank from returning to the Colebrook home although she knew she must. Not only were all her possessions there, but she felt honour bound to ensure her aunt was cared for.

After that, family or no family, she would avoid any further connection with them.

'My dear, you are the only one who knows what Kit looks like. Also, your maid, I believe, is missing. We need you to come with us to London to identify Kit and – what is your maid's name?'

Juliana thought wryly that Tilly was far from important in Sir Alexander's mind. He needed Juliana to help him search for his grandson so he was obliged to humour her.

'Tilly,' she said. 'Her name is Tilly. She will protect Kit as best she can,' she added. 'Tilly is resourceful.'

'Provided they are still together,' Sir Alexander said with a shudder. 'Pettigrew told us of the various houses he and ah ... others own in the rookery, but even he was unsure if the proprietors kept the children together with the women.'

Sir Alexander seemed to be skipping over the horrific facts as best he could in order to spare her feelings. She noticed the finesse with which he avoided naming her uncle and tensed. Had Pettigrew said that Sholto Colebrook was the leader of their revolting enterprise?

Then without ceremony Colly strode into the room, followed in a more leisurely fashion by the marquess and Lord John.

'This is a very early visit, Sir Alexander, is it not?' the marquess enquired, inclining his head in acknowledgment of Sir Alexander's bow.

'Now that we have some idea where to search, we must look for my grandson straight away,' Sir Alexander said, waving his hands restlessly.

'We shall find him.' The marquess was kind but firm. 'I had people out searching as soon as Miss Colebrook apprised us of the situation. And with Pettigrew's additional information, we will find them soon.' He smiled at Juliana. 'I trust you had a good sleep, my dear. We learned very late last night that Tilly and Kit are at a house in Whitechapel.' Then he turned back to Sir Alexander. 'We need to make careful plans if we are to take the villains by surprise.'

Juliana could see that Sir Alexander was taken aback. He had expected to rush off immediately. The old gentleman twitched with anxiety, and although Juliana understood his impatience, she was not sure she could trust him. This man had cut off his only son because the boy had married someone not of his choosing. He might now be remorseful, but he had indirectly caused the deaths of Kit's parents. Although she pitied him, she could not find it in herself to like him very much.

Colly herded her into the breakfast room as if she were a recalcitrant bullock. She understood that he, too, wanted to curb Sir Alexander's impetuosity. From their behaviour she presumed he and the marquess had a plan they did not want the authorities to know about. For her sake they were trying to recover Kit and Tilly without implicating her uncle. She had no intention of joining Sir Alexander on an ill-thought out, fruitless expedition that might jeopardize the marquess's plan.

Having decided thus, she helped herself from the chafing dishes on the sideboard and prepared to sit at the table.

She found Colly at her elbow. He pulled out a chair for her.

'Thank you, Brigade-Major.' She remembered how Lord Brechin had found them yesterday, cuddled together, and avoided Colly's eye.

Colly did not seem to find the situation at all embarrassing. Under cover of the general conversation he enquired, 'Are you well after yesterday's incident?'

She smiled shyly. 'Very well, thank you,' and felt a blush heating her face.

Colly murmured, 'Don't fret about your uncle's wrongdoing, Juliana. It seems there is nothing one can do about awkward relatives.'

'Is there no news of my uncle at all?' she whispered.

He shook his head. 'He has disappeared.'

'Which is tantamount to admitting his guilt,' Juliana said despairingly. 'Nothing the marquess can do will help him now. How much did Pettigrew implicate him in the child-selling racket?'

Colly toyed with his toast. 'I'm sorry, Juliana. Pettigrew was trying to save his own neck. He insinuated that Sholto Colebrook was the prime instigator. However, that did not save Pettigrew. He is on his way to Newgate.'

She put down her knife and fork. 'Then that is the end of my employment. I had hoped … well, I don't like the place. Naturally I wished for something better. But Colly,' she touched his hand fleetingly and felt his skin twitch, 'I *need* employment. I have no money at all. None.' There. Now he knew how desperate she was.

'Excuse me, Miss Colebrook. Can you be ready to accompany Sir

Alexander in fifteen minutes?' the marquess asked. 'And Colly, I think you should go, too, in order to protect Juliana's er … interests.' He nodded to Colly. 'Let us work out how best to go about this thing.' He rose from the table and headed for his study.

Colly excused himself, picked up his coffee cup and followed the marquess.

Sir Alexander said indignantly to Juliana, 'Fifteen minutes? Does he not realize the urgency of this mission?'

'He does, Sir Alexander,' she soothed. 'But he knows more than he is saying. Do have another cup of coffee and I shall be with you in a trice.'

As the three of them climbed into the large carriage, the marquess handed Colly a note. 'These are the names of the men to liaise with, Colly,' he said. Then he turned to Sir Alexander. 'I trust you will be guided by Brigade-Major Hetherington, sir. My men have been searching the rookery all night and have some information which they will pass on to Mr Hetherington.' He nodded to Colly. 'It's in your hands now, Colly.' Then he stood back for the groom to shut the door.

CHAPTER THIRTY-ONE

'IT'S IN YOUR hands now, Colly,' played an endless refrain in Colly's head. The marquess seemed to have unbounded faith in his abilities. That was all very well, but Colly had not been to London for several years. He was unsure of finding the place where Tilly and Kit were imprisoned. The rookeries of London were a complex of interwoven alleyways where even a man well versed in their intricacies could still get lost. From all accounts Rosemary Lane was not a salubrious address, though the driver and groom seemed sanguine enough. The groom was armed with a serviceable pistol and Colly had his own double-barrelled pistol too, of course. Apparently the groom possessed a handy bunch of fives. Colly could truthfully say he did not fall short in that category either.

The men he was to meet were servants from the Trewbridges' London townhouse who 'often carried out extra-curricular errands' for his lordship. Lord Trewbridge had told Colly that fortunately these men knew London 'like the backs of their hands'.

Colly's main problem was to restrain fidgety Sir Alexander. During his time on the Peninsula Colly had met many men like Sir Alexander. If one did not control them, their impatience tended to escalate and infect all those around them.

'It will be several hours till we reach the outskirts of London,' Colly said casually. 'We had best use the time for rest.' He sat back on his seat and, leaning his head against the padded leather headrest, closed his eyes. Of course he would not sleep. But he hoped the others would.

Through his lashes he peered at Juliana. She gave him her little imperfect half-smile and his heart flopped around in his chest as though he had run a mile. Then she leaned forward to speak and her open cloak afforded him an interesting view. Today she was not wearing a fichu, and he let his eyes dwell on the creamy mounds with the dark shadow between. He remembered holding the smooth warmth of those breasts....

'Mr Hetherington, do you know what is happening at the work-house? Who is managing the place today?'

'That question should be more properly addressed to me, young woman,' Sir Alexander broke in.

Juliana sat back, depriving Colly of the best view he'd had in a long time. 'Oh? Have you heard?' she asked Sir Alexander.

'Ah … no. But Captain Easton has been deputized to keep an eye on things.'

'The women will wonder where I am,' Juliana fretted. 'I promised them I would let them know if I found Kit and Tilly.'

'Well, we haven't found them yet, have we?' Sir Alexander snapped.

'We will,' Colly answered, although he did not feel as confident as he pretended.

Four hours later the carriage rumbled over the rough cobblestones heading for Whitechapel. Colly pulled the curtains shut when he saw how many people were gawking at the occupants of the carriage. A carriage with a crest on its panel was not a common sight in this district – at least, not during the hours of daylight. Sometimes during the darkness hours young blades bent on adventure found their ways to the mean streets hereabouts. If they were not taken up by the Watch, their adventures ended with them being assaulted for the contents of their pockets, or in catching a disease from gin-sodden tarts desperate to earn a penny.

Juliana held a handkerchief to her nose. The stench from the open drains was nauseating.

Then the carriage ground to a halt, but their journey was not yet over. Colly helped them disembark, then herded them into an unmarked carriage. It was in this vehicle that they covered the final half-mile into the depths of Whitechapel. When the hired carriage slowed, Colly pushed the door open and told the others, 'Travers will drive you to an inn. Wait there for me. Please do nothing to draw attention to yourselves.' He stared hard at Sir Alexander.

'What about you?' Juliana asked, looking horrified.

'I can look after myself,' Colly replied tersely, jumping down from the still-moving carriage. He *hoped* he could look after himself. He had no idea what to expect.

The driver nodded to him and pointed with his whip towards an inn further down the lane. The carriage rolled forward.

'I hope that young man of yours knows what he's doing,' grunted Sir Alexander, half an hour later, as they sat waiting in the taproom of the filthiest inn Juliana had ever set eyes on.

'No, no. You mistake the matter, sir. We are not— That is to say, he's not mine.'

In spite of his agitation, Sir Alexander's eyes lit with amusement at her disjointed explanation. 'Dear me. You don't seem to know what you mean.'

She waved a hand. 'It's uh … very complicated.'

Sir Alexander nodded sagely. 'Ah, we always make life more complicated than it need be. I advise you, my dear, to sort out your differences. Look what happened to me. Now I have no son and I may not have a grandson either.'

It was the first time Juliana had heard him admit to being at fault. She patted his hand. 'Sir, if anyone can find Kit and Tilly, Colly will.' *I do hope so, Colly, I do hope so. And oh, I pray that you keep safe, too.* She stared through the gloom of the dusty window beside her. It was a little past one o'clock, yet here in the half-dark she could not even see the inhabitants of the cobwebs festooned from each corner.

The taproom door swung open and she glanced up, but it was only a group of rowdy workers from the docks. Juliana shrank back in her seat, trying to hide. This was not the place for a young woman, but the inn boasted no private rooms. Indeed, the arched sign above the entrance saying Rosemary Lane Inn was stretching things too far. Rosemary Lane Inn was merely a squalid taproom with big stables out the back. From what Juliana had seen, the stables were preferable to the taproom. She knew very little about London, but Whitechapel was notorious. Stories about the place had filtered through to the citizens of Porto from the English soldiers quartered there. She had never thought to find herself here.

The door opened a second time and Colly entered, accompanied by two men. They all seemed to be on the best of terms. She watched Colly order up a couple of ales for his companions, then he hurried across the room towards her.

'Juliana, come with me. Hurry. Polking is waiting for us outside a house where Kit and Tilly are being kept.'

Juliana jumped up. 'Polking?' she asked.

'He's the marquess's London footman,' Colly explained. He grasped Sir Alexander's arm as he, too, rose to his feet. 'Sir, please stay here and be very careful. Those two men will explain it all to you.' He signalled to the marquess's men, then grabbed Juliana's elbow and bundled her out to the street. 'We don't know how much time we have. They may be shifted at any moment.'

He steered her along an alleyway behind the inn. The cobblestones were littered with detritus accumulated since the last rain, and Juliana concentrated on breathing shallowly as she had in the hospital. The street lay in shadow. The sunlight could not penetrate the dank alleyways between the high tenement buildings.

She hitched up her skirts with one hand and clasped her cloak with the other. Colly kept his hand beneath her elbow, but when he glanced down and saw her clutching her reticule he exclaimed, 'For heaven's sake! Give me that thing.' Stuffing it into a pocket in his greatcoat he muttered, 'If anyone around here sees *that*, they'll assume there's something in it worth stealing.'

'Then they'd be wrong, wouldn't they?' Juliana snapped. If he only knew how sick of the wretched thing she was. But although it contained such frivolous things as a hairpin and a handkerchief, it also contained a very important item – her penknife. She never went anywhere without that knife. Even though it was small, it was her safety net. She had great faith in that bone-handled knife. It had saved her once before, and it might save her again. Of course it hadn't helped her last night on the Pewsey road because her assailant had anchored her arms to her sides. Just the same, she had derived comfort from knowing it was secreted in her reticule. She had heard injured soldiers in Sao Nazaire talking among themselves and they had maintained that a small knife was virtually useless. You had to get too close to your enemy to do any damage, they said, and that was dangerous. But she knew that most men discounted women when it came to weapons, so women had the advantage of surprise. She smiled grimly as Colly hurried her along the alley. How shocked he would be if he opened her reticule!

'Here,' he said suddenly, and tugged her into an alcove between two shops.

A short man stepped out of the shadows to meet them. 'They're still inside, sir.'

Colly nodded his thanks. 'Anybody else gone inside, Polking?' he asked.

Polking shook his head. 'No, sir.'

'Good.'

Colly didn't need to explain what he meant. There were only so many enemies a man could take on at once.

'How will we see clearly enough to know if it's Kit and Tilly?' she whispered.

'No need to whisper, miss,' Polking said with a grin. 'They won't hear a thing above this row.' And indeed, the alley and street beyond it were in a constant state of cacophony with the clatter of hoofs on cobblestones in the main street echoing through the narrow alleys. The tall buildings along the alleyways channelled the sounds into a roaring commotion. The narrow walkways teemed with a life of their own. Hawkers wandered in the middle of the streets advertising their wares in stentorian cries, and the screams of children playing added their mite to the general row.

At that moment the side door of the building they were watching opened a crack and someone peered out. Tucked around the corner as they were, they could not tell if the person was male or female. The red painted door shut again.

They waited.

And waited.

'Perhaps I should go in as a customer,' Colly said to Polking. 'What do you think?'

'Customer?' Juliana enquired.

Colly regarded her with amusement. 'What do you think this place is?' he asked.

Juliana shrugged. 'I don't – oh!' How stupid of her not to realize they were standing outside a brothel.

'Nah, best just to wait, sir,' Polking said.

All very well for him to say wait, Juliana thought. In the meantime God knew what Tilly and Kit were suffering. She said a quick prayer underneath her breath. She had been praying so much lately that she suspected the Almighty was heartily sick of her.

Colly fidgeted. Waiting did not come easily to him. *A man of action*, she thought.

Then the door opened again and a blowsy, middle-aged tart shoved a dishevelled, battered girl through the doorway and into the alley.

'It's Tilly!' both Juliana and Colly exclaimed.

'Where's the boy?' Polking asked, as another of the marquess's servants joined them.

Puffing and blowing, the other man wheezed, 'We just seen 'im. Leastways, we think it might be 'im. An old codger had 'im. They passed by the tavern as cool as you please. I think it's the same boy we saw this morning.'

'Damn. We'll have to split up,' Colly said. 'Juliana, go with Stebbing here to see if that boy is Kit.'

'But I must help Tilly!'

'I'll look after her,' Colly promised.

Yes, of course he would. 'May I have my reticule, please?' she asked.

'Huh?'

In front of the men she walked up to him and pulled it out of his greatcoat pocket. She held his gaze. 'Thank you. Come on, Stebbing.'

Stebbing raised his eyebrows in amusement. No doubt he thought she was stupid to bother with her reticule. Colly grabbed her hand as she hurried away. 'Be careful, Juliana. Leave everything to Stebbing.'

She pressed his fingers with her gloved ones and rushed after Stebbing, already hovering at the corner of the alley. As they turned the corner they heard a voice shrilling with anger. 'Don't look back, miss. No time,' Stebbing gasped. He was rather stout and Juliana suspected she was much fitter than he was.

They ground to a halt outside the tavern where the third member of the marquess's staff was yelling furiously at a tall, thin man who held tight to the elbow of a scruffy urchin.

Juliana's heart sank. 'Stebbing, that's not Kit under all that dirt.'

'Dash it all,' Stebbing puffed, exasperated. 'Miss, stay here and I'll find out what's going on.'

Stebbing spoke to his friend, then returned to her side. 'That's not the boy we saw earlier, miss. That's a different one. That creature there' – he stabbed his finger in the direction of the thin man – ''e's been back and forth past the tavern three or four times, each time with a different boy. Seems like they use a smokescreen if they think someone's on to 'em.'

At this inopportune moment Sir Alexander burst out through the doors of the tavern and strode over to the urchin. 'Is this him, Miss Colebrook?' he yelled.

The tall, thin man turned to peer in her direction and her heart shrivelled within her. She had *never* seen such evil eyes. They were stone dead in an expressionless face. He looked her up and down without seeming to see her at all. Yet Juliana knew he would never forget her. She stood straight and gave him back stare for stare, but her heart quailed. She was in great danger.

'That bloody old fool!' Stebbing spat. 'Now he's given you away.'

He grabbed Sir Alexander's arm and thrust him back inside the tavern.

'How dare you!' were the last words Juliana heard from Sir Alexander. As she turned back towards the thin man, something hard banged on the back of her head and she felt herself falling. Then a heavy darkness pressed around her.

CHAPTER THIRTY-TWO

SLOWLY SHE DRAGGED herself up through layers of blackness to consciousness. The street noises had stopped. She was lying on a wooden floor in a large, gloomy room. Her head throbbed unmercifully and when she touched the back of it, her gloves came away sticky with blood. At least she thought it was blood. It was difficult to see much at all. Some big shapes, covered in dustsheets, loomed in front of her. She squeezed her eyes shut and opened them again. The shapes were still there. Then she realized she must be in a room where furniture was stored.

'Miss?' hissed a breathy voice.

She froze, then closed her eyes in thankfulness. 'Kit?'

'Yes, miss. Why are you here?'

'I was searching for *you*, Kit. Thank goodness I've found you. Ohh!' She tried to turn around to face him and her head thumped painfully in an urgent rhythm.

'Are you hurt, miss?'

'Just a little. I shall be fine in a trice.' She doubted that. Her heels were bruised and the skin on her arms stung as though she'd been pinched black and blue. They must have dragged her here rather than carried her.

'At least you're not tied up,' Kit muttered.

'What?' Ignoring the pounding pain, Juliana struggled to her feet, using a nearby piece of furniture to pull herself up. The dustsheet on the furniture slithered off and she blinked at the beautiful inlaid table revealed. What a lovely piece of furniture! As she brushed her gloved hand across the dappled walnut, she left a swathe in the dust. This place must be where stolen goods were stored, she surmised. Just how many strings to their bow did Mr Pettigrew, her uncle and the dead-eyed man have? Because she had no doubt that the dead-eyed man was the main perpetrator – the 'man in London' the fearful prisoner had spoken about.

She groped around on the floor. *Please* Lord, surely she still had her reticule? Yes. She'd been lying on it. She breathed a sigh of relief.

'Hurry, Juliana,' she told herself. 'Someone could come in at any minute.' She hauled herself towards Kit hand over hand, using the furniture for leverage. Gingerly she knelt down beside him and stroked his tumbled curls. 'Oh, Kit. You poor boy.' He leaned against her and she held him, just held him. Who knew what the poor little boy had endured? Her arms tightened around him. Her uncle would pay for this. She'd make sure of it. As for Pettigrew, if they didn't have enough evidence against him, well, she'd invent some. She'd lie to the magistrate if necessary.

Something warm dripped down the back of her neck and she put Kit gently aside to fish in her reticule for a handkerchief. She dabbed at the wound on the back of her head and flinched. What on earth had they hit her with? At least her handkerchief was a reasonable size; it belonged to Colly. Even so, it was saturated.

'There's a lot of blood, miss er … ma'am. Are you *sure* you're all right?' Kit asked.

'Don't worry, Kit. Head wounds always bleed a lot.' She should know. She'd treated many of them.

She turned her attention to the ropes that bound Kit's wrists and ankles. Her trusty penknife made short work of them. Kit's eyes opened wide as he watched the little knife sawing back and forth. 'How did you come to have that, miss?'

'I've carried it for years, ever since I got into some trouble in Portugal some time ago. The penknife was all I had, but it worked. I've carried it ever since.'

It had worked all right.

'Do you know what lies outside the door?' she asked, nodding towards the stout ash door at the end of the room.

'Stairs, ma'am – miss – what *is* your name, please?'

Juliana smiled. Kit had an unmistakable lisp.

'Miss Colebrook.'

'Miss Colebrook. A staircase leads straight down to the front door. I been lying here thinking about that,' Kit admitted. He had an amusing patois of good English and servant's cant, no doubt the mixed influence of his mother and the Pirate.

'I'll try the door, though it's probably locked.' Juliana eased herself to her feet, but at that moment they heard a scuffling sound. Grabbing Kit's hand she subsided back on to her knees.

A key scraped in the lock and the door creaked open. To Juliana's terror the thin man with dead eyes stood there, peering at them through the gloom. She clasped her penknife tightly in her free hand and hid it beneath her skirts. The dead eyes swivelled from Kit's hemp binding, now lying on the floor, to Juliana's face where she hovered protectively in front of Kit.

'What a clever young lady,' the revolting animal purred. At the menace in his voice, Juliana felt as though a snake had slithered up her spine. She stood up and held out her ungloved left hand to show him how she had untied the ropes. Dead-Eyes was too wary to come any closer, and she knew he couldn't see in the dimness that the knots had been sliced through.

The pale eyebrows rose. 'Perhaps those dexterous fingers can be put to better use. Come here.' He crooked a long, thin forefinger and the muscles at the bottom of Juliana's stomach jolted. *Hold yourself together, Juliana. Your plan relies on your being as close to him as possible.*

Slowly she sidled towards the creature and for the first time she saw signs of life in the cold eyes.

'I always interview our new young ladies before they are thrust on our clients,' he purred thickly. 'I like to ... warm them up, so to speak.'

Bile rose in her throat. She had never seen an iceberg but she had heard about them, and she had the distinct impression that a huge chunk of iceberg had just washed into the room. 'Warm them up?' She didn't think so. Please, please, please God, don't let him have touched Tilly.

Clutching the penknife in the palm of her right hand, she shuffled closer to him, measuring the distance carefully and also his height. Yes, he was tall. So was she. Flexing her body she moved closer, as if in a trance. His arm shot out and grabbed her.

'No!' Kit yelled behind her.

'Stay back, Kit,' she warned.

'That's right, my dear. You understand. You *want* to be tutored by Benny Ames, don't you?' He tugged her flush against his body.

Struggling not to recoil, she saw he was sweating. His tongue slid greedily over his yellowed teeth and he clasped her left hand like a lover. She kept her right hand hidden in her skirts. Ames's breathing deepened as he tried to rub her left hand over his erection. Even as she struck, he was so lost in a haze of sexual pleasure he had no idea what had happened.

'Hurry, Kit. Run!' she yelled.

This time she was prepared for the blood. It spurted out of his throat in a great arc, dousing the holland covers beside them. Juliana ducked backwards holding the slippery knife handle. The knife blade was buried in Ames's neck. He clutched his throat, his eyes wide with stupefaction.

Juliana's stomach lurched and she dropped the handle. As Ames made the most fearsome gurgling sounds she edged around his flailing body and raced to the door. She hurtled down the stairs and cannoned into Kit. 'Hurry, Kit. Hurry. Get out of here.' She shoved the front door open and pushed him outside.

Kit slanted a glance back over his shoulder as his little legs sped along. 'Where are we going?'

'To the Rosemary Lane Inn. Hurry!'

'But I don't know where it is!' He kept on running all the same, tugging Juliana along by the hand.

Juliana cast a quick glance behind them. The blue door with number 32 painted on it still stood innocently ajar and she could hear no sounds of pursuit.

'Run towards the traffic noise,' she gasped.

A few people glanced at them as they rushed by, but nobody seemed interested in a scruffy boy and a bloodstained, dishevelled young woman running helter skelter up the alleyways. No doubt it was a common sight in these parts.

As they stumbled from the dank alleyway into a wider street she saw a sign stuck on a building façade that said 'Chamber Street'. The steady throbbing of her sore, bruised feet echoed the drumming in her head. Swaying, she knew she was nearly done for.

Kit glanced back and tugged her hand. 'Come on, miss,' he encouraged her, then he raised their clasped hands and stared at the red stains on Juliana's fingers. 'Thank you,' was all he said.

Breathless, she gulped and said nothing, fighting her queasy stomach. Soon it would happen – the reaction. Last time she had shaken as if with the ague for several hours. And when she had finally found herself safe, she had huddled into a ball and cried and cried and cried. She had cried for her mother and for herself, and for all the other women who had been held in the power of men who did not deserve them.

But now was not the time for self-indulgence. She must protect Kit. She lifted her chin and plodded on.

Footsteps pounded behind them. Twisting around, she shoved Kit out of the way.

'Juliana!'

Colly. On a wave of relief so strong it dizzied her, she ran straight into his arms.

CHAPTER THIRTY-THREE

Aeons later she heard his shaken voice mutter close to her ear, 'We must stop making a habit of this.'

Right there in the busy street he held her tightly, soothing her with gentle strokes down her back. 'What happened, Juliana?'

'Sir Alexander called out to me, and Kit's kidnappers must have … where's Kit?'

'Here, Miss Colebrook.'

Colly's arms fell away and, bereft, she stepped back. 'Ah, Brigade-Major Hetherington, may I introduce Master Christopher Mortimer?' she said formally.

Kit giggled, but he held out his hand in the accepted manner.

'Very pleased to meet you, Kit,' Colly said. 'Are you all right?'

Kit nodded vigorously and Colly and Juliana exchanged smiles. Children were amazing. Kit was already bouncing back.

'We'll talk about your … adventures … later, but right now there is someone who wants to see you,' Colly told him. He took Kit by the shoulders and turned him towards the inn where, twenty yards away, Sir Alexander was pacing back and forth, muttering under his breath.

'Sir!' Colly called and Sir Alexander spun around.

'Miss Colebrook! I'm so very sorry that—' Then he stopped as the three of them drew closer and Kit stepped out from behind Juliana.

'My God! It is like seeing your father all over again, boy. Come here.'

Sir Alexander spread wide his arms but Kit, not knowing who this strange old gentleman was, grabbed hold of Juliana's hand. She bent down and took his face in her hands.

'Kit, he is your grandfather. Your father's father.'

Kit stared at her for a moment then transferred his gaze to his grandfather. 'Really?'

He was four years of age. The intricacies of relationships meant little. But there were signs of the man to come. He let go Juliana's hand and walked up to his grandfather. 'Sir?'

Crusty Sir Alexander now had his emotions under control. 'You may call me Grandpapa, boy. They call you Kit, I understand. You will come home with me.' The two of them walked hand-in-hand towards the inn with Kit casting anxious glances back over his shoulder. Juliana nodded to him encouragingly and tried to smile through her tears.

As soon as the Mortimers disappeared inside the doors of the inn, she turned to Colly. 'Tilly?' she asked.

Colly nodded towards the taproom. 'Safe,' he said. 'We had to drag her away from that dreadful woman. The old bit— er, biddy, screeched her head off so we hustled Tilly through some back alleys in case anyone pursued us. Thank goodness for Polking. On my own I would have got hopelessly lost.'

Juliana gnawed on her lip. Tilly might be safe now, but what had happened to her? She drew a deep breath and hurried into the inn.

Tilly was seated in a dark corner. When she saw Juliana she gasped with relief and burst into tears. 'I were that frightened, miss,' she said to Juliana, tears streaming down her face. 'I didn't know what was happening until Mr Polking explained you were looking for me.'

Juliana sat down and stroked Tilly's matted hair. 'Tilly, did anything bad happen to you?' How stupid that sounded. Of course bad things had happened to Tilly and Kit. But with the men standing nearby, Juliana didn't know how else to broach the matter.

Dear, resilient Tilly knew what she meant. She drew a deep, quavering breath. 'I think you'll find Master Kit is still ... fine, Miss Colebrook. I'm sorry I couldn't keep my eye on him all the time. They took him away from me this morning. I fought, but—' She gulped. 'They took me to that house with the red door.' Shivering, she whispered, 'An awful man was there and he kept saying that Kit was useless. All he'd do was cry. So he laughed and said they'd get their money's worth out of me. He ... that man—' She shattered and hid her face in Juliana's lap.

'That man,' Juliana murmured, as she soothed Tilly's fragile back-bone. 'Do you know his name?'

Tilly shook her head.

Several bar patrons stared at them curiously. Juliana returned their stares with a ferocious glare. Colly strode over and stood in front of them, shielding them from curious eyes. 'What is it?' he asked.

Juliana stared mutely up at him.

'Oh, dear Lord!' He understood.

Juliana tickled Tilly's cheek. 'Tilly, tell me, was this man tall and thin? Did he have strange eyes?'

Tilly shuddered and raised her wet face. 'Yes,' she breathed. 'Have you seen 'im?'

'We've met. He had Kit.'

'No! Is Kit—?'

'I don't think so. He seems fine.' Juliana looked up at Colly. 'Sir, at 32 Chamber Street where Kit and I were held prisoner, there is a man who might be ... injured. Would you make sure that he, uh ...' She hesitated. 'We may have to call the Runners after all.'

Colly stared down at her. Then his face softened and he reached out and touched the back of his gloved hand to her cheek. 'Be assured, Miss Colebrook, that I will do what is necessary.'

He spun on his heel and left.

The journey back to Trewbridge seemed to take forever. Juliana's head throbbed and throbbed. Even the slightest bounce in the well-sprung carriage sent shards of pain lancing into the back of her neck. Colly had fashioned a padded bandage from his and Sir Alexander's cravats. As he leaned over to tie it in place he murmured, 'At this rate, Juliana, we will have used up all my cravats within a se'enight. I would ask that you refrain from any more adventures till I can visit Hungerford to purchase more.'

She attempted a smile but it fell awry. She felt sick and her throat was as dry as dust. She licked her lips. 'Wh-what about the other matter?' she croaked.

'All taken care of,' Colly replied, then he sat back, trying to squeeze his lanky frame alongside Sir Alexander's. They were very cramped now the carriage held another two people.

Tilly held tight to Juliana's hand, small shuddering exhalations escaping every now and then, and Juliana knew that her own discomfort was nothing compared to Tilly's pain and fear. The little maid's effervescent spirit was broken. Juliana wondered how best she could help her from now on.

Tilly's eyes had widened when Juliana had whispered, 'I know how it feels, Tilly. Oh, I *know*.' Then Juliana had added, 'The man who did this to you has been taken care of. He will never do that to anyone again.' And Tilly's eyes had widened even more. But she asked no questions, just gripped Juliana's hand tightly, seeking security from her mistress.

Some mistress I am, Juliana thought. *I couldn't even keep one little maid safe.*

Kit and Sir Alexander seemed pleased with each other. Already Sir

Alexander had begun correcting the flaws in Kit's speech and Kit was absorbing the lessons hungrily.

Which reminded Juliana of the Pirate. She leaned forward. 'Sir Alexander, do you remember Minna?'

For a second, Sir Alexander's brow creased, then he laughed. 'Miss Colebrook! Surely you are not saying you've found Minna too?'

'Sir, she has been with your grandson since his birth.'

'No!'

'You will find her very changed. We have not had much time to talk yet, but the carriage accident that took the life of your son' – she broke off to glance at Kit – 'disfigured Minna badly. She is in the Hungerford infirmary.'

Sir Alexander was amazed and to Juliana and Tilly's relief, the rest of the journey was taken up with discussion about the Mortimer family.

CHAPTER THIRTY-FOUR

HOURS LATER, JULIANA was at last able to pull herself free of Tilly's clinging hand. Between them, Juliana and Trewbridge's house-keeper had managed to soothe Tilly with judicious doses of laudanum and kindness. Poor little Tilly had thanked Juliana effusively and said how grateful she was that 'Miss' was a nurse and knew what to do. Unspoken was the message that Juliana knew what to do because she'd suffered the same way herself. And Juliana knew it would be many months before Tilly could come back to the land of the living and feel real again. She would live on the outside looking in until her healing began.

Juliana stood at the window of her bedchamber and gazed out over the gardens. Thus far she had managed to avoid thinking of her own situation, but now dark thoughts and fears crowded her brain. Whatever *she* was, it was a plain fact that her father had been dishonest and her uncle a knave of the first order. If she had thought herself ruined because of the incident outside Porto, her relatives' machinations had now put her well beyond the touch of the *ton*. Colly and the Trewbridges had been wonderfully supportive, but now she must take stock of her prospects. And as far as she could see, she didn't have any. If she had secretly yearned for a future with Colly, now it was not only unattainable, it was impossible. Time to leave here and rid them of their embarrassing guest. She rested her head against the glass and closed her eyes.

The door burst open and the marchioness bustled in. Juliana straightened up and pasted a smile on her face. She bobbed a curtsy. 'Ma'am, I must tell you how grateful—'

'Tosh. None of that, my dear. Now, we have decided you will stay here until things have settled down. But Juliana, I have done something my husband is not best pleased about.' Here, the marchioness pressed a long, pale finger against her lips. 'I am most concerned about Colly's estrangement from his family, so I wrote to his mama.'

'Oh!' Trust the Marchioness of Trewbridge to take the bull by the horns! Juliana could not help but laugh.

'Well, I am best placed to understand a mother's anxiety. And when we receive an answer, I want you to encourage Colly to visit Heather Hill to see his family.'

'But ma'am, Colly might ... I mean, he does not want—'

The marchioness waved a dismissive hand. 'Hah. He has cut himself off from his family for the sake of pride disguised as principles. How like a man! I shall deal with it, and you will assist me.'

Juliana's breath whistled in a quiet exhale. What if the marchioness was subjecting Colly to more rejection? He would be shattered and very angry. She began to understand why the marquess sometimes became perturbed by his wife's impetuousness.

'Ma'am, what shall we do if his family don't want to see him?'

'That will not be a problem,' the marchioness said smugly. 'What is the point of being a marchioness if one cannot pull rank when necessary? In my letter I hinted that I am puzzled and most displeased with their attitude. That should do the trick.'

'I see.' Juliana saw: she saw trouble coming.

Lady Trewbridge settled her shoulders and flicked her skirts, ready to leave on another mission, and Juliana was reminded of an important responsibility.

'Excuse me, ma'am, but would a carriage be available to take me to the infirmary? The place will be at sixes and sevens with no supervisor or nurse.'

'All taken care of, my dear. Captain Easton has things well in hand, I believe.'

'Oh!' Now what was she to do?

'We thought it best for you to have a holiday until the Runners have finished their work. Let things settle down a bit,' the marchioness explained. Juliana understood her to mean: 'until the Runners have found your uncle.'

So she did not have a job any longer. Or anything else.

No home.

No job.

No prospects.

No money.

One thing she had acquired however, was an unsavoury reputation. The Colebrook name would do her no good in future.

'Your clothes have been sent for, so please don't worry,' the marchioness assured her.

Not worry? Only someone born to a position of privilege could say airily 'don't worry' when there was everything in the world to worry about. She hoped they'd bring her hatbox, otherwise she might never see those precious pansies again.

But although her future looked like a huge, empty hole, she still had one duty to perform.

'I must see my aunt,' she said.

'No, my dear, you must not,' the marchioness rejoined firmly. 'What if your uncle should arrive home while you are there?'

Juliana sat down on the bed. She hadn't thought of that. By now her uncle would know what she had done. He would be furious that she had helped destroy his business. He would be out for blood.

The marchioness seated herself on the elegant, spindly chair in front of the dressing-table. 'Juliana, we are trying to keep you safe, but you must be warned. My husband, Colly, and Sir Alexander all feel that your aunt must have known about your uncle's exploits, my dear. She must have decided to ignore it.'

'No doubt she was concerned for the roof over her head,' Juliana muttered.

'Well …' Plainly the marchioness thought the same thing. 'One must be charitable and acknowledge that women such as your aunt are not in a position to do anything, Juliana.'

Juliana sighed. 'No, of course not. But how could she stand by and know that her husband and his accomplice were selling innocent children into lives of depravity? If it were me, I would have tried to find out where the children were being sent and I would have—'

'That is the whole point, my dear. You are not your aunt, and you must not confuse yourself by thinking that everyone who bears the Colebrook name is dishonourable. There is one honourable member of the Colebrook family and that is Miss Juliana Colebrook.'

Juliana blinked rapidly. 'Thank you, your ladyship. But frankly, if I thought the English could pronounce it, I would use my mother's surname.'

'And what is that?'

'Ervedosa.'

The marchioness trilled with laughter. 'My dear, can you see us all getting our tongues around that? You would be "Miss Hervydose" in no time at all.' Then she sobered. 'I have a much better idea. I think Juliana Hetherington sounds best of all.'

Juliana felt the hectic blush blooming on her cheeks and spreading. 'G-good heavens, your ladyship. *Please.* Brigade-Major Hetherington and I are not on those terms. Neither of us intends to marry. And besides—'

Someone knocked on the door. Much relieved to escape an inquisition, Juliana called, 'Come in!'

One of the downstairs maids sidled into the room and bobbed a curtsy to the marchioness. Then she turned to Juliana. 'Excuse me, miss, but Mr Hetherington asks if you would be so good as to meet him in the library.'

The marchioness coughed and smiled a knowing, ironic smile. To her credit she said nothing, but Juliana could see the lady was bursting out of her skin to say 'I told you so.'

'Er, thank you, Molly.' Juliana looked at the marchioness.

'Go,' she said.

Juliana fled.

CHAPTER THIRTY-FIVE

COLLY PACED. THE large library enabled him to stretch his long legs with ease.

How should he go about this? He knew her longing for family, yet he had just received word that her uncle's body had been found, slit from belly to throat near Goodman's Fields. And nobody had seen her aunt since yesterday. The maid, Annie, had told the marquess's man that 'The missus acted a bit strange, sir. Last night it was. She hurried through the kitchen, pushing Cook out of the way, and ran across the fields at the back of the house. James went after her but he couldn't find her. Nobody's seen her since.'

Colly braced himself for some difficult questions from Juliana.

But when she entered the library he could see that, far from seeking answers, she would have avoided this interview if she could. Her borrowed dimity dress swung loosely, showing an entrancing view of neat ankles as she trod towards him.

He bowed, but before he could speak she said, 'Mr Hetherington, I must thank you most sincerely for all your care of me over the past few weeks. I – I seem to be falling into danger wherever I go, thanks to my wretched family.' Her voice lowered on the last word.

He tried to see her face, but she kept her head down. He took a breath. 'I'm afraid I have some more bad news about your family, Juliana.'

She tried to make light of it. 'I did not think things could possibly get worse.'

He stepped closer and took her hand. 'Juliana, your uncle has been murdered. They found his body in London, not far from where we found Kit and Tilly.'

'Oh!' She stared at him in horror. Then, recovering, she said, 'Well, that's not precisely *bad* news, Mr Hetherington. At least he can't hurt anyone else. I mean—'

'I understand.' He massaged her fingers gently. Still the same calluses. Life was not treating Juliana Colebrook any better. Anger welled up in him and he turned away so she could not see how helpless he felt in the face of her hardships. Damn his father to hell. Thanks to the old tyrant he could do nothing except keep a watching brief over the woman he loved.

'Sir? Colly, what is it?'

Juliana laid a gentle hand on his, and he could stand it no longer.

He pulled her close and wrapped his arms around her. 'Juliana,' he breathed into her hair. He closed his eyes, inhaling that enticing citron fragrance.

She did not object to his sudden attack. On the contrary, she snuggled against his chest and he could not prevent himself from swallowing hard and noisily. She murmured something indistinguishable into his waistcoat. Freeing one hand, he tilted her face to his and, as her arms tightened around his waist, he gently turned her face aside and brushed a kiss against her ear. He would not take advantage of her unhappy state to push for more. She shivered with pleasure and he greedily absorbed the sensation like a man savouring a piquant snuff. Then tired of fighting himself, he pulled her even closer, flush up against his hard – and getting harder – body. And waited for his face to be slapped. Nothing happened.

Instead, convent-bred Miss Colebrook wriggled invitingly against him as she stretched up to stroke his face.

God, it felt *so* good. It felt as if she really cared for him. For a second he nearly succumbed, then warning bells clanged. What did he think he was doing? And in the Marquess of Trewbridge's library, for God's sake!

He began to draw back but her lips were parted in expectation, and he couldn't resist kissing her. Just once. As he leaned forward she murmured, 'Colly.'

Quite a few women had murmured his name, but none had ever said it as if he were the most important man on earth. As he felt the soft lips meld with his, he knew a heady relief. At last! He settled in to feast.

'Oh, sorry. Excuse me.'

John Trewbridge's voice scraped across Colly's skin like a flaying knife. He jerked back. 'What...?'

The library door closed.

Juliana stared up at him, her eyes huge. 'Was that – was that Lord Brechin?' she stammered.

'I'm afraid so. Better John than the marquess, however.'

'Yes!' Juliana agreed fervently.

And now they were well apart, a gate-legged table separating them. Juliana looked a trifle dishevelled. He glanced down. He did not look precisely unruffled himself. How the hell was he going to wrestle himself back into a manageable state? Fifty buckets of ice chips might do it.

'Oh God, I'm sorry Juliana. I—'

She shook her head. 'It was not all your fault, Colly. It takes two to – er – do this sort of thing.'

Even now, she made excuses for him. Why did she persist in thinking so highly of him? She was an amazing woman.

He smoothed down his sleeves and fingered his cravat. 'I – I need to find John,' he said desperately.

She put out a restraining hand. 'Please, before you go, could you advise me what I should do? The marchioness has invited me to stay at Trewbridge for a while.'

Colly smiled. 'I think that is an excellent idea. I know the marchioness has been asking among her friends if anyone needs a companion. So—'

She interrupted him and he saw the fear in her dark eyes. 'But I cannot wait forever for the marchioness to come up with a prospective employer. I have no money.'

'I understand. I shall ask Captain Easton to send you what the infirmary owes you.'

She bit her lip. 'Thank you. But I doubt it will be very much. I only worked there for two weeks.'

'Oh, Easton implied it was a reasonable sum,' Colly lied. Easton had said nothing of the sort, but Colly intended to subsidize her wages. If he was careful she would never know.

'I must return to the Colebrooks' house to check on the servants and see if my aunt is well.'

'I'll come with you,' he offered.

She did not protest but said simply, 'I would feel safer that way.'

He felt ridiculously pleased. 'Come, I had best find John,' was all he could manage.

CHAPTER THIRTY-SIX

W HEN JULIANA AND Colly arrived at the Colebrook house the following day, however, four brawny village lads were carrying her aunt's body into the stillroom. James was conspicuous by his absence.

Cook stood by, wringing her hands. 'Miss Colebrook, thank goodness you've come! I did not know what to do because ... well, they say the poor lady did it herself.'

Juliana nodded. Guilt nudged at her. If only she'd got here sooner. She *knew* her aunt had been unhappy. 'I understand, Cook. Thank you very much for taking the responsibility. How did it happen?'

'Some village lads found her body floating in the river down towards the ford, Miss Colebrook. The doctor sent them out to search.' Cook sniffed into a man's huge handkerchief. 'They say that last evening she walked past some of the village lads who were swimming there and just waded in. Nobody could stop her. She was carrying heavy stones in her pockets, and when the blacksmith tried to grab her she dived under the water and—' Cook shrugged and a tear dribbled down her face. 'And this morning James and Annie up and left. They're not from these parts. They've headed back to London.' Cook's usually florid face was pale and faintly puzzled, as if the world she knew had changed and she could not understand what she must do next.

Juliana thought of something that would calm Cook's frazzled nerves. 'Would you find some ale for these kind gentlemen?' she asked, hearing the whispers and the steady shuffling sound behind her cease. 'Then we must decide what to do.' She looked helplessly at Colly. 'Can you...?'

'I'll see to everything downstairs, Juliana. Perhaps you'd best go upstairs and ensure that everything is in order.'

And in her aunt's bedroom she found it. Aunt Colebrook had perched a letter jauntily on her dressing table, as if, having decided to end her life, she felt relief and amusement in walking away from her problems.

Holding the note, Juliana noticed something else. There were very few personal belongings in her aunt's room. She had seen inside the room only once, but she was sure there had been a jumble of knick-knacks on the mantelpiece. Now the marble mantelpiece was bare. And her aunt's clothes were strewn about as if a whirlwind had passed through. She wasn't sure, but she didn't think her aunt would normally have left her bedchamber in such disarray. But, of course, the circumstances were anything but normal.

Juliana scanned the note again. And blinked. She put the note in her pocket to read again later.

Upstairs on the attic level she looked in her own room. All was intact. She returned downstairs and pushed open the door to her uncle's bedchamber. Shocked, she stopped on the threshold.

The bed hangings flowed in shredded tatters from the tester to the carpet. Garments lay spread across the room, slung on chairs and across the bed, even on the windowsill. No brush set, nail paring knife or any personal items were left on the dressing table.

It looked as though Annie and James had taken payment in lieu of wages. They must have hired a carrier from Melksham.

In her uncle's study the desk drawers stood open and empty. Juliana remembered that an expensive jade paperweight had held down her uncle's papers. It was gone. And the gold penholder he had fiddled with as he'd told her she was 'nothing like her father' had disappeared.

Colly spoke from the doorway. 'Is everything all right, Juliana?' Then his face twisted. 'Well, as right as it can be under the circumstances.'

'My aunt cannot be buried in hallowed ground.'

'No.'

'It is very strange. When she received a message saying that my uncle was dead she—' Juliana broke off.

'She what, Juliana?' He took her hand as her face puckered and she handed him the piece of paper.

'Read it,' she whispered, searching for a handkerchief. Already she knew the lines off by heart.

Juliana, I will never sleep in hallowed ground. It does not concern me. At last I shall have peace.

Now that we are gone, you are the last of the Colebrooks. I do not know the legal requirements, but as Sholto died before me, I think I have the right to leave everything we own to you. However, you must check with Mr Beck, our solicitor.

Sholto was of the opinion that he would live to a great age like his father, and he refused to make a will. He did not wish to tempt fate. I have no idea if your inheritance is of much value, as Sholto never discussed his business affairs with me.

From what little my husband let slip when we first met, your father and uncle's upbringing was vicious and unpredictable. I can only presume their adult behaviour reflects that. I can no longer live with myself for having stood by and watched my husband's cruel destruction of the lives of others.

Your aunt, Emmeline Colebrook.

'Poor Aunt,' Juliana murmured.

'Poor you,' Colly retorted, 'if you are left to deal with this wretched household. We will have to find out the whereabouts of this Mr Beck.'

'I shall have to stay here. I cannot return to Trewbridge and leave Cook on the premises alone. We'll never see James and Annie again, not after what they've done.'

'How do you mean? What have they done?'

She showed him the damaged rooms. They stood in the doorway of her uncle's room and he pursed his lips in a soundless whistle. 'I can understand them stealing some knick-knacks, but it seems pointless to vent their spleen on a dead person.'

Juliana grimaced. 'He was not a kind employer,' was all she said.

Colly grunted. 'He probably had a hold over them or some such thing,' he said.

'Yes,' she agreed. 'He was that sort of man.'

Colly paced around the room. 'There is much to be done here, Juliana, but first of all I shall find Mr Beck. We will be guided by him.'

Thank goodness for Colly. She had no notion how to arrange her aunt's burial or how to close up a house. Worst of all, there was no money to pay off Cook. However she knew very well how to lay people out, and it was up to her to see that her aunt looked respectable.

Colly pulled her close. 'Are you all right, my d— Juliana? This is very trying for you.'

She nodded against his cravat. 'Are you going into Melksham?' Her voice was muffled.

'Yes. If Beck is not based in Melksham, I shall go on to Hungerford.'

'It would be best to try Hungerford first. Uncle Sholto and Pettigrew used Prior's Bank in Hungerford.'

He put her back from him and examined her face. 'How do you know that, Miss Efficiency?'

She smiled wanly. 'Tilly once told me that Annie saw them coming out of the bank together.'

'Very well. But Juliana, you cannot stay here alone. I've arranged for one of the lads downstairs to stay here today. This afternoon, no matter what happens, I'll convey you and Cook back to Trewbridge. It might be very late, because I don't know how long I'll be.' He paced restlessly along the hallway and back again.

'D-do you think some of Uncle Sholto's associates might come calling?' Juliana asked, swallowing hard.

'It's possible. With Ames and your uncle dead and Pettigrew in Newgate, there are probably very few players left. But who knows? It would be best if you and Cook kept the doors locked today.'

Juliana grimaced. The early September day was stifling.

She followed him out to the Trewbridge carriage and watched till the dust clouds kicked up by the carriage had faded. It had been wonderful having his support today, but she must not rely on it. Soon she would be on her own again.

She went back inside and locked the door.

CHAPTER THIRTY-SEVEN

I N THE EVENT, it was the larger of the Trewbridge carriages that arrived first. Cook was 'putting together some odds and ends for a wee snack' as she put it, when they heard carriage wheels in the driveway. To Juliana's surprise, Tilly, Lord Brechin, his valet, Lady Brechin and her maid all alighted from the carriage. Quite a contingent.

Juliana opened the door. 'Good heavens! What brings you all here?'

'Chaperons!' Marguerite said, laughing.

Juliana rolled her eyes. 'If you are referring to Mr Hetherington, he's in Hungerford.'

'Not any more. He should arrive here very soon. He sent us a message from Hungerford and told us that things have become very, er ... difficult for you.' Here Juliana laughed at Marguerite's masterly understatement and Marguerite grinned. 'So John decided we should come to help.'

Juliana cast Lord Brechin a grateful look which he deflected with a vague smile.

Colly followed hot on the heels of the Brechins.

Half an hour later the entire company assembled in the drawing room.

'Not a very welcoming room, is it?' Marguerite said.

Juliana laughed. 'The whole house is depressing. I hope your bedchambers are acceptable. Tilly and Cook did the best they could, and poor Amy has been slaving away rushing up and downstairs trying to find enough bedding for us all.'

'How is Tilly?' Marguerite enquired.

Juliana shook her head. 'Not good. But she wants to keep busy.'

Marguerite nodded in understanding.

'Your uncle's claret is outstanding,' Colly reported, after taking a tentative sip.

'Probably smuggled,' his loving niece said. 'He knew how to look after himself.'

'Not when it really mattered, he didn't,' Colly muttered. He had not told Juliana how her uncle had been killed, and he intended to avoid the subject unless she pressed him.

Mac, John's valet who had been his batman on the Peninsula and who took all sorts of tasks in his stride announced, 'Dinner is served.'

And although the rest of the house was run-down and shabby, Cook rose to the occasion. With no Sholto Colebrook to pull in her reins, she delighted in creating an excellent dinner.

'What are your plans for tomorrow?' John asked Juliana.

She grimaced. 'I doubt the vicar will entertain the idea of a Christian burial, so I'd best speak to the undertaker,' she said. 'Aunt should be buried at the crossroads.'

'I don't think it will come to that. I'll take care of it. That's why we came,' Lord Brechin said, very reminiscent of his father. 'Colly, what did this Mr Beck have to say?'

'It's probable that Juliana will inherit all this,' Colly said, grinning at Juliana's look of horror. 'Juliana, your aunt was correct. It seems you are the last of the Colebrooks. According to Mr Beck, your uncle's bank account is not to be sneezed at, either.'

'No!' Juliana snapped. 'I will not take that money.'

'I think you'll have to. It might take some weeks, but eventually the money will be yours.'

'Then I shall give it away. I could not bear to profit from money obtained through the misery of helpless children.'

'You could donate it to the poorhouse,' Marguerite suggested, helping herself to some of Cook's fine Spanish cream.

'What an excellent idea, Marguerite!' Juliana exclaimed. 'That's what I shall do. But I will give it for the benefit of the children only.' She could not repair the damage her uncle had done, but she could help other children, those whose parents could not afford the necessities of life.

'Will you sell this place when probate is granted?' Colly asked.

'Heavens, yes! I cannot afford to run a large household.'

'The income from that will be a good dowry,' John commented, watching Colly.

'I do not intend to marry,' Juliana said, crunching down firmly on a bite of celery.

'Neither did I,' Marguerite muttered.

Colly's eyebrows shot up. He stared hard at John.

'Yes, things were difficult for a while,' John said, answering Colly's unasked question.

Juliana's gaze moved from John's face to Marguerite's. 'Was there a problem?' she asked, puzzled.

'Aside from the obvious one, you mean?' Marguerite sounded most belligerent.

Juliana cringed. She must have hit a raw nerve. 'I don't understand. What is the obvious one?' She was confused. She had heard nothing about Marguerite's family. Perhaps they were unacceptable to the Trewbridges?

'There, Marguerite. Hoist with your own petard!' John crowed. He grinned at Juliana. 'Thank you, Juliana. I had to work hard for months to persuade her that her limp was not important to me.'

'The limp?' Juliana said. 'Gracious, I hardly notice it, Marguerite.'

Marguerite reddened. 'I'm sorry, Juliana. I know it sounds petty, but when your whole life has revolved around "Marguerite's leg" you become very sensitive about it. John was not at all sympathetic.'

'"Better a limping leg than no leg at all", was what I said,' John intervened.

'I did not speak to him for a week,' Marguerite admitted.

'And was that all that kept you from marriage?' Juliana asked, unable to contain her curiosity.

'No. My mother, you see, had decided that as she could not marry off a daughter with a limp, she'd have me as a prop in her old age.' Marguerite pulled a face. 'I did not look forward to it, let me tell you. Mama is umm ... very difficult.'

John snorted into his syllabub. Marguerite speared him with a glance.

'Sorry, darling,' he apologized, grinning. 'I am awed at your understatement. The old harridan would have had you waiting on her hand and foot.'

'Yes.' Marguerite shuddered.

It seemed that a lot of people had embarrassing relatives, Juliana mused.

Colly tossed her an 'I told you so' look, which she ignored.

'What is *your* objection to marriage, Juliana?' Marguerite enquired.

'My relatives,' she replied tersely.

'But you haven't any now, have you?' Colly said.

She threw him an impatient glance. 'I mean the sort of people they were. No respectable man would marry a woman from a family such as mine – a father who was a thief when it came to *discovering* questionable antiquities, an uncle who was a criminal of the first order, and an aunt whose guilt forced her to suicide.'

175

There was a short silence.

'But your mother's side of the family is very respectable,' Colly said quietly into the hiatus.

In spite of everything, she smiled. 'Yes. They are nice people. However I am in England and it is my English relatives who count.' She grimaced.

'Tell us about your Portuguese family, Juliana,' Lord Brechin encouraged.

My, he *was* like his father. Before she knew it, she found herself recounting tales of her childhood. The shabby English dining room became fuzzy around the edges and her narrow point of focus became Portugal – the harsh sadness of the *fado*, Portugal's lazy warmth flowing counterpoint to its strict formality and the brassy brightness of its sun. She came to herself with a bump when Colly commented, 'After the sale of this house you will become a woman of means. If you wanted, you could return to Portugal.'

Opening her mouth to refute his suggestion, she glimpsed the pain in his eyes. Did he not want her to go? So why had he said that? She stared at him.

John smoothed over the awkward moment. 'We might be able to find your relatives in Brazil. I'm sure my father has contacts there. After all, he has contacts everywhere.' He rolled his eyes and everyone laughed.

Indeed, when they returned to Trewbridge after Aunt Colebrook's burial, Juliana found that the Marquess of Trewbridge *did* know someone at the newly established English consulate in Rio de Janeiro. So she penned a letter to her relatives and the marquess franked it and sent it off to Brazil.

She reflected how easy it was to organize things if one were titled, or rich and powerful – or all three. At Melksham, when she'd been faced with the insurmountable problem of dealing with an aunt and uncle who could not be buried in consecrated ground, John had organized everything. Workers from the village were hired and the Melksham house received a more thorough cleaning than it had for some years. Several gardeners tamed the neglected gardens, then the house was closed up and the key despatched to Mr Beck. Cook was ecstatic when she found she was to be employed at the Brechins' manor house at Westbury. When Juliana tried to thank John Trewbridge for sending Cook to his home which was rarely occupied, he brushed her thanks aside saying, 'Anyone who can cook like that is a treasure. She will earn her keep.' So Juliana had given up worrying. Who was she to stand in the way of furthering Cook's career?

On her first night back at Trewbridge Juliana discovered that it felt very odd to have no burdens weighing upon her shoulders. It had been many years since she'd been worry-free. She could not remember when she'd last felt so ... rudderless.

Something else was odd, too. Her grumbling stomach had ceased grumbling. All she felt now, after a delicious dinner *chez* Trewbridge, was the faint reminder of a niggle. It had begun to settle down on the day Colly accompanied her to her uncle's house. Her stomach seemed to have decided that if Colly and the Trewbridges were happy to shoulder her problems, then it had nothing more to complain about.

Clambering into the luxurious bed she wondered why she felt so useless. Was it that nobody needed her? What was she going to do with herself? She stared at the ceiling, wondering if her uncle's money was really going to be hers. If that happened, she imagined Uncle Sholto would scream his anger all the way from Hell. She stifled a giggle. *How* he would hate to know that the niece who had 'too much to say for herself' was trying to ascertain the most practical way of spending his money! She stroked the silk sheets. Such luxury. But she must not become used to it. The Trewbridges' warm cocoon of friendship was only temporary, for as soon as the claim on her uncle's estate had been settled, she must move on.

She climbed back out of bed and parted the floor to ceiling velvet curtains. A nightjar squawked unmelodiously in the Lady's Garden beneath her window, quite drowning out the ecstatic, soaring notes of a nightingale. For a few precious moments she imagined herself back in Portugal, hearing in the nightingale's melody the bell-like trill of a chamariz. Homesickness never went away, she thought. It was like an aching tooth. Always there. But she must put Portugal to the back of her mind. She was in England now.

The marchioness had mentioned a pleasant friend who might need Juliana's services, but at the moment the lady was sojourning with her daughter in Tunbridge Wells. Lady Trewbridge had said airily, 'Anyway, Juliana, if the claim on your uncle's estate is settled, you will not need to become a companion after all.'

Could the nurse from Sao Nazaire become Miss Colebrook of Ivy Cottage somewhere in England? Of course she could. So many possibilities. What had she been thinking? There was plenty to do.

The most important thing was to tell Colly about Benny Ames. Colly had been kind-hearted enough to allow her to recover from her London experience, but she must tell him what had happened. He had risked everything for her. Padding across the cold floor she went to her hatbox and took out her herbal notebook. It fell open naturally at the centre page and she lifted out the three pressed pansies. Holding them to her cheek she felt a little comforted. With the pansies clasped in her fingers she crawled back into bed and pulled the bedsheet up around her neck. She and Tilly would never forget that revolting man. She could only be thankful that Kit had not suffered his attentions. Such world-weary eyes that man had had – as if he had seen everything evil the world had to offer yet his jaded appetite demanded more. She knew he had killed her uncle. Although Uncle Sholto's body had not been found till two days after that creature had died, Colly had told her that Uncle's body had lain in the gutter in an alley off Rosemary Lane until someone had seen fit to inform the authorities. He must have been murdered as soon as he reached London to report that the child-selling ring was under investigation. Even as they scoured the streets of Whitechapel searching for Kit and Tilly, her uncle already lay dead. Colly had not told her of the manner of Sholto Colebrook's death and she would not ask. It was enough that the man's worthless life was over.

But because of him – the last of her father's family – she must leave Trewbridge. If any of the local gentry heard about her family, Colly and the Trewbridges would be looked at askance for befriending her. She had seen the way these English set such store upon reputation.

In the event that Mr Beck disproved Juliana's claim she would find Tilly a place in another household and then quietly disappear into a town such as Bath where old ladies sought dutiful companions. She sighed. She could be dutiful, surely? From what the marchioness had told her, some of those ladies could be hard taskmasters. Her wretched independence had ill-prepared her for tending selfish dotards, but at least she'd have a roof over her head. She could not wait for a reply from her cousins. It might take months.

Everything depended on Mr Beck's decision.

She touched the pansies delicately with a long finger. 'What do you want to do with your life, Juliana?' she asked herself. In the darkness the walls threw back two little words – two impossible little words.

CHAPTER THIRTY-EIGHT

COLLY STRODE TOWARDS the stables. He had much work to catch up on since the last few days had been spent on his own interests. Granted, the Trewbridges were the most generous of employers and had taken Juliana's cause as their own. But he could not presume upon their generosity any longer.

First, he would arrange for the empty tied cottage to be cleaned and repaired. Now that their interloper had been despatched home to Cornwall with, as John had put it, 'a flea in his ear', they could prepare the cottage for one of the new workers Colly intended to employ. The marquess and John had endorsed his plans to expand the cattle-breeding programme on the home farm, and institute grain crops on a couple of outlying farms where good fertile land was lying fallow.

He must also look over the big gatehouse that had been unoccupied since the last steward retired.

'Buildings first, people next,' he muttered to himself. It was an old axiom of his father's about preparing for new employees. It was about the only thing he and Colly had agreed upon.

He passed a colourful flowerbed of London Pride and pinks. Juliana would like those. He'd have some taken up to her room.

'Sir!' A footman hurried towards him. 'Mr Hetherington?'

Colly waited for the man to catch up to him. He knew his long legs ate up the ground much faster than most people's.

'You have visitors, sir. In the large drawing room with her ladyship and Miss Colebrook.'

Colly's eyebrows rose. If Twoomey had seen fit to show the visitors to the large formal drawing room, then there must either be a very large group of visitors, or else the butler wished to impress them with the grandeur of the salon. The Trewbridges preferred the smaller room.

Perhaps some of their army friends had descended upon them. That would be fun, but they would be more likely to ask for John than for Colly. It was early for a morning call but ex-army men were notorious for not keeping to the prescribed rules of polite behaviour. He sighed and retraced his steps, wondering if he was going to get any work done today. The footman pattered behind him. Colly had still not got used to the deference with which the Trewbridge servants treated him. If his father could see them, he would be amazed.

Then Colly stopped dead on the threshold of the big room. Good heavens! It *was* his father.

Here. Now. And his mother and his grandmother. No William, however.

His eyes flicked to where Juliana sat beside the marchioness and he felt the sharp fangs of betrayal bite.

'You knew of this?' he asked her, ignoring everyone else in the room.

Into the fraught silence Juliana whispered, 'Only since yesterday. I did not have time to—'

He cut her off. 'Really?' He was unable to keep the derisory tone from his voice.

'You must not blame Juliana,' the marchioness said. 'It was my idea.'

'I do not doubt it, ma'am,' Colly said bitingly. 'But Juliana—'

'Colwyn!' his father barked. 'How dare you speak to the marchioness like that?' His father had been seated in a wing chair near the marchioness but he leapt to his feet to give Colly a dressing-down. He hadn't changed a bit.

'Enough, sir.' The marchioness could bark too. 'Colly, please be seated.'

To his annoyance, Colly found himself obeying her like a lapdog. Naturally he had to obey his employer's wife, but in his anger, for one dangerous minute he considered defying her. Simmering, he concentrated on reining in his temper. There was no point in doing battle when you were so irate you could not think straight.

'My boy.' With a footman's assistance his grandmother had risen and was bearing down upon him. He jumped up again and hugged her.

'Grandmama! Dearest Grandmama, why did you not continue to write? I—'

'Hush,' his grandmother cautioned. She jerked her head in his father's direction.

'I thought as much,' he muttered, for her ears only.

'One of my own servants, too,' she explained. 'When I found out, I sent him to your father with a note telling him that I had thrown the fellow out and he might like to employ the spy himself.'

Colly grinned. He could see a few wrinkles on the old lady's face that hadn't been there five years ago, but then, he had a few more wrinkles now, too. She looked tired. No doubt travelling in a closed carriage with his father was responsible. They must have left very early. But he was pleased to see his grandmother still retained her fiery spirit.

'I'm proud of you, boy,' she said loudly. 'A brigade-major, Miss Colebrook tells me.'

He flicked a glance at Juliana. Her back was ramrod straight against the back of the red velvet sofa. Her glorious hair glowed against the rich fabric and, although her eyes were downcast, he could see the hurt in the hunched shoulders and the elbows held tightly against her sides. Well, she deserved it. How dare she conspire with the marchioness against him? Friends did not betray each other. The marchioness was … well, a marchioness. But he would never have thought Juliana would do this. She *knew* how he felt about his family.

Concentrate, Hetherington, he told himself. *Find out what is going on*. But he found it difficult to tear his eyes away from Juliana's bowed head and tried to swallow a trace of guilt. Had he been too harsh?

'My boy,' his mother husked. To his knowledge, his mother had never raised her voice. Even when he and his brother had been naughty and their tutor complained, she had been patient, almost long-suffering.

'Mama,' he said gently. He had always been gentle with her, even when he was still in leading strings. He had barely been able to toddle when he discovered that she received a constant stream of harangue and pointless gabble from his father. His first memories of his mother were ones where she sat silent, meekly listening to one of his father's monologues. As Colly grew older he had often wished she would show some spirit when his father made a scathing comment about one of her bosom friends, or was speaking rubbish about the political situation. For Lady Hetherington was very knowledgeable about the important issues of the day, having been brought up in a politically aware household.

And perhaps that was the crux of the matter. Mama seemed to have a wide circle of associates, whereas his father did not have her easy talent for making and keeping friends. And as much as Ambrose Hetherington fancied himself to be *au fait* with the revolutionary ideals of Mr John Wilkes and the far-sightedness of Lord Grenville's support of Catholic emancipation, he could never understand the motivations which drove politicians to go out on a limb and saw off the branch. Yet his wife observed such extremes with an amused tolerance that came from an educated understanding of men in power, and from the natural distance with which she observed life's foibles.

'Colly,' she murmured again. '*How* I have missed your dry comments and reliable kindness. When your grandmama told me you had joined the army, I—' She broke off to swallow hard. 'Never mind. Here you are, safe and sound.' She blinked away a tear and he took her gloved hand and kissed it.

'Mama. I thought about you every day. How is my little sister?'

His mother smiled. 'Not so little any more. She is turned seventeen.'

'She's a baggage,' his father broke in.

Lady Hetherington raised her eyebrows at this, and kept hold of Colly's hand. 'She is quite the young lady. I doubt you'd recognize her,' she said, smiling, and Colly, dismayed, found himself feeling uncomfortable as he always had when his parents disagreed. They seemed to take a disdainful delight in holding opposing opinions.

'She did not come today?'

Sir Ambrose answered. 'We had a carriageful,' he said resentfully. 'Your grandmother *would* come.'

'I wrote to your grandmama as well,' the marchioness explained from the sidelines.

Then to Colly's horror, the marchioness took her fire straight into the enemy's camp. 'Have you found out the truth yet from Miss Blevin?' she asked Sir Ambrose, as if she were discussing the exorbitant price of coal or the latest of Mr Watt's inventions.

'What truth?' Ambrose Hetherington spluttered.

'The truth about who her baby's father is, of course,' the marchioness replied impatiently.

'Well I ...' Sir Ambrose floundered, out of his depth.

The marchioness pressed her advantage. 'But why not, Sir Ambrose? After all, it is as plain as the nose on your face that Colly would not do such a thing.' She managed to instil a large amount of incredulity into her question, leaving everyone in no doubt of her opinion.

Colly looked around the room, trying not to show how eagerly he awaited his father's answer. His grandmother perched on the edge of a chair, her eyes never once leaving his face. His mother's head was bowed as she examined her gloved hands. Two very different women, but both with his interests at heart. How could he have forgotten that?

Miss Colebrook's eyes were fastened on his and for a moment he thought she would speak, then the door opened.

The rest of the Trewbridge family trooped in, followed by Twoomey and a footman bearing trays of wine and refreshments.

It tickled Colly's sense of humour to see his father leap to his feet again and fawn over the marquess, who favoured him with a brief nod. Instead, the marquess addressed Colly.

'Colly, do introduce me to your – father, is it?' he asked. Not *Sir*

Ambrose Hetherington. Not a person in his own right. But a person attached to Colly, and therefore acceptable at Trewbridge.

Colly knew an evil moment of smug satisfaction.

Then the marquess motioned John to come forward. 'Sir Ambrose, I'd like you to meet my son, John, Lord Brechin, who had good reason to be grateful to Colly during a couple of skirmishes on the Peninsula.'

John bowed towards Sir Ambrose then faced the ladies. 'And who are these ladies, Colly?'

Colly sensed his father's ill-concealed displeasure. He obviously couldn't understand why the Trewbridges had befriended his son. Colly didn't care. Not one bit. He had spent half a lifetime trying to appease his father for some unknown sin, all to no purpose. He was tired of living his life to spite his father, because the Marquess of Trewbridge had just brought home a simple fact to Colly. *He* was not his father. He was Colwyn Ellett Hetherington, who had always been honest, who had acquitted himself well in wartime, and who now held a responsible position in the household of the Marquess of Trewbridge. And if his father could not abide him then it was regrettable, but it did not matter greatly. The world would continue to turn.

Colly felt as if somebody had freed him from bondage. Well, almost. He would like to hear his father's reply to the marchioness's question. If Father was so sure Colly was the culprit, what evidence did he have to back that up? Or if his father had any doubts at all, why had he treated Colly that way? Why hadn't he searched for the real culprit?

Colly glanced across to where the marquess smiled down at his wife. Thank goodness. His lordship was not going to chastise her about taking the law into her own hands. Much as Colly deplored the way the lady went about things, one could not doubt her courage. Of course, he tempered the thought, it was easy to be courageous when one was a marchioness.

'Now,' Lord Trewbridge said conversationally when the company was settled, 'how can we clear Colly's name?'

Both Sir Ambrose and the Dowager Lady Hetherington spoke at once. The lady's 'Quite easily' cut across Sir Ambrose's 'Personally, I don't see the need—'

Everyone stared at Colly's grandmother.

'Easily?' the marchioness asked.

The dowager gave a snort of amusement. 'All one has to do is look at Amelia Blevin's child. He is the spitting image of your brother, Colly, right down to the drooping eyelids and jet-black hair. Anyway, Amelia has already admitted it to her parents. She sees herself as the future

Lady Hetherington. But the joke is on her. She thought you were the easier catch, Colly, but you refused to marry her. And now William, the culprit, ignores her. She must have suspected he would not come up to scratch so she tried you first.'

'*William*?' Colly was aware his voice had risen, but he couldn't help himself. 'B-but William believed in me. He—' Then he remembered how William had turned on him. He spun around and glared at his father. 'You suspected this at the time, didn't you? *Didn't you?*' His body shook with the effort to restrain himself from planting his own father a facer. 'Yet you threw me out. Why? I don't understand. I don't care what you think about me any more, but I want to know *why*.'

'Because,' the dowager's voice said clearly, 'the fool knows that you are far more suited to run Heather Hill than William is. You had to be got out of the way so William could succeed. But instead of doing that sensibly, like giving you one of the minor estates, *my son*,' and here his grandmother's voice dripped scorn, 'elected to throw you to the wolves.'

Colly blinked, unable to say anything. Of all the scenarios he had envisaged, lying lonely and unhappy beneath the skies of Spain and Portugal, this was the last thing he had expected.

'Mama! Please,' Sir Ambrose bleated in distress.

But Colly's mother leaned across and held her mother-in-law's hand. 'She is quite right. It was despicable. Colly could have been killed and all for naught. And William has not precisely shone with all the opportunities he has been given.'

'It makes no odds,' Sir Ambrose shouted. 'He is still the future owner of Heather Hill and that's all there is to it.'

'I know,' Lady Hetherington said, as if this was a road they had travelled many times before.

'Good grief, Father!' Colly said. 'All you had to do was tell me to back off. I would have found a way to survive. Found a position with another stud farm perhaps or …' He shrugged, nonplussed.

'Yes, and you'd have gone into competition with Heather Hill, wouldn't you?' his father demanded.

Colly blinked. If he'd had his father's goodwill he'd have gone further east to the good horse breeding and racing country of the downs – Suffolk or Norfolk. His father did not know him at all. 'Rubbish,' Colly said.

Then he glanced around and saw that the Trewbridges had tactfully withdrawn to the far side of the room. He stalked across to the marquess. 'I – I'm sorry about all this, my lord,' he said. 'We had best take this discussion into another room.'

'On the contrary, Colly. It is we who shall leave. We came to lend support, but I see you have the situation well in hand.' The marquess's eyes twinkled.

Colly ran a hand through his hair. 'I wouldn't say that, my lord. It was easier fighting the French than trying to make head or tail of this family business.'

'You have my sympathies, but I have confidence in you. Will you come with us, Miss Colebrook?'

It seemed to Colly that Juliana had to tear herself away. She obviously wanted to stay; he would rather she did not. Who knew what else his family had in store for him? He shuddered as he envisaged Juliana listening to the Hetheringtons airing their dirty linen.

CHAPTER THIRTY-NINE

JULIANA DID SO want to hear what was resolved between Colly and his parents, but of course it was none of her business. She paced restlessly along the pebble paths of the Lady's Garden, telling herself she was selecting blooms for the brass urn in the foyer. And if it so happened that she frequently cast her eyes towards the arbour leading to the main driveway, so what?

After being closeted with his family for a couple of hours, Colly emerged to wave goodbye to the Hetherington contingent. Then he strode towards the stables.

Juliana watched out the corner of her eye as Colly loped away from the house. Escaping his demons, no doubt.

Goodness, how surprising families were!

And although Colly was angry with her, she was annoyed with him, too. Could he not understand that as a guest here she would have been seen as conspiring against her hostess if she'd warned him his family might arrive?

She refused to let him think of her as a traitor. She would tackle him as soon as she could get him alone.

Four hours later she was still waiting. Soon it would be time for her to change her dress for dinner. She glanced out the window. Rain threatened above the Cotswolds.

She put down her sewing and excused herself to Marguerite and the marchioness. Then she went upstairs to fetch her cloak. She found Tilly there, trying to dress up Juliana's dinner dress with a length of beading.

'Tilly, you should be resting.'

'Miss, I'd far rather be working. That way I have no time to think.' Tilly's vivid little face worked for a moment, then with an obvious effort of will she controlled herself. She settled back onto her stool in front of the big windows, straining to use the last light from the dying day.

'I understand, Tilly, but please use a lamp. That is very pretty. Where did you find the beading?'

Tilly essayed a smile. 'Lady Brechin's maid told me to take what I liked out of the big sewing cupboard in the hall. They're ever so kind here, Miss Colebrook. I wish we could stay.'

So did she. But it wasn't possible.

Torn between consoling Tilly and confronting Colly, Juliana hovered, clutching her cloak.

'Ah, there you are, Tilly.' Mrs Willis, the housekeeper, bustled in. She cast a questioning glance at Juliana. Juliana shook her head. Mrs Willis folded her lips and said briskly, 'Come along. We are waiting for you in the maids' room.'

Tilly jumped up. 'I forgot! We are all to meet before helping our ladies to dress. Is that all right, Miss Colebrook?' She glanced at Juliana, hesitating. The old Tilly would have dashed off without a care. Juliana nodded and hurried off in search of Colly.

She found him sitting on a stone bench outside the wall of the Lady's Garden. He gazed into space, rubbing the old scar on his thigh, oblivious to her approach. However, when she sat down beside him he snapped out of his reverie.

'Juliana?'

As he turned his face towards her, she received a shock. The hazel eyes were devoid of emotion. She had seen those intelligent, expressive eyes warm, humorous, even chilly, yet now they were empty. He looked as if he had sustained a blow to the head.

She reached out and touched his arm. 'Colly, what happened? Tell me.'

He turned his hand under hers and gripped it like a drowning man clutching a spar. If she didn't know how capable he was, she would have thought *she* was rescuing *him*.

He drew a deep breath and stared down at their clasped hands. 'When William and I were away at school, things between us were fine. It was only when we went home in the holidays that we seemed to rub up against each other. Now I know why. My stupid father fanned the flames.'

Juliana nodded. 'I heard him say he thought you were not being fair to William. I think that's a very odd way of looking at it.'

'You'd have to live with my father to understand. His entire life revolves around Heather Hill. His father trained him to take over the reins when he was twenty-five, I believe. Anyway, he decided William should do the same. Except that William didn't show much aptitude and Father didn't know what to do.'

'And you *did* show plenty of aptitude,' Juliana said with satisfaction.

Colly glanced at her sideways. 'Apparently. So when Amelia dropped her bombshell, Father grabbed the opportunity to get rid of me.'

Juliana shook her head. 'Couldn't he have done it another way? A kinder way?'

'That's what my mother and grandmother said. But he is what he is. Very much an all or nothing person.' Colly sighed. 'However, I am partly to blame. I knew something wasn't right that day, yet I never stopped to ask questions. I should have realized that if Father was hesitant, then something was very wrong. He is always so damned *sure* of himself. But my pride ...'

'Your feelings were hurt,' Juliana excused him. 'It is perfectly understandable.'

Colly grimaced. 'You should have heard him when we all ripped into him. He changed tack and got all maudlin and began calling me his "dear son". Of course, Grandmama couldn't help herself. She went on about how Amelia thought I'd be a softer touch so she tried me first, but that Father queered her pitch by getting rid of me.' Colly's mouth hitched up at one corner. 'Then Father asked Grandmama that if she suspected that, why didn't she speak up? And Grandmama laughed madly and said he had never listened to anyone in his life ...' Colly cast his eyes up.

Juliana giggled. 'No wonder I saw you rushing out to work as if the hounds of hell were after you. You must have been glad to escape the drawing room.'

'Lord, yes. I thought they'd never go.' He sighed. 'To add to the drama they told me that Lieutenant Davidson and his aunt called to see me. Davidson assumed I'd be living at Heather Hill. That was when my parents learned I had returned from the Peninsula.' He smiled wryly. 'My unfilial behaviour in not contacting them was another thing held against me.'

'Davidson?' Juliana enquired. 'Dear me, are we never to be free of him?'

Colly grinned. 'The Davidsons must have been surprised at the odd reception they received.' Then he scraped his feet impatiently. 'Right up till the minute they left, the family kept issuing invitations for me to visit Heather Hill. At the moment it is the last place I want to go. I know it's wrong of me but it will take me a very long time to forgive Father. And Mother also, because she knew his reasoning and never bothered to ... oh, well. It's best forgotten.' Then he laughed. 'Of course I'll visit Grandmama as soon as possible. Otherwise she'll bombard me with letters or send a carriage to collect me.'

'You are very lucky to have her,' Juliana said quietly. 'I would give a lot to have someone believe in me the way that lady believes in you.' She thought of the love on the old lady's face when she'd first set eyes on Colly in the drawing room. The power of her indignation and her forceful championing of Colly had gone a long way towards setting things to rights with his parents. Oh, he was lucky.

CHAPTER FORTY

AT THE DESOLATION in her voice, Colly turned to look at her. And what he saw made him ashamed of himself.

'I'm sorry, Juliana. Very sorry. But when the marchioness blethered on airily about my parents coming to visit, I could have strangled the both of you. How could you not understand that the last time I saw my father, he was busy washing his hands of me? And my mother did not say goodbye at all. She found it too difficult to do, and disappeared rather than face me.' He hesitated for a moment. 'I am ... disappointed in Mama. She didn't try to prevent me from entering the army because she knew I needed to get away from Heather Hill. But it irks me that she never tried to dissuade Father from some of his more irrational notions.'

'I doubt it was a conscious decision, Colly,' Juliana replied. 'Perhaps she found it easier to let things slide by.'

'That is very like Mama. You are a very quick judge of character, Juliana.'

'I have had to be,' she said matter-of-factly.

He stood up, still holding on to her hand. 'Come on. I want to talk to you where we cannot be overheard.' He strode across the open yard to the high wall beside the stables. When she stumbled, he cursed himself for being an impolite care-for-nobody. He slowed. 'I'm sorry.'

'Where are we going?' she puffed.

'Here,' he growled, backing her into the office next to the tack room. He braced one arm against the wall and rested the other on her shoulder. 'Juliana, tell me about the man in London. I *must* know in case there are official enquiries.'

'Yes. I – I understand. And please let me thank you—'

He brushed his hand through the air in negation.

She flicked him an upward glance, then fixed her gaze on the chain from his fob watch. She took a breath. 'Well, when I woke up, I found Kit.' And she told him in detail all that had transpired while he had been bringing Tilly to the inn.

'The knife,' Colly said. 'Who did it belong to? Where did you get it?'

Juliana stared hard at the watch chain. 'I had it in my reticule.'

Colly felt his jaw slacken. 'Uh. So that's why you wouldn't move without your reticule?'

She nodded.

He chose his words carefully. 'Do you always carry a penknife in your reticule?'

'For some years, I have.'

'And have you had much cause to use it?'

'Yes.' Her terse answers hid a wealth of bitterness.

'I see.' He pulled her close and whispered into her hair, 'You are the bravest woman I know.'

She relaxed into him and his heart, already at a trot, stirred to a canter. He wanted her warmth closer. With one arm protecting her, he used his other hand to unbutton his jacket and waistcoat. Then he pulled her flush up against his body. His eyes drifted shut. This was what he craved. Closeness to another human being – to her, specifically. For so long he had put aside the possibility of a normal, loving relationship but today he'd discovered he no longer had to live out in the cold.

'What did that animal try to do to you?' he asked her huskily. 'Tell me.' She needed to unburden herself in order to heal and he needed to know the truth if the authorities should question him.

'It wasn't just about *me*, Colly. It was what I thought he'd done to Kit and to Tilly. Luckily Kit is untouched. But poor, poor Tilly. I'm glad I did it. Glad!' She stood back from him and gripped his sleeve. 'He told me he liked to *warm up* the new young ladies in his care, and oh, Colly, the expression on his face when he said that! I knew he'd done unspeakable things to others. I saw eyes like that once before,' she whispered. Then she stepped back into his embrace and clung, as if trying to press herself right through his skin.

Colly tried to concentrate. She needed him to be kind and protective and understanding. But holding her close like this— No! She needed gentleness. He struggled to listen to the papery, ashamed whisper. 'Tell me,' he urged. 'Where did you see someone else like that?'

'It was outside Porto when I travelled to work at Sao Nazaire. My maid deserted me. She hated the whole journey and wanted to return to Coimbra. It was our last night before entering the city, and we camped well back among the trees on a slope above the Douro. I took a pot and clambered down to get water and, as I returned, I heard the clink of harness. She had taken one of the donkeys and most of our belongings. If only she had waited just one more day! I was so frightened on my own. As well as the English soldiers quartered in Porto, I'd been warned that some French deserters were in the vicinity, trying to cross the border into northern Spain and then to France.'

She paused, and he set his teeth: he knew what was coming.

'I did not dare light a fire. I had some apples and I was peeling one when they burst through the trees. There were three of them – deserters from the French army. Two were Germans. They were reeling drunk. But it was the third man who terrified me. He was a French officer, a captain.'

She shivered and he eased her down on to the ottoman in the corner of the office. It was comfortable but none too clean, although Colly doubted that Juliana noticed. She was in another world – a terrifying world of remembered helplessness and paralyzing fear.

'What did he do?' he asked, although he already knew. Oh, God. No wonder she was cautious around men. No wonder she'd been petrified when he told her about the accusation against him.

'At first it wasn't what he did. It was the look on his face.' Her breath quickened. 'The other two were so drunk they could hardly stand and after a few minutes they just dropped down and slept. Every now and again one would mutter in his sleep, then he'd roll over and begin snoring again.'

'But the captain...?' Colly prompted. He hated pushing her this way and, of course, he didn't want to hear it, but she needed to tell someone so she could put it behind her. Rather the man who loved her than anyone else.

'H-he *hunted* me,' she said angrily, 'as if I were prey. He laughed as he prowled between the trees, chasing me. He could easily have caught me, but he wanted me to run. When I realized that, I stopped running. He would have caught me anyway, but my conscience still pricks at me that ... that—'

'You did the right thing,' Colly assured her. 'Otherwise he might have been rougher when he caught you.'

A sob escaped her and Colly's heart contracted. All this time she had blamed herself for making it easy for her attacker to capture her.

'That is what I told myself. I even thought he might just make game of me then let me go.'

'Instead?'

'He caught me from behind and gripped me with one arm. With the other he – he pushed up my skirts. He made me bend over—' She drew in a breath. 'It hurt,' she said baldly, then stoically continued. 'When he had finished he spun me around and around, having a game with me. I was so dizzy I fell over and I looked up and saw his eyes close to for the first time. It was then I realized it wasn't a game he was playing. He'd done this before. It was a sickness with him. I was going to die. He pulled his pistol out and tried to push the barrel up between my legs, and all the time he muttered soothingly, as if he thought I was *enjoying* it! *Deus*, Colly—'

Two fat tears trailed down her cheeks. All he could do was hold her. He felt so damned helpless and useless. Anger vibrated through him in waves and he struggled to bring it under control so she couldn't feel how much he wanted to jump up and bash something. Anything. Preferably the Frenchman's head.

After a time she sniffed and sat up, unable to meet his eyes.

His hand shook as he proffered his handkerchief.

She took it gratefully. 'Thank you.'

'Can you go on?' he asked.

She nodded, gazing down at the handkerchief as she rolled the edges between her forefinger and thumb. Then she continued, rather as if she were reciting a lesson for her governess. 'He dragged me back to where the rest of my possessions were and, out the corner of my eye, I saw the knife lying where I'd dropped it when he chased me. As he shoved me down on the ground I wriggled closer to the knife. He never even saw it. Not then, not later. Instead, the *filho da puta* laughed when I wriggled. "Oh, I *like* that", he said. "Do it again".' Her voice wobbled and she cleared her throat. 'I grabbed the knife with my left hand and I plunged it into his neck.'

'Of course you did,' Colly murmured. 'It was all you *could* do.' Considering the details of her story, he was surprised when she rested her head on his shoulder trustingly and sighed.

'I have told myself a hundred times that I did the only thing I could. But ... to take someone's life!'

'Did he try to grab it?' Colly asked. He prayed she had not had to endure a life and death struggle with the French captain.

'No,' she said, closing her eyes. Then she covered her face and muttered, 'At first he was so intent on ... and then the bubbles ...'

'That's enough,' Colly said. He'd seen many a dying man. She had no need to struggle through the ordeal of giving him the details. 'What about his companions?'

'They heard nothing!' she said incredulously. 'They were so drunk they slept through the whole thing. I hid behind the trees, waiting for the captain to die and I was terrified the others would wake up. Then I

... pulled the knife out.' She grimaced. 'I had to do it in case the others chased me and I had to ... had to use it again.'

Oh, God, Colly thought. *One penknife against two army deserters.*

'I stole a pistol from one of the German soldiers,' she went on. 'Then I grabbed my things and set the donkey free. I hoped that when they woke up they'd follow the donkey.'

More like cut their losses and bolt, Colly thought.

'Then I ran towards Porto as fast as I could,' she finished. She fell silent.

He thought of the fearful horror of it all. Running through the dark not knowing where she was going, terrified the soldiers might pursue her, wondering who else might be in the vicinity, and worst of all, her body bruised and bleeding and sore.

He tucked her against his side. 'You are an incredible woman, Miss Juliana Colebrook.'

'I am a murderess twice over,' she answered, her chin tucked on to her chest; then she began to cry in earnest – great, racking sobs that shook her whole body.

'It was done in self-defence, Juliana. It was not murder.'

She was not listening. Making no attempt to hide her face, she sobbed and sobbed.

Colly let her be. A cleansing was long overdue. For both of them in fact. They had both been through a form of catharsis today.

Holding her hand, he felt the cold ball of anger he'd clasped to his chest for so long begin to dissipate. Compared to what this courageous woman had gone through, his dislocation from his family was trivial. And, strangely, he had begun to feel a sort of resigned pity for his father. How difficult it must be for one of his ilk to have an heir who didn't measure up to his impossibly high standards. And to be married to a popular and intelligent woman whose distant and martyred air extended also to her husband and children. Colly shook his head. He could never marry a woman like that. No, he would marry the woman sitting beside him. The one who tried so hard to be tough, but who, inside the protective shell she'd created, felt far too much. She had not retreated to the safe confines of a convent when her life had tattered into shreds. His Miss Colebrook had straightened her shoulders and stumbled staunchly into the future. And the courage of her when she'd offered to share a cabin with him on the boat even after she'd heard his story! He hated upsetting her further, but he must ask about the man in London.

'Juliana?' He stroked her hair.

'I know. You want to know about Benny Ames.'

'Who?'

'The man with the cold eyes. He called himself Benny Ames. I should have told Sir Alexander that.'

'The less Sir Alexander knows, the better. We must keep that man's death a secret.'

'I would do the same thing again, Colly.'

'I know, my love.' He rocked her to and fro. 'Tell me,' he whispered. He wanted her to tell the story not only so he could ensure there would be no repercussions, but also to free her from her self-imposed guilt. Since that day in London he'd seen a helpless, lost expression in her eyes. Now he'd heard what had happened to her outside Porto, he knew she believed she was as opprobrious as the rest of her family.

She stared into space for a moment, assembling her thoughts. 'Kit was terrified. When Ames said he wanted to warm me up like all the others he captured, I knew that if Kit and I were to survive, I had to do something quickly. It was a miracle Kit was still untouched, but Tilly told me he gave them a lot of trouble, screaming and trying to escape. So they began instead with Tilly, poor girl. It was my fault they caught Tilly. I should *never* have sent her out searching for Kit. If only I'd been able to find her before they took her to London.'

'Hush. You did all you could.'

She told him how Ames had staggered about, clawing at the knife blade in his neck, trying to dislodge it.

He nodded. 'Yes. I found him lying in a huge pool— Never mind, you don't need to know that,' he said, when he saw her tremble.

'Was he ... was he still alive?'

Colly hesitated. 'Barely. It was only a matter of minutes.' He had done nothing to aid Ames at all. It had crossed his mind that depressing his foot over the man's throat would be a merciful way to end it. But he hadn't done so. Why should he accord that animal a merciful death? He had waited, his eyes locked with Ames's, and kept guard until the last laboured breath gurgled from his throat. Fishing the knife blade out of the man's throat with slippery, bloody fingers had been the hardest part. But he had wanted any official enquirer to assume the man's death was the result of a falling-out with his conspirators after Kit and Juliana had fled.

'Sweetheart, how much did Kit see?'

At the endearment, Juliana rubbed her cheek against his waistcoat. 'Not much. I told him to run as fast as he could when Ames grabbed me.'

'I've already warned him that the Runners or his grandfather may question him about it. But he just shrugged and said he'd seen nothing,' Colly said, grinning. 'He's a bright lad.'

She sighed, a huge sigh of thankfulness, and leaned limply against him.

In the distance a bell rang.

'Dinner!' they exclaimed in unison.

'We must hurry.' Colly urged her to her feet.

She pulled a face. 'I do not feel in the least like eating.'

'Nor I.'

They scurried across the open yard where a blustery wind scattered raindrops from the darkening sky.

'Juliana, if anything unexpected arises out of all this, I shall deal with it, I promise you,' Colly said as they parted in the foyer.

'Thank you,' she whispered and fled upstairs.

He watched her for a moment, admiring the straight back and proudly held head. At the top of the stairs she glanced back over her shoulder. Ignoring whoever might be passing through the foyer, he blew her a kiss. He was rewarded with the slightest of smiles.

No, it would not be long before she was his.

CHAPTER FORTY-ONE

THREE WEEKS LATER Juliana found that she had indeed become a woman of means. Earnest Mr Beck assured her that all was in order for her to take over her aunt and uncle's property. Advertisements in *The Times* and *Morning Post* had brought forth no other legal claimants. It had been a simple exercise to ascertain there were no more Colebrooks of their particular line because a family tree was inscribed on the first page of the family Bible in her uncle's study.

Juliana had snorted when she heard that. 'The family *Bible*?' she asked Mr Beck, trying to suppress a snigger.

'Yes, Miss Colebrook.' Mr Beck did not see anything untoward about owning a family Bible. Of course, he had no idea what sort of family he was dealing with. 'Your uncle was the senior and last remaining member of his line, so he held the Bible,' the solicitor said, shuffling a heap of papers together. He obviously did not want to waste too much time on a simple transaction from which he would not make a large fee. He hustled her into his carriage and took her to the bank in Hungerford where he introduced her to the bank manager.

But apart from changing the name on the account and withdrawing a few pounds, Juliana left the bulk of the money in the bank. She also refused Mr Beck's advice on investments. He was stunned when she asked him to make arrangements to sell the house. 'B-but all this money, Miss Colebrook! Will you not use it to bring the house up to scratch?'

'No thank you, Mr Beck. I'm not yet sure what I shall do. I've made no plans. But you can rest assured that most of the money in that bank account will go to charity.'

Mr Beck's parsimonious soul was rattled. Aghast, he protested.

Juliana knew she would need a business associate, someone she could trust – apart from Colly – because she had plans that did not include him. So she set to work to explain to Mr Beck why she felt uncomfortable about inheriting her uncle's savings. The stuffy little man was horrified.

'Now can you see why I am reluctant to use it for my own ends?'

'I can indeed, Miss Colebrook. And might I add that I'm impressed. Another person might well turn a blind eye, under the circumstances.'

Good, she had him on her side. She smiled. 'I'm afraid I have some more work for you, sir. When the family house is sold, I intend to use the proceeds to purchase a small cottage or something of that nature. There must be sufficient monies left over to maintain a small household.'

Mr Beck nodded sagely as he tooled his carriage through the busy streets of Hungerford.

'The money for the upkeep of the house was inherited from family funds, so I'm happy to use that,' she explained.

'I trust you will be guided by my advice, Miss Colebrook.'

She smiled. Hopefully he would take that as a yes. She was not sure where she would go but it would be best for her peace of mind if she left the Hungerford area altogether. Now that Colly's father had come to his senses, Colly could, with a clear conscience, feel free to court a nice young woman. But that nice young woman would not be Juliana. By no stretch of the imagination could she be called *nice* – not when one took into consideration the fact that she had killed two men, even though Colly insisted she had done it in self-defence. Nor was she the pure, innocent lady of leisure society decreed he must have. If the authorities ever investigated the kidnappings and Ames's death more closely, they might enquire into her background. Thanks to Colly they would not discover her part in Ames's murder, but the ensuing gossip about the way her aunt and uncle had died rendered her unacceptable in the best circles. She had learned enough about English society to understand that everyone, from chambermaids to owners of great houses, thrived on gossip. And as a child she had learned from her father how rigidly English society adhered to its self-made rules. No. She was too old and too dark-skinned and she was a member of an iniquitous family. Heavens, she was even unsure which knife to use when eating fish! Worst of all: what if it got about that she had accompanied Colly as his wife on board the *Maximus*?

She must not allow Colly to continue their friendship. He needed to resume his rightful place in society. Association with her would not help him the way marriage to a carefully reared young Englishwoman would. Because she loved him she would let him go. No one had earned his happiness more than Colly Hetherington. A lump grew in her throat as she thought of how the Trewbridges and Hetheringtons would hold up a bevy of beauties for him to choose among. In time he would forget the half-English, half-Portuguese nurse who had caused him so much trouble. His bride would be a pale, pure virgin who would know instinctively who was important, and who was not – someone like Lady Richelda. That lady would be confident in her knowledge of fish knives and whose title was the oldest. She would have a large dowry to enable Colly to purchase the estate he so longed for, not a silly little inheritance sufficient to buy a mere cottage. And she would have smooth, white hands. She would stroke those elegant hands across Colly's scars. (It was to be hoped she would not flinch.) Juliana prayed that this mythical, perfect creature would appreciate all his good qualities – his kindness, his gentle toughness and his innate sense of responsibility, because that young lady would be the luckiest person in the whole of England.

'Is there anything else I can do for you, Miss Colebrook?'

Good heavens! She had ignored poor Mr Beck for the entire journey back to Trewbridge. 'I'm sorry, Mr Beck. I was wool gathering. Please allow me to offer you some refreshments.'

She must not let Colly suspect what she was planning. She dreaded his reaction, but she knew she was doing the right thing. For Colly, anyway. Ugh! Why did doing the right thing always feel so bad?

CHAPTER FORTY-TWO

INSTEAD OF COMPILING a list of repairs for the empty cottage and the gatehouse, Colly found himself sitting at his desk gazing into space, wondering where he could find a romantic setting to ask Juliana for her hand in marriage. He wanted romantic, damn it all, because Juliana had had very little of it in her life. She *deserved* romantic. Perhaps the Lady's Garden would be appropriate? She loved flowers and that was perfumed wondrously at this time of year. Although most of the roses were well past their prime, a few hardy ones remained and the musky scent of clouds of pinks wafted on the breeze. Or maybe the summer-house would be better for a proposal. That was it. He'd arrange for—

There was a light tap on the door and Twoomey bustled in. 'Sir, your father is here to see you.'

His *father*? Now what? He hoped there would be no repeat of the maudlin contrition he'd had to face the other day. Unfilial it might be, but he had hoped it would be many months till he had to face his parents again.

'Thank you, Twoomey. Please show him in.'

'I think it best to tell you, Mr Hetherington, that Sir Ambrose is er … not in the best of humours.'

'Good Lord, Twoomey. You unman me.'

Twoomey's lips twitched. 'Yes, sir.'

The butler scarcely had time to step back out of the way before Ambrose Hetherington rushed into the study.

'What do you have to say for yourself, boy?' he demanded.

'Ah … about what?' Colly enquired cautiously. 'Have a seat, sir.'

'Mmph.' Sir Ambrose flung himself on to a ladderback chair and it rocked alarmingly.

'Sir?' Colly enquired again.

'You'll have to marry the girl.'

Colly wondered for one startling moment if his father was a mind-reader.

'Which girl?' he asked.

'That dark-eyed foreign woman who was here last time we called,' his father shouted.

'Her name is Juliana Colebrook,' Colly said with narrowed eyes.

'Whatever her name is now, it'd better be Hetherington as soon as possible.'

'I've had that in mind for some time. Why the urgency, Father?'

He had not called his father by that title for many years and for a moment Sir Ambrose's eyes snapped shut. When he opened them again, they glistened. But he took only a minute to recover. 'There's a filthy rumour flying about. We received a note yesterday. Unsigned of course.' Sir Ambrose all but spat the words.

'If it's a rumour, ignore it. But what does it have to do with Juliana?'

'The note said that you and she travelled from Portugal as husband and wife.'

'Hell!' Colly exclaimed unguardedly.

'Colwyn! You didn't! My God, wasn't the last débâcle enough for you?'

Colly stood up and strode towards his father. 'Must I remind you that the débâcle before was not of *my* making?' In contrast to Sir Ambrose's voice, his was quiet. But Sir Ambrose must have heard the steel beneath the measured words, for he subsided, refusing to catch Colly's eye.

'Well then,' he responded meekly, 'I can see from your attitude that you admire the gel, so instead of hedging about, marry her. Then all will be well.'

'That will not be necessary, sir.' A third voice joined the conversation. Colly and Sir Ambrose whipped around. Juliana stood in the doorway. 'Excuse me. I saw you arrive, Sir Ambrose, and I wish to speak to you regarding your son.'

'Eh?' Colly asked, startled into rudeness.

Juliana ignored him. 'Sit down again, Sir Ambrose.' She patted a settle invitingly and Sir Ambrose sat, looking puzzled.

But not nearly as confused as Colly was. What was the little minx up to? Juliana disposed her skirts and Colly noticed she was wearing a new dress. Very nice it was, too. Instead of the worn drab gowns she'd been wearing since he met her, she was now garbed in a deep-blue gown of some silky fabric. It was reminiscent of her evening gown and Colly was very fond of that evening gown. Without a fichu it showed a lot more of Juliana than he was used to seeing. He hoped she had consigned her prim, boring fichus to the dustbin. Thank goodness she had broken down and used a little of her late uncle's money.

'Your son,' she said to Sir Ambrose, 'is the most honourable man of my acquaintance. When I cajoled him into acting as my husband' – here, Juliana's voice hitched a little – 'he did not like the situation but felt obliged to help me. I was responsible for the masquerade and—'

'Hush.' Colly had recovered his senses. He was exalted that she loved him enough to protect him from his father – in fact, he was damn near jumping for joy – but he did not want her to incriminate herself. After all, he hoped his father would soon become her father-in-law. Then he reminded himself to temper his enthusiasm. One never quite knew with Miss Juliana Colebrook. He had caught her looking at him once or twice recently with a serious, remote look on her face that he was unable to read. 'Thank you for championing me, Miss Colebrook,' he said politely, trying to take the heat out of the discussion. 'I'm sure my father understands. No doubt the anonymous letter gave him a severe shock.'

'It did,' averred Sir Ambrose, wiping his forehead with a large hand-kerchief.

'I think we both know this originated from Davidson, don't we, Juliana?' Colly murmured, touching her hand briefly. He noticed his father flick a quick glance at them, then look away. He could have sworn he saw a smirk edge the corners of his father's mouth, but he wasn't sure.

'Well, whatever the circumstances, you must fix it,' Sir Ambrose said.

'May I see the letter, Father?' Colly asked.

Sir Ambrose fished inside his coat pocket and produced a much-folded piece of paper. 'Here. It's couched in terms that reek of blackmail.'

Colly scanned the lines. And raised his eyebrows. 'Yes. I see what you mean. Leave it with me. I cannot spare the time to make enquiries today. I have work to do and the Trewbridges have been more than generous in giving me time to get my affairs in order.' He hoped Juliana would not object to being called an affair. He tapped the letter. 'I know where the writer of this letter lives and tomorrow I'll see what he has to say for himself. It will have to be an overnight trip.' Colly pocketed the letter.

'You're sure about his identity? Wouldn't do to go flourishing this around the wrong people, m'boy.'

'I shan't flourish it, Father. I shall make discreet enquiries.' Lord, his father must think him an idiot.

Colly smiled at Juliana. 'You may rest assured, Juliana, that we will settle this matter.'

Juliana looked at him, her chocolate eyes full of secrets. 'Very well, sir.' She turned to his father. 'Sir Ambrose, nuncheon will soon be served. Might I tempt you to stay and eat with us?'

By dint of gentle persuasion and a hand beneath his elbow urging him on, Juliana edged Sir Ambrose out the door. She cast Colly an eloquent glance over her shoulder and he was hard put to it not to laugh aloud. Her expression said, 'I shall get rid of him for you.'

He settled back to work and this time accomplished all he had set out to do. Three hours later, feeling quite smug about his achievements, he strolled out to find Twoomey hovering in the foyer. 'Ah, there you are, Twoomey. Is my father still here?'

'No, sir. He left some time ago.'

'I see.' Colly was not surprised his father had not said goodbye. Juliana had no doubt prevailed upon him to leave Colly alone to get on with his work. She was a gem. Her years of nursing stood her in good stead when it came to dealing with difficult people.

'Is Miss Colebrook available, Twoomey?'

'No, sir. She left with Sir Ambrose.'

'*What?*' For one dreadful moment Colly's whole world skidded sideways.

'Well, sir, Sir Ambrose and Miss Colebrook were getting on like a house on fire at nuncheon. Next minute I heard Sir Ambrose offering Miss Colebrook a ride in his carriage as far as Heather Hill. Then Miss Colebrook mentioned purchasing tickets on the stage for Keynsham, but Sir Ambrose said it was no bother, he'd convey her to Keynsham anyway. Then Miss Colebrook asked Tilly to pack her a valise.'

Twoomey must have listened assiduously to every word.

Colly rallied. 'Did she, by Jove?' he exclaimed. 'We'll see about that! I know what she's up to.' Then he recalled who he was talking to. 'Ah, Twoomey, have you seen Lord Brechin anywhere about?'

Twoomey directed him to the stables, and Colly, feeling like the worst employee anyone could ever have, set out to beg John for even more time off.

But John just laughed. 'Been expecting you, old boy,' he said, grinning. 'M'mother warned me you'd be on the warpath when you discovered how neatly Miss Colebrook gave you the slip.' Then he laughed even harder. 'Take the small carriage.'

'Glad to afford you entertainment,' Colly said stiffly. 'I should get as far as Heather Hill tonight, anyway. The weather is clear. Tomorrow I hope I can find Juliana in Cheltenham or thereabouts.'

'Bring her back here, Colly. Tell her you shall have the gatehouse when you marry. That might stand in your favour,' John said, grinning. 'And Marguerite and Mama can at last plan your wedding. It will be a great relief all round.'

'Know-it-all,' Colly muttered under his breath. He bolted from John's knowing grin and hurried to his bedchamber to pack a change of clothes. For a man who detested the word family he was hell bent on creating one of his own. Yes, he would eat his words later. Right now he must catch up with his skittish intended. As he stuffed a spare shirt into his valise he said aloud, 'Get used to it, Miss Colebrook. You belong with me.'

Half an hour later he tooled the Trewbridge carriage along the Bath road towards Heather Hill.

CHAPTER FORTY-THREE

HE ARRIVED AT Heather Hill as dusk settled. Bath was as busy as an anthill and he'd had to weave his way through an endless procession of doddering old carriages carrying doddering old people doddering home from taking the waters. Then he'd had to bypass Royal Crescent altogether and had driven around the park instead, which was a shame. The new, unfinished curves of golden sandstone buildings were one of the things he had reminisced about as he trudged over the bloodied snow through the pass at Corunna, and waited, battle ready, heart pounding, on the heights above Fuentes de Onoro. But he would see the finished crescent another day. Perhaps he would bring Juliana to see the Sydney Gardens.

The pair of Trewbridge blacks would be pleased to rest overnight in his father's stables. Heather Hill boasted the finest stables in the south of England. At least, he hoped that was still the case. He slowed the horses to take the curve around to the back of the house.

He was in two minds about staying here. He no longer saw it as home, but neither did he hold the bitter animosity towards his family that he had carried until only last week. Oh, he did not find it easy to forgive his parents, but he did not intend to let their machinations rule his life from now on. Neither did he look forward to meeting William, but he very much wanted to see how Felicia fared.

He jumped down and flexed his fingers, then looped the reins over the holding post. Carefully he stretched out his injured leg. Cramp was setting in and he massaged the thigh as Dr Barreiro had taught him to do.

'Well, I never!' exclaimed a voice behind him.

He spun around. 'Mersey!' Tom Mersey and he had played together in the stableyard two decades ago.

Tom grinned. 'I come runnin' when I heard the carriage, but you're the last person I expected to see.'

Colly shoved his hand out. 'Tom, you're a sight for sore eyes. I presume you're head groom here now?'

Tom shook his head. 'Nah. Yer brother imported some fancy Irish groom from Dungarvan last year so I'm just one of the under-grooms now.' He changed the subject. 'I can't tell you how glad I am to see you, sir!'

'But Tom—' Colly stopped. The cheerful mask pasted on the craggy face belied the misery in Tom's shrewd eyes. Colly didn't ask any more questions.

'I'll come out later and blow a cloud with you,' he promised. 'And when I'm well settled at Trewbridge I'll find you a more conducive position – that is, if you want it. Would you leave Heather Hill?'

'Oh, I'd leave Heather Hill all right,' Tom said. 'Working at the best stud in the south of England might sound fine, but I've had enough o' this place. I'd be right glad to leave.' Then he collected himself. 'That is … do you mean it, sir? Could you find another position for me?'

'Certainly. Just give me a couple of weeks and I'll contact you.'

Tom's face lit up like a beacon. 'Bless you.'

'In the meantime, Tom, we'd best get this pair rubbed down.'

'Lovely high steppers,' Tom commented, running his hand down a glossy flank. 'Are they yours, sir?'

'No such luck. They belong to the estate where I work as steward. Trewbridge,' he explained when he saw Tom's curious look.

'*Really*, sir?' Tom flicked a glance at the insignia emblazoned on the carriage door. 'Don't hear much about it, but what I do know is good. Was it Trewbridge you were thinking of, to find me a position, I mean?'

'One of the Trewbridge estates, anyway,' Colly told him.

'Strewth! How many have they got?'

There was the scrunch of feet on gravel and they both turned.

William Hetherington stood, arms akimbo, framed in the centre of the archway like a painting. He glowered at Tom.

Colly nodded and made no attempt to approach his brother. 'William,' was all he said. As far as he was concerned, his brother was a gutless cheat. He did not intend to bother with him. Mild civility would have to paper over the cracks of familial duty.

But William surged forward with his hand held out. 'Good Lord, Colly! You've grown even taller!' His jocular tone rang false. Colly extended his hand and brushed William's fingers, but William was having none of that. He tried to pull Colly towards him but Colly stood rigidly still and favoured William with a grim smile.

William tried again. 'God, I've missed you!' he exclaimed.

'Why?' Colly flashed back. 'Running out of people to blame for your misdeeds?'

Tom Mersey choked and disguised his bark of laughter by crooning to the horses in a sing-song voice.

William's face purpled. 'If all you've come to do is rake over old scores, then damn you! I can't be bothered trying to make amends.' And off he stomped towards the house.

Colly knew that William would have had no idea how Colly's life had changed after he was thrown out of Heather Hill. William wouldn't have given a thought to the shame Colly had borne amongst his own set of friends, and the fear of having nobody to turn to and nowhere to go. William's hand was smooth and white; his mouth softly petulant. No. He had remained here, coddled and safe, whilst Colly had been biting down his blazing anger at the injustice done him in a country far away from everything he knew. William would neither know nor care about Colly's struggles to carve out a life for himself. As for fighting the French far away in Portugal and Spain, William couldn't even begin to understand what army life entailed.

Colly snorted to himself. That was over. He had come here to find out what his father knew of Juliana's plans. He was merely using Heather Hill as a convenient stopover point. Juliana came first, and always would.

He grabbed his valise and strode towards the house, expecting a frigid welcome.

But his parents were pathetically glad to see him. 'Welcome, m'boy,' his father said, hand outstretched. And this time Colly did not reject the overture, because if he read the situation right, the old boy now had Colly's interests at heart.

'Hello again, Father,' he said, laughing. A footman stole up beside him and took away his valise. 'Er, thank you.' This time he did not recognize the retainer. He raised his eyebrows and Sir Ambrose nodded.

'Yes, he's new. Your brother is determined to fill Heather Hill with people *he* has selected.' Ambrose Hetherington smirked. 'He's hoping I'll shuffle off this mortal coil soon, then he can take over altogether.'

'Good grief, Father! He's a trifle premature.'

His father burst into nervous laughter. 'So his sister told him yesterday. Caused a bit of a furore. Felicia was sent to her room.'

'Since when does William have the ordering of the household, Father? What is going on here?' Colly demanded. Heather Hill was no longer any of his business, but something here was not right.

His father's face worked alarmingly, then he got himself under control. He began pacing about in a restless manner that Colly recognized. 'Colly ... I, well, when you left—'

Colly interrupted. 'I didn't *leave*, Father; you threw me out.'

'Well, yes. Let me explain. Even when you were small, your horsemanship was superior to your brother's. And when you came down from Eton, I saw you could run the Heather Hill stud without any help from me. Your business skills seem to be intuitive. I suppose the Trewbridges are getting the benefit of that,' his father added gloomily. 'So William leaned on you. While you made the important decisions, he spent all his time in London. But Colly' – here his father stopped to stab a finger in Colly's direction – 'William stood to inherit the estate and most of all, the stud stables. He *had* to learn to stand on his own two feet.'

Colly smothered a smile. Not much chance of that while the old man still lived.

Ambrose Hetherington shot an anguished glance at Colly. 'You had to be sacrificed, Colly.'

Colly stared at his father. 'Why on earth didn't you just say so in the first place?'

His father flushed with embarrassment. 'Well, when I told you to leave, I didn't mean *leave forever*.' He glared at Colly who grinned back.

'You're damned lucky I didn't ask Grandmama to finance me into a stud farm right next door to you. Lord, yes. I could have called it Hetherington Hall,' he mused.

Ambrose Hetherington stared at his son in horror. 'You wouldn't have, would you?'

'In those first few days I just might have. But once I'd simmered down, I knew I couldn't do it. Anyway, Grandmama didn't lend me enough money to purchase an estate. It was just enough to purchase a majority.'

'Damn fool woman. You might have been killed!'

'Nearly. Several times. But that's over with now. Let's forget all that. I just met Tom. What's happening with the stud?'

Ambrose Hetherington thumped down on a brocade chair. 'When you left, I gave William free rein.'

Colly did his best to keep his face straight. His father's idea of free rein and other people's ideas of free rein were two different things.

'I told him he'd better get used to running the stud. I wasn't feeling too well in those days, you see.' He cast a glance at Colly from beneath beetled brows.

This time Colly had to work really hard to subdue a snigger. Ever since he could remember his father had suffered from imaginary ailments that he predicted would carry him off any day. The bouts of illness often occurred when his will was crossed.

'I thought by handing over the reins to William before I died I was doing him a favour. With my guidance he could develop the skills to manage everything competently. Instead, he turned into a tyrant,' Sir Ambrose gloomed on. 'He concentrates on petty household matters that do not concern him while harvests languish and good staff leave. He's made a right mull of it. Comes to me for advice then does the opposite of what I suggest.'

Colly was stunned. William had always been very much in the old man's pocket, but now the tables were turned.

There was a rustle behind him and someone grabbed his hand. His mother. 'Darling boy. So pleased to have you here.' She stood on tiptoe to press a kiss against his chin. He held her hand for a moment. When he was a child she'd never touched him or given any demonstrations of love. It was sad that he'd had to go far away before she could bring herself to touch him.

'And Felicia? Where is she?' he asked.

'I'm here, Colly.'

A little vision in blue slipped into the room. *This* was his young sister?

'Felicia!' He opened wide his arms and she ran to him.

'Dear Colly, how I missed you! We've all missed you.'

'Sweet little Felicia, I thought about you often as we slogged through Portugal.'

Her hazel eyes blurred with tears as she clung to his arm. 'Grandmama kept me apprised of where your brigade was posted. I have a map with coloured pins stuck all over Spain and Portugal.'

'Do you, by God?' their father interrupted.

They ignored him.

Colly smiled. 'I wish I'd known. It would have been such a comfort to think of you marking our progress across the Peninsula.' She clung harder to his hand in a silent message of sympathy, then stepped back into the shadows. The innocent-eyed hoyden he used to know had never behaved in such a subdued manner, but, as he'd speculated, it seemed she had been tutored in the ways of young ladies. Such a shame. He thought of Juliana who would never fit the current description of a young lady yet who was undoubtedly a lady. Felicia must spend some time with Juliana. That way she would have another yardstick to measure against.

'I'm sorry you missed dinner,' his mother said. 'I've ordered a tray to be taken to the conservatory. At this time of year it is very pleasant.' As she spoke, she threaded her arm through his.

'Certainly, if you don't mind watching me eat.'

His father, recovering rapidly, winked and said, 'I know what, or rather who, you came here for.'

Colly grinned. 'I hope you know the trouble you've caused me, bringing Miss Colebrook to this part of the country.'

'Son, I did it because she was adamant about this Davidson chap. She was sure he'd written that letter. I couldn't dissuade her from setting out for Keynsham so I thought it best to lend her our carriage and keep her under my thumb.'

For once, Father's arbitrary thumb had come in handy. 'Thank you, Father. I agree with Juliana that Davidson is the most likely candidate for a little gentle extortion. That letter was couched most genteelly.' Colly laughed. 'If you knew Davidson better, you'd understand what I mean. He is a very deliberate, careful individual.'

'Yes. He called on us,' his mother said, her lips quirking.

His father wanted to know the ins and outs, however. 'But what was Miss Colebrook *really* up to, Colwyn? She fluttered around saying goodbye to all and sundry as if she didn't expect to return.'

Colly sat down and accepted the plate stacked high with food that his mother had selected for him. He felt most uncomfortable eating in front of his family. In fact, he felt rather like an exhibit in a sideshow.

Selecting a slice of partridge, he tried to avoid his father's question, but Ambrose Hetherington stood, waiting. Finally Colly was forced to answer. 'She knows I intend to ask her to marry me, and because of her family she has a bee in her bonnet about not being good enough for me.'

'Congratulations, m'boy!' His father was beaming.

Colly blinked. 'I didn't think you approved of her, Father.'

'Rubbish. Didn't get the time to know her when we first met. I spent several hours with her today and I've come to like her very much. Don't let her slip through your fingers. What an interesting life she has had!'

Colly sincerely hoped Juliana hadn't told his father everything; the old boy would have an apoplexy.

'Very courageous gel,' Sir Ambrose warbled on. 'Took the bull by the horns and admitted that travelling from Porto with you was all her idea. And when she told me why, I couldn't condemn her for it.' He shook his head. 'All alone like that, with no family to turn to. Doing a little nursing to keep the wolf from the door.'

Thank goodness. Juliana must have fed his father an expurgated version of her background. He wondered what she would think of her father's notion that she had been 'doing a little nursing'. Fourteen-hour working days amidst filth and blood had become watered down to 'doing a little nursing'.

Felicia was hovering at his elbow. He smiled at her. 'Felicia, did you meet Miss Colebrook while the horses were being changed?'

'Yes, indeed. She explained about the locket. Oh, Colly, were you very much hurt at Fuentes de Onoro?' Her gamine face was screwed up with anxiety, and he wondered again at the fey, delicate young creature she'd become.

'It wasn't pleasant, but thanks to Dr Barreiro and Miss Colebrook, I've recovered enough to lead a normal life again.' He left it at that. He could not possibly find a way to tell these sedate English people living sedate English country lives about scars that chafed, about nightmares where he relived the agony of being dragged on to a dray with the other injured, or about dying men begging for water.

Feeling hunted, he cast his mother an anxious glance. She came to the rescue.

'Don't tease Colly now, Felicia. You can see he's tired. Perhaps if he can persuade Miss Colebrook, they could stop here overnight on their way back?'

Colly had other plans for Juliana. They did not include spending the night under his parents' roof. He shook his head. 'I doubt it, Mama. I must hurry back to Trewbridge because much work awaits me.'

'Good to see you take your tasks seriously,' his father grunted. Colly was amused. How did his father think he had survived almost five years in the army if he didn't take his tasks seriously? Then, with newly acquired intuition, he realized his father was upset that he did not intend to stop at Heather Hill on his return journey. Of course, the old boy would never admit it.

'There will be a next time,' he assured them all. 'But I am not a man of leisure.' Then he said goodnight and hurried off to meet Tom Mersey before they could think of any more ticklish questions.

CHAPTER FORTY-FOUR

NEXT MORNING HE avoided any unpleasantness by leaving before breakfast was served. He had no desire to sit at table with his brother. His father waved him off saying, 'Nice to see you settling down.'

Gathering up the reins, Colly smiled ruefully. 'Don't know if she'll have me yet.' He desperately hoped Juliana would agree to marry him, but he could only persuade her, not coerce her. She must come willingly or not at all. 'Think positively, Hetherington,' he told himself. He knew many of Juliana's reservations about marriage stemmed not from the excuses she was making, but from her deep-seated fear of intimacy. Her only experience had been bitter as gall and he must carry her past the fear and show her the exciting reality of love-making – the giving and the receiving and the belonging. She loved him, he was sure of it. He smiled as he thought of one or two instances where she had given herself away.

He could not remember Lieutenant Davidson's precise address, but it was not difficult to track him down. An ostler at the first inn he came to waved a hand towards Whitchurch.

'The Davidsons? A rum ol' couple they be. Over towards Whitchurch, last house before the smithy.'

More difficult to find out was where Juliana was staying. Eventually he discovered she had booked into the Old Bank Inn. According to mine host, the lady had hired a job-carriage to take her to Whitchurch early that morning.

Colly made some arrangements with the obliging proprietor, and a large amount of money changed hands. Then he strode outside and flicked a coin to the boy holding on to the horses' heads. Leaping back on to the seat he set the horses in motion. He knew that Davidson would no more hurt Juliana than he would fly to the moon, but from the hints he had dropped when he was drunk, his aunt might be a different proposition. So Colly approached the Davidson home carefully. A one-horse hired carriage was pulled up by the roadside, its job-master waiting on the box, arms folded, his head nodding in the morning sun.

'Good morning,' Colly said as he drew up beside it. 'Did Miss Colebrook hire you?'

The driver glared at him suspiciously. 'Who wants ter know?'

'The name is Hetherington. Brigade-Major Hetherington,' Colly added for good measure. 'I'm a friend of Miss Colebrook's. I arranged to meet her here. Shall I pay you off now? I'll be taking her back to Keynsham.'

The fellow looked truculent but Colly respected him for it. The man was right to be cautious.

'No ...' the job-master said at last. 'I'd like to see Miss Colebrook first. We agreed on a price.'

Colly's eyebrows rose. An honest job-master! Scarcer than hen's teeth.

At that moment raised voices rang out from behind the stone wall separating the Davidson property from the road – Juliana and Lieutenant Davidson's voices.

Colly jumped down from his carriage and looped the reins over a handy iron spike that had been rammed into the ground. Over his shoulder he said to the job-master, 'I'd be obliged if you'd keep an eye on this pair. They belong to the Marquess of Trewbridge.' That should assure the driver of Colly's bona fides, provided the man believed him, and why wouldn't he? The Trewbridge crest was emblazoned on the carriage panels.

Davidson's voice had stopped but Juliana's continued. It sounded as though she was giving Davidson a severe dressing-down. Colly strode around the curve of the driveway and came to a halt. A garden seat, placed between two beds of hydrangeas, faced the driveway. Davidson, standing beside the seat, had not noticed Colly. Neither had Juliana who was pacing back and forth in front of the erstwhile lieutenant.

'And another thing, Lieutenant, please remember that if it were not for Brigade-Major Hetherington and myself, you would not be here.'

Colly agreed. Davidson's dogged insistence on bivouacking his company well before dusk on an exposed ridge had encouraged a small, hungry group of French soldiers to try their luck at relieving Davidson and his men of their rations and arms. Although the French had been beaten off by sheer weight of numbers, Davidson had paid dearly for his mistake. His slow reactions had ensured he would never ride or dance again. As Colly had dragged Davidson away from the fracas and into the shelter of the surrounding trees, he, too, had had his old wound reopened by a sabre-wielding Frenchman. Worst of all, Davidson's sergeant, who had argued against the bivouacking site, was felled by a shot from a French musket. For the rest of his life, Davidson would have to live with that.

'I would rather not have survived,' Davidson muttered, head downcast, his injured leg stuck out to one side.

'¿*Por qué te quejas*? How *dare* you! I nursed hundreds of men who struggled desperately to survive, only to succumb to infection weeks later. And you, you great ninny, all you can do is spread rumours and feel sorry for yourself. What is wrong with you?'

Colly stepped back behind the hydrangea bushes.

'You don't understand. I – I didn't mean to let the cat out of the bag about you and Hetherington, I promise. But my aunt screamed and raved and demanded information she could use. Sh-she makes a tidy sum out of—'

'You mean she blackmails people, don't you?' Juliana harangued. '*Inferno*! What a family!'

Davidson continued miserably, 'She was going to throw me out. We used to live in London, you see. Plenty of secrets there,' he added. 'But when my uncle became ill, we moved here for the cleaner air. My aunt misses going to social events and listening to secrets – you know, all the *on dits*.'

'The rich pickings, you mean,' Juliana interrupted crossly.

Behind the hydrangea bushes Colly's brow creased.

'I ... oh hell!' Davidson sounded terrified.

'Portland? Portland Davidson! Who is that woman?' demanded a strident voice.

'It's *her*,' Davidson whispered. 'You must go, Miss Colebrook. Hurry!'

'I don't think so, Lieutenant.'

Colly peered from behind the hydrangeas and saw a buxom woman bearing down upon them. She waved a parasol in Davidson's direction. 'This is not your house, Portland. How dare you invite strangers here?'

'Sh-she's—' Lieutenant Davidson stammered.

'Who is she? I'm asking you, Portland, who *is* she?'

Lord, poor Davidson, Colly thought. So this was the relative who had purchased a lieutenancy for Davidson. Probably with the intention of getting rid of him.

Colly saw Juliana step forward. 'I, madam, am Miss Colebrook. I knew your nephew on the Peninsula.'

Colly saw Davidson close his eyes. Now the fat was in the fire.

'Colebrook? Colebrook? Why, you're that dreadful women who—You dare to come here? Portland, get rid of her!'

The aunt sounded frightened. Good. No doubt she had never before been confronted by one of her victims. Blackmail victims usually lie low. Colly grinned to himself. Juliana seemed to have things well in hand.

'You!' she said now, pointing at Davidson's aunt. 'I believe you are responsible for attempting to blackmail Brigade-Major Hetherington. Let me tell you' – here Juliana stalked towards the woman – 'that Brigade-Major Hetherington is the most decent man I know,' she stated in a tone that brooked no argument.

Behind the hydrangeas, Colly felt his face reddening.

'It was my idea to pretend to be married. I had my reasons. They need not concern the likes of you. But you will *not*' – here Juliana leaned forward to stab her finger in Mrs Davidson's chest – 'annoy the Hetheringtons any further. Do you understand?'

Colly noted that Davidson wisely kept his distance from the women.

'Or?' demanded the woman, her voice rising. 'Or what will you do, you – you sloe-eyed foreigner?'

Then Juliana really let fly. Colly heard some indistinct words that sounded like Portuguese swear words. He thought he'd better rescue Davidson and his aunt before Juliana annihilated them. As he stepped forward she was saying, 'You know, Lieutenant Davidson, I feel sorry for you. With this terrible woman for your aunt, you'll never be a real man like Mr Hetherington, if you live to be a hundred. Oh!'

She'd finally spied Colly and stopped in the middle of her tirade. Colly stepped to her side and threaded her arm through his. 'Well met, my dear.' Then he nodded to Davidson as if he were paying a social call. 'Davidson.' He ignored the aunt and turned back to Juliana. 'In the event, these histrionics are unnecessary since we're to be married shortly. I've come to take you home, my dear. It was not necessary to take matters into your own hands, you know. My father and I planned to call on Lieutenant Davidson within the next few days.'

Davidson blanched. 'See here, I'm sorry about this misunderstanding—'

'It is no misunderstanding, Davidson. We understand perfectly well. You and your aunt are trying to extort money from either myself or my father.' Colly's impatience began to rise. He didn't have time for this. He wanted to go far, far away with Juliana and leave the world behind.

'No, not me! I would never do that to you. I am conscious of the debt I owe you both.' And to Colly's consternation the wretched youth hung his head and sobbed.

Juliana made a *moué* of distaste.

Colly sighed. He walked over to Davidson and clapped him on the shoulder. 'I shall take one of your problems away, Davidson.' He smiled at Juliana. 'Are you finished here, my love?'

'Oh, ah, that is to say, I have a carriage waiting,' Juliana muttered.

Good, she was beginning to understand he'd not come all this way just to pass the time of day. 'Yes, indeed you have. And when you have paid him off, he can be on his way. Let us go.' Then Colly's conscience smote him. He couldn't walk away and leave the miserable Davidson without offering him a crumb of comfort. 'Davidson?' he said, over his shoulder.

'Sir?' Davidson scrambled to stand up straight. Old habits died hard.

'I shall seek out an occupation for you if you wish,' Colly murmured.

Fortunately Mrs Davidson was stumping away from them down the gravel path towards the house, the back of her neck red with fury.

'*Sir*!' Davidson exclaimed in heartfelt tones.

'I can make no promises and it may take some time, but I'll do what I can. Don't mention it to your aunt, or you might find yourself without a roof over your head. By the by, how is your penmanship?'

Davidson's eyes lit up. 'Tolerable, sir.'

Colly urged Juliana towards the gates and Davidson attempted to follow them, but Colly shook his head.

'Not now, Davidson. I have things to do. I shall send a carriage for you ah … the day after tomorrow.'

The lieutenant dropped back behind them, still proffering his thanks as they passed the curve in the driveway.

When they reached the carriages, Juliana stopped. 'Where are we going?'

'Back to the Old Bank Inn so we can sort out why you are running away from me.'

'H-how did you find out?'

'Twoomey told me that Tilly requested a couple of footmen to fetch your trunk from the attics. He was wringing his hands at the prospect of never seeing you again. You've made a great conquest there. Then the marchioness informed me that on your departure you had thanked her most prettily for her many kindnesses and presented her with a small gift. Apparently I am the only one at Trewbridge who was not informed of your plans.'

'I am far too much under an obligation to you all. It was time to leave.' Her voice was terse and she looked over his shoulder at something of interest on the horizon.

'And you were not going to say goodbye to me?' Colly could not help letting the deep-seated hurt leach into his words.

Juliana's voice broke on a sob. '*Deus*, Colly. I could not.'

He took her in his arms. It would be all right. She hadn't *wanted* to leave him.

'Where were you going after you'd seen Davidson?'

'To Chippenham,' Juliana mumbled into his lapel. 'I have rooms booked at the Hare and Hound. Mr Beck is going to – to purchase a cottage for me in the vicinity.' She sniffed inelegantly.

'I see.'

'Look 'ere, you two. I'm not waiting all day,' interrupted a stentorian voice. They had forgotten the job-master. 'Miss, do you want this carriage or not?'

'Not,' Colly answered.

'I don't think so, thank you,' Juliana said. She flicked an anxious glance at Colly which was not lost on the job-master.

'Are you sure, miss? If you don't want to be bothered by this major fellow 'ere, I'll dispatch him for you. Or at least I'll try to.' The driver eyed Colly.

'I'm quite sure. Thank you.' Stifling a watery laugh, Juliana turned towards the Trewbridge carriage. Colly lifted her in, then he unhitched the horses and leaped on to the seat. They edged past the job-carriage and headed in the direction of Keynsham.

CHAPTER FORTY-FIVE

JULIANA CLUNG TO the carriage strap. Colly had set a brisk pace. She peered out the window. They were bowling alongside a very pretty river and in no time at all the carriage slowed, getting ready to turn.

Butterflies as big as bats swirled in her stomach. She knew what he wanted. Of course she wanted the same thing, but ... He had already done so much for her. In leaving him, she had sought to do something for him. Well, that's what she'd been telling herself. She chewed her lip.

The door opened. 'Coming down, or are you going to stay there all day?' Colly asked.

'Oh!' She hadn't noticed they had stopped, let alone heard Colly alight. She held out her gloved hand but Colly simply spanned her waist with his hands and lifted her down on to a clean corner of the inn yard. A boy holding the horses' heads pretended he hadn't noticed, but a grin split his face from ear to ear.

Colly stepped aside for her to precede him into the Old Bank Inn's foyer.

Juliana felt the rhythm of her heartbeat accelerate. How absurd. This was Colly. She was safe. But of course safety was not the issue.

'May I go with you to your room?' Colly asked her diffidently, his face a frown of anxiety. 'I'd far rather do this in private, Juliana, because a man doesn't need an audience when he – when he tries to propose.'

Juliana's heart jumped. Oh! If only ... She gave him a nervous half-smile. They'd spent more than two weeks together in the close confines of a cabin so she'd look ridiculous if she said no, wouldn't she? 'That's fine,' she whispered, knowing her smile was a frail, frightened thing. She was going to disappoint him.

But when he ushered her into her bedchamber she stood amazed on the threshold. 'Oh, Colly!' She clasped her hands underneath her chin and spun slowly, taking in the big bedchamber crammed with hundreds and hundreds of flowers. Late summer flowers flourished on every table and in every nook and cranny. Peonies and poppies rubbed petals with lavender and snapdragons. Dahlias jostled for position with delphiniums, all grouped in the colours of the rainbow. The heady perfume reminded her of the Lady's Garden at Trewbridge.

'Good,' Colly commented with satisfaction, shrugging out of his greatcoat. 'They got it right.'

'*Right*? It's exquisite!' She flitted from vase to vase inhaling the scents and exclaiming over the fresh cool blues and butter yellows. Then she turned to Colly. 'You did this for me?'

He spread his hands. 'Of course. There isn't anyone else I'd want to do it for. Never will be.'

'Dear Colly.' She smiled mistily and sat down on the edge of the big bed before she fell down. It bounced invitingly. 'I do love you so but ...' She trailed off as he sat down beside her and she felt herself sinking deeper into the brocade cover.

He took her hand. 'Running away solves nothing, Juliana. I don't care about your awful relatives but I'm grateful they're dead,' he added, grinning. 'As to the other matters, they are finished with. There is nothing to connect you to either incident. But there's something else you haven't thought about yet.'

Puzzled, she looked an enquiry.

'You will have a dowry when that property is sold. Do you realize you might become a magnet for fortune hunters?'

'Good heavens!' Juliana felt her jaw slacken. She hadn't forgotten Lord Brechin's comment that her property would be a respectable dowry, but she *had* forgotten that some of the officers she had nursed had told her that in England, money could sometimes gloss over a person's faults. She had looked forward to being a woman of independent means but she hadn't realized how 'respectable' she had become overnight. How ridiculous people were. As if mere money could determine one's true qualities!

'I am not looking forward to despatching the queue at your doorstep,' Colly said gloomily.

Juliana couldn't help it. She giggled. 'Ah, but you would be first in the queue. I seem to remember you had designs on me long before I inherited anything.'

He brightened. 'So long as you remember that, Miss Colebrook.' Then he turned to her and set to work untying the ribbons of her bonnet. He cast the bonnet aside and, kneeling on the rug, began on the ties of her cloak.

Juliana tried to quell the fluttering in the pit of her stomach. She looked down on his bent head as he concentrated on disentangling the cloak strings. Very few people got to look down on Colly Hetherington. She stretched out her gloved hand to stroke the springy dark brown waves of hair.

There was a muffled curse from Colly. Her cloak ribbons had become knotted. His lean, brown fingers were shaking, making matters worse.

She stripped off her gloves, then leaned over to pick up her reticule. And presented him with her brand new penknife.

He tilted his head back in shock and gazed into her eyes. Then grinned. 'What a sensible idea,' he said as he sliced through the ribbons. Her cloak joined the discarded bonnet.

Still on his knees before her, he laid his face on her lap. Gazing straight ahead like a sightless person, she ran the tips of her fingers over his head, savouring the texture of his hair and the curve of his head down to the nape of his neck. Her fingers stilled. He was hers. She desperately wanted to be his. Why was she making things so difficult? Colly would cut off his arm before he hurt her. She knew that. She took a deep breath and tossed her fears and scruples over her shoulder. And could have sworn she heard them thud on the carpet.

'Yes,' she said.

He glanced up and grinned. 'I haven't asked you yet.'

She tugged on his hair, smiling, and the hazel eyes darkened. He stood up and hauled her into his arms.

'Sweet, let me hold you, warm you.'

'*Sim*, yes, please,' she whispered, burrowing into his chest. She, who had always been so independent, would always need this man. She craved this addictive feeling that only Colly could engender – a sensual mix of security and smouldering excitement. She felt his mouth on her hair and then, slowly, he brushed soft, seductive open-mouthed kisses on her nape and on her cheek, trying to coax her to raise her face.

Smiling, she tilted her head back and exposed her throat so he could lavish those soft, sweet kisses on her neck. Her smile grew when he followed each kiss with a murmur of pleasure. 'Dearest Colly,' she whispered. She curled her arms around his neck. 'Kiss me properly, *meu amor*,' she demanded.

He drew in his breath and she felt a quiver of laughter shake his body. 'Yes, my lady. Anything you say, my lady.'

And then he kissed her 'properly'. Oh, *how* he kissed her. He began at the corners of her mouth, placing soft, warm kisses there. Surrendering to the seductive sweetness she opened her mouth, and

Colly knew exactly what to do. One hand was employed in steadying her head as he kissed her deeply, delicately tipping her teeth with his tongue. His other hand smoothed down her body from her neck to her thigh and back again as if he were committing the curves to memory.

Juliana shivered. Oh yes. She wanted to make love with him.

'Juliana,' he murmured, as he took her hand and pressed a kiss on to her palm, 'I always knew it would be like this.'

'So did I,' she assured him fervently. 'But I was so frightened …' She trailed off and bent her head.

'And now?' he asked anxiously, his hands grasping her elbows to pull her close.

She looked up into his face and smiled. '*Eu quero fazer amo com você*,' she whispered, stroking a hand down the side of his brown face.

He blinked. 'Uh?'

She giggled and he tickled the side of her neck. 'I said I want to make love with you.'

'It sounds more romantic in Portuguese,' he admitted. 'And when the time comes, all will be well, you'll see.'

'I know, *meu amor*, I know.'

CHAPTER FORTY-SIX

JOHN TREWBRIDGE WATCHED as Colly lifted Juliana down from the carriage. He smiled with satisfaction when Juliana clung to Colly as she was lowered to the ground.

John strode forward to greet them. 'Colly, so pleased you caught up with Miss Colebrook. You'd best put the poor girl down. You're crushing her.'

Grinning, Colly turned with Juliana in the crook of his arm. He thrust out his free hand. 'John, Miss Colebrook has done me the honour of agreeing to become my wife.'

'Congratulations to you both!'

Colly released Juliana and said, 'It must be nigh on dinner time. If you can contain your curiosity till then, my lord, we will tell you our plans.'

'Plans? No need. Mother has everything organized. You are to have the gatehouse and she wants to talk to you about a licence.'

Colly blinked. 'I had thought to have banns read.'

John laughed. 'Best leave it to Mama. You might make a mull of it.'

When dinner was over, the marchioness chivvied Colly and Juliana outside to walk in the Lady's Garden to watch the stars come out.

Juliana sniffed appreciatively. 'It smells like the inn chamber this morning,' she commented, as they wandered past a bed of musky stocks.

'That was the idea,' Colly said, smiling down at her. 'I originally planned to propose to you here, but you ran away.'

Juliana raised her chin. 'I thought it was for the best.'

'Not for *my* best, Juliana. I could live without you if I had to, but it wouldn't really be living. I would get by, but there'd be very little joy in life.'

She rubbed her cheek on his shoulder. 'It is the same for me. I planned on buying a cottage where Tilly and I might live out our days.

After all, it was much more than I ever thought to have. I decided I would help the local people when they became ill. Growing medicinal herbs seemed like a fine idea too. I've never been in one place long enough to do that.'

'You may grow all the herbs you like at the gatehouse. Maybe one day we might purchase a place of our own, but until then we are nicely set. And the folk at Trewbridge and in the village will be very grateful indeed for your nursing skills.'

She smoothed his cravat. 'We are very fortunate, Colly. You have managed to establish a bridge with your family and I am well rid of mine. How odd that we set out to do the very opposite.'

He bent to pick a poppy for her. 'We shall make a family of our own. Even if we are not blessed with children, you and I will be a small family. And if we are fortunate enough to have sons and daughters, we already know how *not* to treat them.'

Juliana smiled. 'True. And we have friends who are every bit as good as family. Better, in fact.'

'Indeed. My darling, I am so glad you forgave me for giving you a black eye at our first meeting. I shall never forget waking up from a cloud of laudanum and seeing your bruised face—'

'Hush, Colly. You were in agony at the time and had no notion what you were doing. Believe me, many patients hit me harder.' She tried to make a joke of it but he would not be pacified.

'No one, *no one* will ever hurt you again, Juliana,' he said fiercely.

'I know, *meu amor*. I trust you to protect me always.'

Hidden from the house they stole a quick kiss before walking on.

'I should like to invite Grandmama and Felicia to visit from time to time, if that should suit you.'

'Of course. They are my favourite members of your family.'

'Mine too,' Colly agreed. 'I will do my filial duty by my parents but I shall keep well away from William. They do not seem to be very happy at Heather Hill, do they?' Colly tucked the bright orange poppy behind the comb in her hair and admired the result against her rich, dark tresses.

'No. I was only there a short time, but saw that your sister would prefer to be anywhere rather than Heather Hill, and your mama seems to lead her life separately from the rest of the family. And, of course, I received an earful of your father's remorse all the way from Trewbridge to Heather Hill,' she ended, laughing.

Colly shook his head. 'It's strange, but after being away from them for so long I can see how uncertain my father has always been around my mother. Mama may have our best interests at heart, but she does not show it. And Father is a person who has to be shown that he is needed. However, I doubt my mother will change.'

'No,' Juliana agreed. 'I think your father is destined always to be chasing a star which is just beyond him.'

Colly folded his arms around her, needing her warmth, her strength. 'You are very insightful, my Angel of Sao Nazaire. I wish we had met many years ago.'

'We would have been two very different people then,' she said wisely. 'You would not even have glanced at me.'

'Rubbish. I would not have been able to resist your chocolate eyes and glossy hair. It is more likely you would have passed me on the street and ignored me. I do not possess the Portuguese address and ease with women.'

'I would have looked,' she said with confidence. 'Remember my height. Oh, I would have looked. I would have said to myself, "Juliana, there is a man you can look up to".'

They laughed. Then she leaned into him and kissed him. 'And you really are a man I can look up to, Colly.'

Colly held her in his arms and thanked his lucky stars he had met her. It had taken a long and dangerous journey to bring them here, but at last they were home.